IN THE HELLO AND IN THE GOODBYE

MELISSA WHITNEY

ABOUT THE BOOK

Can distance bring breaking hearts back together? For Colm and Evie, they hope that the miles between him in Costa Rica and she in California can help them find each other again. Colm and Evie never made sense. She's a pumpkin spice latte. He's a large black coffee. But for the last five years they've been utterly in love. That is until a tragic night a year ago. Now Evie's big smile no longer reaches her eyes and far too often the seat beside her is empty.
When Colm leaves to teach in Costa Rica for sixty days the distance magnifies the growing emotional gap between them. They must choose to say goodbye or fight for each other. Colm proposes an experiment to long distance date in order to find each other again. Will the miles help them erase the space between them? Or are second chances only found in the romance novels...and not in real life?

For Liam
You'll always be my Gigantor and I'll always be your Donut.

A NOTE FROM THE AUTHOR:

Dear Reader,

This is a fictional story. It is not based on actual events or people. Real life locations portrayed in the book may have both fictionalized and actual details in their description. However, this remains a work of fiction.

Any similarities to actual people and places is mere coincidence. Real locations in this book may have fictionalized details. While the people, events, details about actual places, and even some of the locations are fictionalized, this book is deeply personal. It is inspired by the relationship I have with the love of my life, my husband Liam aka Gigantor.

This book portrays a relationship of a man on the spectrum and a neurotypical woman. As a neurotypical woman with a disability (legal blindness) and wife of a man on the spectrum, I hope that I offer a positive representation of individuals on the spectrum. Like Colm, individuals on the spectrum are far more than their Autism and I hope I did his character justice.

This book is a romance with a guaranteed happily ever after (HEA) that will, hopefully, make you swoon, smile, sniffle, snort, and, sometimes, fan yourself. However, it does deal with some themes, topics, and issues such as grief and loss, impact of parental divorce, gaslighting, and pregnancy complications. As well, the book discusses and depicts consensual sexual acts on the page. These topics may be triggering for some readers. As a trained social worker, I endeavored to tackle the things discussed in my book in a thoughtful and sensitive manner. My dear reader, please do what you need to in order to take care of yourself.

I hope after reading this book that you fall in love with Evie and Colm as much as I did with them while writing their story.

Always,

Melissa (aka Liam's Donut)

PART 1

IN THE HELLO AND IN THE GOODBYE

CHAPTER ONE

In The Hello - Colm
The First Hello - Five Years Ago

Could this coffee line move any slower? Colm clenched and unclenched his fists as a young brunette ahead of him cooed about all things pumpkin. It was only August twenty-seventh and the heat of summer still gripped, but Jitter Bean Coffeehouse was already peddling autumn.

"I love a pumpkin chai!" she gushed to the older man that stood between them in the line.

The old man chuckled his agreement.

I am in the lesser-known tenth circle of Dante's Inferno.

"OMG! I love my pumpkin lip gloss. I stock up every fall," she giggled. Her pink dress hugged hips that were positively pulsating with joy, and the happy wiggle called his attention to her apple-shaped bottom.

Does her body always vibrate when she's happy? God, he needed coffee.

The coffee was vital not just because it was 6:48 a.m. on the last Tuesday before returning to The Land of Bad Excuses for Forgotten Homework, but because in two hours he'd be giving a talk to future special education teachers at his alma mater. Jonathan, his freshman roommate-turned best friend-turned associate college professor, roped him into it. Far too often, Jonathan talked him into things with his "hey buddys" over one too many cold beers.

Despite his chosen profession requiring him to speak to classrooms full of junior high students who only gave him half their attention, he hated getting up in front of people. You could call it his kryptonite, although he was more Clark Kent than Superman. On the outside he would appear cool as a cucumber, but inside was a tornado of anxiety. Tight chest, throat dry, his words elusive. A nervous jitter would vibrate through him the entire time. Still, he did it.

"Good morning. How are you?" The brunette's greeting to the barista oozed cheer, pulling Colm away from his musings to study her as if drawing the map of a newly discovered continent. Her thick dark hair hung loose against a paper white blazer. The fitted skirt of her dress stopped just below the back of her delicate knees. The fabric caressed each curve of her body creating a silhouette that was sexy, yet sweet.

Colm forced his eyes to the rows of mugs, tumblers, and bags of coffee for sale. No matter how the fabric luxuriated over her shape, staring was impolite. Besides, this woman was annoying, verbally fluttering between the barista and the old man chattering about seasonal treats while people waited.

Less chit-chat and more ordering, please.

"Hello. What would you like?" The brunette had spun to face him. Her big smile sucker-punched him with its brightness and stole his breath. Her eyes sparkled with anticipation of his response.

"What?" *Why was she asking? Also, do smiles come that big?*

It was the type of smile that erupted like a volcano, happiness flooding all over like joyful lava.

Her dainty fingers fiddled with a gold butterfly necklace that dangled inches below her collarbone. When Jonathan asked if he was a tits or ass man, he'd normally choose ass. But in that moment, collarbones clinched the title of the sexiest part of a woman. There was an urge to press his lips against this little chatterbox's collarbone and make her purr.

Colm blinked away the thought. It wasn't like him to objectify a woman. Even if she had a smile that paralyzed him with its brilliance.

"To drink. What would you like? My treat." She bit her lower lip, eclipsing that big smile.

He wanted to untuck that lip and free that smile. *Keep your hands to yourself…* He shrugged, shoving his hands into the pockets of his grey slacks.

"Isn't she a sweetheart?" The old man turned with admiring eyes. "Evie here is buying our drinks since we've been waiting so long."

That big smile had a name. *Evie.* The corners of his lips tugged up as he stared at her Mediterranean blue eyes.

"They have the best pumpkin chai. That's what Stanley and I are getting. You can join our pumpkin patch…" she paused with a nervous giggle, "…or do your own thing."

Evie batted her eyelashes, peering up at him. At six foot five he towered over her. The top of her head, covered in shiny hair that his fingers itched to touch, would rest snug below his chin.

Dude, stop being creepy and order a goddamn drink!

"Large coffee…black," he said clearing his throat.

"Perfect." That big smile blasted him, causing an unfamiliar flip in his stomach.

In all the dates and two girlfriends he'd had since he was seventeen, nobody had ever made his stomach rumble like a herd of stampeding rhinos. That was something that only happened in the romance novels that Jonathan read, convinced they contained secrets to wooing the ladies. It did not occur in real life, but it was happening to him right now.

Spinning on her pointy pink heels, Evie ordered their drinks.

Evie. Each syllable of her name hummed like the notes of a new favorite song. Colm had never met an Evie. The name wasn't as rare as his own, but unique enough to not be common. Just like her smile.

While he splashed cream and two sugar packets into his coffee, his gaze flicked back to her. There was a desire to retreat, yet also a desire to remain.

He'd said thank you when she ordered their drinks, but nothing more. Mom had raised him right. Respectful, though he lacked the smoothness Jonathan had to chat up a pretty girl. He was Clark Kent, after all.

Hesitation lurked as he glanced at Evie, who still waited at the end of the counter for her drink. The alluring melody of her voice tangoed around him. He wanted to talk to her. He wanted to ask her to join him.

She's sunshine. You're a storm cloud. With a self-defeated shrug, he pivoted from where Evie waited for her drink.

In the sea of early morning patrons munching on stale pastries and drinking fancy coffees over laptops and cell-phones, he located an isolated table tucked in the corner. He tried to focus on his breathing and ignore the distracting soundtrack of hushed chatter, chairs being pulled out, and the hissing espresso machine. The outside world often drained him. He drank up the solitude with his coffee while reviewing his notes for his talk.

"Hello." A honey sweet voice pierced his concentration.

Evie stood in front of his two-person table, an unabashed grin on her pretty face. Her delicate fingers clenched her coffee cup. *Evie* danced around the cup in fat cursive letters. Writing wasn't prone to dance, but damn if her name didn't appear to be doing just that.

"Hello." It was a statement punctuated with questioning.

"This place is as busy as the cantina from *Star Wars*." She gestured around at the full tables and clusters of waiting customers. "Except way fewer bounty hunters. At least, I think. There *are* a few sketchy looking folks in here."

Colm nodded, not getting the reference. "I've never seen *Star Wars*."

"I thought the sci-fi fairytale was a rite of passage for all millennials?"

"My mom never let me watch anything that she deemed killy."

"Killy?"

"Violent."

Evie tipped her head to the right and scrunched her face. "I wouldn't say it's *that* killy."

He smiled at her use of his mom's word, "killy." As if she was learning his native tongue. Learning him.

"Well, there was something about shooting wombats that mom found objectionable," he explained.

She nodded. "Makes sense. Animal cruelty shouldn't be tolerated. Come to think of it there are some other red flags with those movies. Like the weird incest angle when you find out Princess Leia is Luke's sister."

Quiet settled over them as they stared at each other. Was it seconds? Or hours? He wasn't sure.

"So…" There was another bite of that pink bottom lip and an anxious tug of her necklace. "Feel free to say no, but would you mind if I sat with you?"

Colm blinked at the empty seat across from him. When was the last time a stranger asked to sit with him? Especially such a pretty one. There were people on the bus or at the movies that asked if a seat was taken, but never to sit *with* you. Sitting with someone implied sharing a space versus just existing in it.

Evie's face pinched. "Sorry. I know it's weird for a stranger to ask to sit. But at least I'm not offering to show you my puppy in my windowless van," she laughed with a slight wince. "I'll go. Have a good day." She turned to leave.

"Wait…sit." The words slipped out like a plea. Maybe they were. There was something about this little chatterbox that made him want her to stay.

"Are you sure?" she asked, looking skeptical. "I don't want to intrude. Although I kind of already did. My bad. I had a plan to kill time here and all these people are putting a wrench in that. Drives me nuts when a plan doesn't go… well, *as planned*," she giggled.

Something in her uncertain giggle and the fact that she was a planner like him endeared her to him. "Sit." He motioned to the seat with a soft smile. At least he hoped it was soft.

Don't be creepy. Don't be creepy.

"Thanks. I'm Evie Johnson." She held her hand out.

"Colm Gallagher."

His hand enveloped hers. It was warm from holding her drink, but something told him that her hands would always be warm. Her smooth hand fit snug in his big rough one as if her hand was always meant to be in his.

There was that stomach flip again. Ridiculous! Thirty-year-old men weren't supposed to react like a teenage girl seeing BTS, but then, he never fit the mold. Why should this be different?

"Colm? Like Colm Feore?"

"Who?"

"He's an actor. Been in a bunch of stuff, but not like a household name. Not like Chris Evans. Oh, golly *The Nanny*

Diaries is one of my favs!" Her face contorted. "Sorry. I'm sputtering about Chris Evans when you asked about Colm Feore. Stay on topic Evie," she simpered. "Colm Feore was in the *Chronicles of Riddick*. Truly terrible movie, but my mom has a thing for Vin Diesel, so I've seen all his movies—thrice. My mom even has a Chihuahua named Diesel. Dreadful dog. He bites."

"Vin Diesel?" Listening to her rapid speech was like riding a tilt-a-whirl at the carnival. Your equilibrium was off kilter, but your heart sped with happy excitement. He did not want to get off this ride.

"Yeah. Mom loves sexy bald men. Vin Diesel and Bruce Willis are her fantasy men. Although neither are sexy to me."

"What's sexy to you?"

Pink rouged her cheeks. "Chris Hemsworth."

"Thor?" There was a knowing arch of his right brow. How often had Jonathan told him that he looked like a clean-cut version of the God of Thunder?

Evie's blush deepened. "Back to Bruce Willis. We watch *Die Hard* every Christmas."

"Oh," Colm said, cringing inside at his less than smooth response.

"Do you have a movie you watch each Christmas? Oh wait, do you not celebrate Christmas? That might have been insensitive of me to ask." There was a lip-biting frown on her face. "Although you can still watch Christmas movies even if you don't celebrate. My friend Leo's boyfriend Martin is Jewish but lives for the Hallmark Christmas movies. If it has a princess from a made-up Eastern European country where they speak with British accents falling in love with a Christmas tree farm owner, he's there." Evie's face twisted in self-reproach. "Sorry. I'm babbling again. Not even giving you a chance to answer."

"*It's a Wonderful Life*," he offered.

How strange that the sputtering ways that he'd found grating in line now seemed delightful. Evie's entire face lit up as she talked, and her voice was like an orchestra of inflections.

"Oh. That's a good one."

A cheeky grin covered his face. "Yup."

"That face. Colm Gallagher, are you *not* a fan of the story of George Bailey's redemption?" There was a glint of playful accusation in her eyes.

"The guy makes poor financial decisions and we're supposed to applaud that," Colm guffawed.

Mom would get so annoyed when he'd snark back at George Bailey, "Yeah, why did you have all those kids?" during their annual Christmas Eve viewing of the film. Colm related more to Mr. Potter and never understood why the only member of Bedford Falls with a sound business plan was vilified. Mom would grumble, but they'd watch the movie each year with peppermint hot chocolate and caramel popcorn. It was tradition. And he never broke from an established plan. That is, until today. Evie wasn't on his plan for today.

"Can I admit something to you?" Evie bent close. Her vanilla-lavender aroma wrapped around him like a hug.

Inhaling deep, he smiled. "Sure."

She wagged a warning finger. "You can't tell anyone or I'll…well I'll think of something terrible. Like buy you decaf and say it's regular the next time we have coffee."

"Diabolical." Colm liked the sound of a next time slipping from her heart-shaped mouth.

"I'm an evil genius." She winked. "When that little girl at the end says 'Daddy, Teacher says when a bell rings, an angel gets its wings' I find her voice as painful as a root canal. Like it's supposed to be cutesy, but it totally ruins the moment for me."

"I feel the same way about Tiny Tim in every version of *A Christmas Carol*."

Evie tapped her cup against his in a toast to them both being terrible humans.

"Colm. I like your name. How did you get it?" she asked, her fingernails skating across the smooth surface of the table.

Evie's fingers were delicate and long with a pale pink sparkle polish. There was no ring. Again, his stomach did something men's bellies shouldn't do.

"I was named for my grandfather," Colm said, trying to figure out a not-obvious way to display that there wasn't now, nor had there ever been, a ring on his finger.

"Oh, good old Pop-Pop Colm." That big smile danced with mirth. "That's sweet that she named you after him."

"There's no Pop-Pop Colm, but a Grandfather Bill. My Grandfather was from Northern Ireland. Mom wanted an Irish name in honor of him but didn't want to be so on the nose by naming me after him. I don't know." He shrugged, sipping his coffee.

"I like that. It's *super* clever and *totally* original of your mom."

Most people would snark about how that didn't make sense. Nobody ever got his mom's reasoning behind his name, but Evie did. There was no sarcasm in her words, just an earnest admiration. To Evie, his mom was ingenious, not fanciful.

Something about those blue eyes told him that she could understand him, though there was no logical explanation for why he thought so. That made him uncomfortable. Decisions were made with research, facts, and lists, not with the gut. Especially when the gut was somersaulting like a backup dancer.

"I bet it must have been hard to find those pens with your name on them in gift shops as a kid. I could never find

Evie, but sometimes I could find Evelyn. Evelyn is my birth-name, but I go by Evie. I'm named after a character from a book my mom read in high school. Fun fact, she doesn't remember the name of the book or the plot, but still named me after that character."

"Huh," he said.

Really? Huh? So smooth, man.

Colm never wanted to be smooth as bad as he did right now. To have all the swagger of Jonathan, who could chat up women at the bar like a modern-day Casanova. To be able to flow between topics, easing into a comfortable current of conversation.

As she spoke, he continued to nod and give one-word answers or grunts. More grunts than were appropriate for a non-neanderthal. He should have just said his name was "Ugg" with his monosyllabic answers.

Evie talked about her job as a hospital social worker. Colm nodded.

She asked what he did. He said "teach," and sipped his coffee. When she asked what he taught, he said "kids." They both cringed and she changed topics.

Evie talked about moving from Kansas City to Long Beach three years ago. Colm said, "Oh."

When she asked if he grew up in Long Beach, he said, "Nope" and didn't elaborate.

Evie talked about wanting to get a corgi. Colm wasn't sure what sound he made, but it was either a huff or a "Ha" in response.

I have no game. He sighed, closing his eyes.

"So, you're a coffee guy," she said, her smile collapsing in mortification. "I'm being awkward. Of course, you're a coffee guy. You ordered coffee. Sorry. I get nervous meeting new people. Look at me chattering away like a train with no brakes. Sorry…I'm clearly annoying you."

Whatever had fluttered in his stomach earlier now gave him a swift kick, telling him to reassure her and bring back that smile. God, he wanted to drink up that smile.

Drink up? You sound like an Ed Sheeran lyric.

This little whirlwind of cheerfulness shouldn't be darkened by his cloudiness. Even if his cloudiness was a mere trick of the mirrors of how people saw him.

"You're not talking too much," Colm assured. His eyes met hers, hoping to soothe her uncertainty.

"Phew." She wiped her brow with goofy theatrics. "Can I get you to sign an affidavit to that for my friend Leo? He'll never believe that someone said I didn't talk too much."

"Gladly." There was a playfulness to Colm's tone that he hadn't heard in a very long time. Dare he call it flirtatious?

"I was worried when you weren't talking that I was mowing you over with my blathering. I know I can do that at times. Like I only have one speed when I talk." Concern sobered her sweet features to serious as she spoke, "It's okay to tell me if I am. People tell me I talk too much all the time."

The idea of anyone making Evie feel bad for talking sparked a desire to get a list of their names and rage through the city like Liam Neeson seeking revenge on her behalf. Of course, he lacked Liam Neeson's particular skillset. The only skill he had would be quiet intimidation and pop quizzes.

Everyone would get a pop quiz!

While he wanted to protect Evie from sadness dulling her effervescence, this was another thing they shared. Neither quite fit the expectations of others. One too much. One not enough.

"People say I talk too little," he offered.

"So, it's not me?"

"No, it's me," he sighed, looking down. There was no

Colm scribbled in ink dancing on his cup. Just another way he didn't fit in.

"Then it's us." Evie reached across the table, her warm hand resting on his in solidarity.

"Ok." He placed his other hand atop, blanketing hers. "Then it's us."

CHAPTER TWO

In The Goodbye - Evie
Present - Five Years Later

E vie stood on the bow of the Queen Mary, ocean breeze pressing airy kisses on her cheeks. In her gauzy sky-blue dress, skirt waltzing in the summer air, she was the vision of Lady Mary Crawley. At least that's what she told herself as she weaved through the well-wishing and toasting guests at Josephine and Mandala's Royal Wedding themed reception. The aloof bluster of the eldest Crawley sister from *Downton Abbey* was needed for yet another event attended alone.

It's not that Evie couldn't attend things alone. Teachers used to joke that Evie could make friends with the plants in an empty room. It was the Monroe gift of gab, inherited from her mom's family. Dad had once told Evie she was like a hot summer day—at first welcomed, but prolonged exposure left you drained, sweaty, and seeking shade. As companionable as Evie was, her relentless chattering exasperated some, leaving her sitting alone at cafeteria tables in school or on couches at parties.

The days of empty seats beside her and her eyes wandering around a room looking for someone to talk to should be a mere memory now that she had Colm. He was supposed to be the person filling the seat beside her with an amused smile at her runaway train verbal antics. The person that didn't seek shade away from her.

"Good afternoon, my fair Evie." Leo smacked his lips against both of her cheeks.

For eight years, Leo Gonzalez had been the Pooh to her Piglet. The jam to her toast. The Beyoncé to her Kelly Rowland. Whatever cliché used for the best of friends would fit.

They all worked together in the emergency department of Grace Memorial Hospital. Leo was the charge nurse marching his troops into medical battle with his trusty tablet and yellow crocs, Josephine the no-nonsense attending physician, and Evie the social worker with pockets full of encouragement and candy.

"You look smashing," he awed in a spot-on British accent.

"You too, darling." Evie's accent was less Judi Dench and more Madonna, but it fit the vibe.

"I still can't believe Josephine is a married woman." The ice of his old fashioned clunked against the almost empty glass as he sipped it. "For years she was all 'marriage is an archaic institution developed by men to hold women back.'"

"She did say that, but I think the love of a good woman like Mandala softened her stance. Plus, they are so perfect for each other," Evie said, tightening her grip on her hat as the Pacific breeze threatened to snatch it away.

"True. Mandala has the patience of a saint." His eyes flicked to where a smiling Mandala listened to Josephine's mom go on about something. "Speaking of saints, what time is Colm's flight?" His gaze dropped back to Evie.

"Ten p.m."

Leo whistled. "Two months in Costa Rica and he's going to spend the entire time setting up a special education program. I'd be spending it at the beach working on my tan and catching some waves."

"He's so dedicated."

It was one of the things that she loved the most about him. Most days he'd come home from teaching wrung out like a battered washcloth from giving so much to his students. Still, there was a quiet anger brewing in her belly that he was leaving for two months. Leaving her.

"Ready, gorgeous?" Leo asked, holding out his arm to escort her into the reception room.

"I hope Martin doesn't mind that I'm stealing his man," Evie giggled, taking Leo's arm.

If Colm couldn't be here, at least her table would be full of friends. Leo and Martin, the one couple Colm never complained about double dates with, would be at their eight-person table, along with two other nurses from work, Jane and Alex and their spouses, and some new doctor that would start at Grace Memorial next week. The lucky chap scored an invite to what Leo dubbed the wedding of "the quarter" because he'd gone to medical school with Josephine.

The reception featured an ocean of women in bright colored fascinators and men in tuxes seated at white linen tables bedecked with gold candelabras. The soft light colluded with the sunlight streaming through large windows to wash the space in a quintessential romantic glow.

No fascinator for Evie. Josephine had demanded an over-the-top big white hat saying it went perfect with the drama of Evie's dress. It was Josephine's day, after all. Plus, Evie enjoyed any excuse to wear any hat. The bigger the better!

Colm would tease her about her hat fetish. Where some women had shoes or purses for every outfit, she had a hat. Valentine's Day two years ago Colm took her to Mad Hatters, a hat shop along the downtown ocean front, telling her to buy a hat perfect for a picnic. After buying a black hat with a red bow that matched her red dress, they sat at a stone picnic table that overlooked the waterfront sharing yellow curry with tofu and spicy eggplant from their favorite Thai place. As the sun dipped goodnight, he bent with a kiss, saying, "My little chatterbox," making her cheeks blush.

He still made her cheeks blush and belly somersault, but he could also make her heart frown and sometimes, cry. Especially moments like this. Alone at this table full of couples. The empty seat beside her where he should be sitting, which was soon to be occupied by some random nobody instead of her somebody.

"Hi. I think this is my seat."

A deep baritone tickled Evie away from her thoughts of Colm. She looked up into a pair of ashen eyes rimmed in gold.

"Hello." She smiled.

He was tall, but not as tall as Colm. Perhaps only six foot, which was still a mountain compared to her five foot five inches. Where Colm's gaze was restrained, this man's eyes seemed to play. Where Colm's smile was guarded and a sparse gift that she was often the sole recipient of, this man's smile was open and generous.

"I'm Wyatt Kurtzman," he said, holding out his hand in greeting.

"Evie Johnson." She took it, noting its warmth.

"Nice to meet you. May I?" He gestured to the empty seat beside her. Colm's seat.

"Of course." The corners of her lips ticked up a little higher.

CHAPTER THREE

In The Goodbye - Colm
Present - Six Hours Later

The apple-shaped clock in the kitchen ticked closer to 7:45 p.m. The rideshare to LAX needed to be hailed. Colm had procrastinated long enough. The plan was to cue up the car in the app at 7:40 p.m. to ensure an on-time departure.

"Damn it," he grumbled as the clock clicked 7:46 p.m. Things were not going according to the plan today, despite it having been drafted, discussed, and agreed upon.

It had started off well. His last morning home was spent sitting across from Evie eating avocado toast and fresh fruit. Queen Elizabeth, their three-year-old corgi, snoozed at their feet as Evie sipped her homemade English Toffee latte and he drank his coffee. The smell of the coffee melded with her vanilla-lavender aroma like a hybrid coffeeshop/garden/bakery, three of his favorite places to go with her. It was perfect. Just as planned. He had a plan. *They* had a plan.

After breakfast together, Evie spent an hour getting ready

for the wedding, rolling her silky hair into fat curls. Colm tried to touch them as she stood in her robe applying lipstick at the mirror, but she'd swatted him away half-annoyed, half-playful. That big smile of hers not reaching her eyes. Evie's smile and expressive eyes always told the story of what was happening inside.

Most people would only see Happy Evie. The nurturer, always ready with a smile, encouraging words, and a purse filled with tissue packets and snacks. Colm got to see all of Evie.

Frazzled Evie came out when tiny things went wrong like the restaurant being out of what she'd wanted. It was adorable how she'd spin at the little stuff but be the steady captain of a burning cruise missile destroyer in any emergency.

Angry Evie came out infrequently, but when she did… watch out.

Scared Evie second-guessed herself and tugged with anxious fingers on her butterfly necklace. Colm tried to soothe that Evie away with a squeeze of his hand, wrap of his arm around her, or press of his lips.

Then there was Sultry Evie, whose voice dropped low and sexy as she murmured, "Come to bed." Colm hadn't seen that Evie in a while.

Quiet Evie retreated deep inside herself, escaping when the world swirled around her like a hurricane that didn't allow her to grasp onto anything for safety. He wanted to be her anchor, helping her weather the harsh winds.

And there was Goofy Evie, who would place her hands on Colm's lips doing an impression of him answering her questions in the way she'd want them answered when he was stunned into silence or taking too long to mull over the question.

They were all his Evie and he loved each of them. He loved her.

Lately, though, something had shifted. Quiet and Scared Evie had been coming out more and more over the last twelve months. Her smile didn't reach her eyes as often. The comfortable silence when they'd sit in the same room, her reading a romance novel while he did a crossword, was now laced with a choking tension.

Today, as Evie got ready for the wedding that tension permeated the townhouse. The culmination when she went to leave.

Heels tapped against the hardwood floor announcing her presence. "I'm all dolled up for the wedding."

"Ok," Colm said, his back to her, double-checking his packed suitcase against his list.

She cleared her throat, "I'm leaving."

"Ok. Have fun," he mumbled, his eyes fixed on his checklist.

There was a rustle of fabric and light shifting of feet behind him. Then the clack of heels down the stairs, scamper of four stubby furry legs following, and slam of the door.

Why didn't I turn? Colm clenched his jaw. He told himself it was because he was so focused on his list. On making sure nothing was missing. But those were just excuses so he wouldn't have to face the real reason: that she was getting ready to go to another event without him.

He should have turned around to look at her. To have seen her in her new dress. To allow his eyes to devour her effervescent smile and calm sea eyes. Knowing she was beautiful and experiencing it were two different things. So was experiencing the lit Christmas tree effect of her face when telling her she was beautiful.

Letting out a long breath he looked down at his phone. Her message mocked.

My Little Chatterbox: Sorry! Home soon.

That was two hours ago. *When was soon exactly?*

As the clock moved to 7:48 p.m., he hailed his ride. Suitcase and duffle by the door, he stood waiting. Frustration crawled through him as each minute ticked away. Evie was late.

She had agreed to be home by five. Now, the image of her that he'd carry for the next sixty days would be of her swatting him away, instead of her big smile beaming as he told her she looked beautiful.

Colm lowered to his haunches to give Queen Elizabeth some goodbye ear scratches. At least while he was gone she'd be here to snuggle, protect, and keep Evie company. Even if she did more sleeping than guarding.

"You're a terrible guard dog, but you'll take care of…" He swallowed hard. "…mommy."

Evie had always been obsessed with both corgis and Her Majesty the Queen. For months he'd researched corgi rescues. Evie loved the breed, but only wanted to rescue, not purchase from a breeder. It made him love her just a little more, that she'd sacrifice something she wanted in order to do the right thing. After ten months of calling area rescues daily, a litter of abandoned corgi puppies showed up. Queen Elizabeth was the only girl in the small pack of three-month-old pups. As soon as he saw her Evie-sized puppy grin, he knew she was their dog.

Evie had worked late at the hospital that day. When she walked in, Queen Elizabeth greeted her wearing a tiny red bow on her collar. Evie burst into happy tears, scooping the puppy into her arms. Colm held a weeping Evie, who held a licking Queen Elizabeth.

Letting the memory dissolve, he rose. "Be a good girl. Goodbye," he said, grabbing his luggage and walking out the door.

His driver was three minutes away. He always wanted to be outside when the driver was close. It was something he and Evie had in common. They hated to keep people waiting. Tonight, they'd had a plan, and she'd kept him waiting.

She should be here, beside him, peppering him with questions about his trip while he responded to each one with a wry grin.

She should be here beside him painting a portrait of the wedding with the vivid colors of her words while he soaked up the image with adoring eyes.

She should be here beside him reminding him about texting her when he arrived at LAX, then when he got to the gate, when he boarded, when he landed, when he got through customs, when he arrived where he was staying, and for every morning and night until he was home. And he'd say "of course" and kiss her with each request.

Instead, he was alone. An empty space beside him where she should be. The frustration grew as his ride inched closer.

"Colm!" A tipsy melodic voice called from the backseat window of a white SUV pulling up in front of the townhouse. "Thanks, Roman. You're a doll. Five stars," Evie gushed, jumping out of the vehicle and running to Colm, her arms open and ready for an embrace.

"You're late," Colm grumbled, his arms at his sides as Evie's encircled him.

Three hours late and she was tipsy. Three hours late and he'd worried. Three hours late and now here was his car.

"I'm sorry. I lost track of time. There were so many people I hadn't seen in a long time, and Josephine's parents…" she trailed off, looking down at her feet. The downcast eyes were a trademark of Quiet Evie, who churned with regret and self-flagellation.

"It's fine," he said with a firm line etched on his face.

There was a moment of quiet standoff. Even Evie's

expressive eyes were quiet. *What was she thinking?* His mouth opened but closed again as he saw the impatient gaze of the driver, who stood beside the open trunk, waiting.

"I love you. Goodbye." He placed a quick kiss to her forehead and grabbed his bags.

"I'm sorry I broke the plan," her voice wobbled.

"Me too," he muttered.

Evie's soft features flinched. The same flinch as *that* night.

Standing beside the open backseat door as the driver hoisted his luggage into the trunk, he studied her. Her curls had loosened into mere waves that fell past shoulders exposed by the off-the-shoulder flutter sleeves of her dress. He wanted to sweep those soft strands away and press his lips against her collarbone. He wanted to gently nip at her glossy pink lips, causing that little whimper she'd sometimes make with hard kisses. The thin fabric of her dress hugged every curve, and he wanted to trail his lips down the entirety of her body. Her eyes brimmed with looming tears, and he wanted to run from the car to hold her and whisper it was alright.

It wasn't alright, though. It hadn't been alright for a while.

"You look beautiful." Colm swallowed the lump of everything that roamed the halls of his sad, worried heart.

"Thank you," Evie whispered.

"Goodbye." He sighed and got in the car.

As they drove away, he did not turn around. He did not want to see what he knew was there—Evie crying. The almost-smile cut him, but her tears on the sidewalk as he left would destroy him.

CHAPTER FOUR

In The Hello - Evie
The First Date - Five Years Ago

"That's the one." Leo whistled, his angled face filling the screen of Evie's phone.

"Are you sure? It's not too short, is it?" She twisted in front of the mirrored closet door.

The blue sleeveless sheath dress draped around her curves, the hem falling mid-thigh. The tightness and length of the dress made her feel too va-va-voom. She didn't mind a little sexy-adjacent but attempted to stay clear of sex kitten territory.

"Babes, Josephine helped you pick out the perfect first date dress. Coffeeshop Cutie will want to do dirty things to you in that little dress. I want to do naughty things to you, and I prefer hairy masculine legs," he crooned.

"Best only be *my* hairy masculine legs," Martin shouted from somewhere offscreen.

"Of course, babe," He tilted away from the screen. Martin's were the only legs, lips, and arms Leo craved but he loved to play the precocious flirt. It was all false bravado for a lovestruck Leo.

"There will be no naughty things on a first date," she *tsked*.

"Have you told your mom about Coffeeshop Cutie?"

"HA!" Martin hooted from off screen. "Of course she's told Diane. She's probably calling her after this to get her opinion on the outfit."

"Martin, do you want to join us instead of playing peanut gallery from the kitchen?" Leo snarked, twisting away from the phone with a slight eyeroll before turning back to Evie. "So, what does Diane think?"

"She hopes you and Josephine don't talk me into wearing anything too *sexy-sexy*."

Of course she'd called her mom about Colm. Evie told her almost everything. They talked daily and had an ongoing text thread. Today's thread was dominated by recipes of all the things mom made in her new air fryer over the past week with a sprinkling of questions about Evie's upcoming date. And no doubt tomorrow morning they'd have an in-depth recap, like sportscasters analyzing post-game footage.

"How does she expect to become Grandma Diane if you don't get a little *sexy-sexy*?" Leo quipped, combing his long fingers through his wavy black hair.

"You're a bad influence."

"You say that, but when Coffeeshop Cutie has his tongue down your throat and hand on that tight little ass, you'll thank me."

"As soon as you're off the phone, I can stick my tongue down your throat and grab your tight little ass," Martin purred. He appeared on the screen with a wicked wink of his hazel eyes as he pressed his lips against Leo's temple.

A deep crimson shaded Leo's almond skin.

"On that note, I'm heading out. Thanks for the fashion advice. I'll let you two grab ass! Bye guys." She blew kisses.

"Oh, you are a bad influence. Our little Evie just swore," Martin teased, wrapping his arms around Leo's broad shoulders.

"Bye babes. Text us after the date to let us know you got home safe." Leo air-kissed back.

Twenty minutes later, Evie parked her car. Her navy heels clicked against the sidewalk as she made her way to Mama Gurga's. The Belmont Shore Italian café was a renovated craftsman-style house turned restaurant. Little places like this had popped up more and more in the last few years, offering a cozy feeling with homemade food. It was the type of place where the owner moseyed around asking customers how they liked the meatballs. "It was my grandma's recipe from the old country," they'd boast.

"Hello." A giant grin stretched across Colm's face as he greeted her beneath the red pinstriped awning.

"Hi." There was an honest-to-goodness hitch of her breath.

The muscular frame of his body was clearly visible beneath his pale blue shirt and navy slacks. No man had ever made her belly flip like this. Before Colm there'd only been boys that captured her gaze. But he was *no* boy. The broad shoulders, height, Viking physique, and low timbre of his voice was all man.

Keep it cool, Evie.

"You look beautiful," he murmured.

"Thanks." A heated flush crept up her body. "You look handsome."

His emerald eyes smiled. "Shall we?"

Evie bit her lip and nodded. The palm of his hand rested at the small of her back guiding her into the café. She liked his hand there and wondered if it could be permanently fused in place.

Can I super glue his hand?

The herby aroma of garlic, oregano, and basil greeted them. Delicate light from tiny gold shade lamps and the orangey-purple glow of the setting sun streaming through the windows bathed the room in rom-com-worthy mood lighting. String quartet versions of popular love songs glided around the room as if violinists played beside each red checkered linen-draped table.

"This place is adorable. It's straight out of a 'How to Romance the Ladies' handbook," Evie gushed, taking the chair Colm pulled out for her.

"I hope so. I did thorough research," he said, tugging his short blond hair as he took his seat across from her.

"You did research for our date? What was the criteria for settling on this place?"

Since moving to Long Beach three years ago, most first dates were at the bar down the street from the hospital. Evie never committed to anything beyond a drink for a first date. After most, she'd regret not just staying home in her University of Missouri hoodie binging *The Vicar of Dibley* with Thai food.

The fact that he'd done research reinforced her gut feeling to skip the drinks and proceed directly to dinner. None of her past dates put this level of effort into planning.

"Well…" He snapped his fingers below the table as if each snap unlocked his thoughts. "…It needed to be first-date appropriate. Romantic, but not over-the-top. No hot air balloons or gondolas in the canal. It needed to be quiet, as I don't like loud and wouldn't want to spend the night shouting 'What?' like an old man in a Miracle Ear commercial. It needed good food with lots of options, because I wasn't sure if you had any dietary preferences or restrictions. Finally, it needed a pumpkin dessert."

"Pumpkin dessert? Why?" Evie said, bemused. The thoroughness of his research made her head spin in such a delicious way.

"At the coffee shop you were talking to that older man about all things pumpkin. They have a pumpkin cheesecake here that my friend Jonathan says will change your world."

"Do I want my world changed?" she mused with a wry grin.

She imagined there were hearts floating around her like a Looney Tunes character falling in crush. At that moment Colm went from Coffeeshop Cutie to her crush. He wasn't just a good-looking man that asked for her number and called the next day, but the man that spent the three days since researching the perfect spot to take her.

"I don't like change, but I'm willing to risk it for you." Colm fixed his gaze on her, the green in his eyes as lush as a clover field after a rainstorm.

"You don't like change? Like all change, or just the bad kind?"

"All change."

"Well, change is hard. Even if it's good. Like moving here from Kansas City was a big change. It was good, but it still took adjustment."

"Yeah." He nodded. "The big changes are hard, but it's the little ones that drive me bonkers."

"Like when you have a plan with friends to go to the movies and then at the last minute they say, 'Let's go bowling instead'?" she offered.

"Yes!"

"I totally get it. I have an apple-shaped clock in my kitchen that was my papa's. I've had it since I was thirteen. It hung in my bedroom, then my college dorm, and now my apartment."

Tiny crinkles kissed the edges of his eyes as he smiled at her. "I have the same alarm clock my mom bought me when I was twelve. It sits on my dresser, even though I've used my cell phone for my alarm for the last six years."

"You use your cell? Look at you, embracing change."

"Huh." His forehead creased.

The ping-pong of conversation and stretches of smiling silence filtered throughout dinner. There was the small talk about where they were from. Colm grew up in Orange County. It was just him and his mother after his dad left when he was ten. There was more to that story, but Evie didn't pry. There would be time to pry later, perhaps during their fifth date. She'd decided there'd be a fifth after he placed the last stuffed mushroom from their shared appetizer on her plate.

Evie's parents were divorced as well. This wasn't unusual for millennials. People with intact parents were the greater oddity. As normal as it was, she knew just being like everyone else didn't mean it hurt any less.

She fluttered from different topics sprinkling in a barrage of questions while they ate. Did he like cats or dogs? Dogs. When was his birthday? November 21st. Where was his dream vacation spot? Alaska. What music did he like? Classic Rock. Who was his best friend? Jonathan and his mom. What was his favorite book? *In Cold Blood* by Truman Capote. Was he a vegetarian because he ordered the veggie lasagna? He was. How many siblings did he have? None. Just his mom's cat Prudence, an orange tabby that kneaded her claws into his jeans each time he'd sit on her couch. Three ruined pairs of jeans later, she'd secured his dislike of the feline species.

At times Evie stopped, got quiet, and looked around the room. It was difficult to find a balance. There was a pulsating need to just keep speaking. Don't stop. If you stop, they'll stop. They'll leave.

Colm answered her questions, but there would be long pauses, his face scrunched in consideration before answering. A snapping of his fingers beneath the table was the preamble to each of his responses. Each of her questions seemed to be swirled in his brain like a new glass of wine.

"Am I talking too much?" she fretted.

"No. I like your chatterbox ways," he smirked, reassuring her. "As you know, I'm not a big talker. I tend to be in my head most of the time or so focused on what to say that I can't keep up with the conversation. Yes, you talk a lot and jump from topics like an Olympic hurdler, but you ask a lot of questions. Most people take my quiet or one-word answers as disinterest. You just keep asking. I like that. It makes me feel like you want to know…like you want to know me."

"That was *way* more than a one-word answer." Evie smiled.

"Look what you've already done to me." His tone low and flirtatious.

"I hope I'm a good influence." She batted her eyes, skating the pad of her index finger over the rim of her glass.

"I suspect you are."

OMG! There will be a tenth date. The seductive cocktail of earnestness and flirtation in Colm's voice left her feeling crush tipsy.

"So, what made you want to be a teacher?" she asked, taking a bite of her chicken piccata. There was a little bit of guilt about eating meat in front of him.

"The answer I give most people is summers off."

"What answer do you want to give me?"

"The truth. Always the truth." Those emerald eyes locked to hers. Eye contact with Colm was like a skittish rabbit. When you finally caught it, you'd soak in its silky softness.

"Ok." There was a breathy tremble to her voice.

"As a kid I always felt like I didn't quite fit in. There never seemed to be anyone that got it. Just people telling me all the ways in which I could make myself fit in…how I could be normal. I guess I wanted to be that one adult that listened and understood. Especially for the kids in special ed. There's an extra layer of feeling like not belonging that seems to wrap around them."

"Were you in special ed? Is that why you relate?" Evie flinched as the question ran screaming from her mouth like a prisoner escaping.

Evie! Don't ask someone if they were in special ed!

He chuckled and covered her hand with his, rushing relief through her. "It's alright. It's a logical question. No, I wasn't, but I understand feeling like an outsider. Like you're in this labeled box that gets moved around the room never finding its place."

"I think you've found your place with your students. They're lucky to have you. I would've loved a teacher like you when I was a kid."

"I bet your teachers loved you."

"Well, yes and no. I got a lot of 'needs to learn appropriate times to talk' on my report card. Other than that, I guess I was just a boring regular student."

"I doubt you were ever boring or regular." He smiled, his eyes finding hers again.

The heat deepened on her cheeks. *Yep, there'd be some tongue in that goodnight kiss tonight.*

The pumpkin cheesecake was indeed world-changing. How had she gone her twenty-six years without its creamy cinnamon spice and glazed pecan topping goodness? The facial expressions and moans she made while eating may have been a little illicit. There was an amused slant of Colm's grin as their forks cut through their shared piece.

"I may leave you and go home with this cheesecake," Evie jested, licking her fork. "How have I lived my whole life without this?"

"I was wondering the same thing." Colm's eyes flicked from the almost finished dessert to her, making her heart race.

CHAPTER FIVE

In The Goodbye - Colm
Present - The Morning After The Wedding

The humidity was palpable. Sweat pasted his T-shirt to his back as the taxi bumped down the streets of San Ramón, Costa Rica. The air conditioning wasn't working, of course. Nothing had gone to plan. The flight that was supposed to leave LAX at ten p.m. didn't leave until midnight. The bus from San José was thirty minutes late. Apparently, everything was going to make him wait. Each delay more salt in the wound of waiting for Evie to come home last night.

As the taxi moved past downtown's rows of commercial buildings and an oversized Catholic church, golden rays streaked across a sky almost as blue as Evie's eyes. Colm cringed at the memory of the threatening rainstorm he saw there last night. The eyes that had flinched when he'd said, "Me too."

He should have said something last night, something other than what he had said. Words were always something that stuck in his throat. Sometimes he'd be able to dislodge them, but so often they'd just stay there until they were swallowed—or vomited out.

"Bienvenido Colm," an older woman with grey streaked black hair greeted.

Duffle flung over his right shoulder, Colm lugged his suitcase up the stone steps to the front door of the yellow brick house. Lush green vines with fat-petaled white flowers crisscrossed the house he'd call home for the next two months. While in San Ramón, he'd stay with one of the teachers at the school, Señora Garcia Ramirez, and her family.

"Señora Garcia Ramirez?" Colm asked, reaching the uncovered stone porch.

"Please, call me Sylvia while you're here." A welcoming smile crinkled her eyes as she led him into the house. "This is my husband Antonio, and our youngest Ricardo. Our oldest, Letitia and her husband Miguel will be here this evening for a dinner in your honor."

"Yes, the entire family will be here to welcome you," Antonio said, reaching out his hand to Colm.

"Señor," Ricardo greeted.

The teenager looked like a miniature version of his father with floppy black hair and bushy eyebrows. Only he didn't have Antonio's impressive mustache and beard.

Colm never could grow facial hair. He'd go three days without shaving with no real effect. There was no sexy stubble. Evie was the only one that noticed, teasing him that kissing him was like sandpaper. He'd rub his face all over hers and she'd squeal with laughter.

I guess everything is going to make me think of Evie, even a man's mustache.

"*Mucho gusto. Hablo Espanol*," Colm cleared his throat finally addressing the family in Spanish.

Sylvia smiled, tapping Colm's bicep. "We can speak English. I'm sure after your trip, your brain would want a rest. You'll have plenty of time to speak Spanish."

"Ok." Colm nodded.

"Antonio will show you to your room to unpack and rest a bit. Then we'll have lunch. Does that sound okay?"

"Yes. Thank you."

Colm followed Antonio up a small set of stairs leading to a long hall. At one end was a small guest room with a double bed draped in a mustard yellow blanket. The bathroom was shared and at the other end of the hall. Besides Evie, Colm hadn't shared a bathroom with anyone since living in an apartment off campus with Jonathan their senior year. After a year of catching Jonathan with the current week's love of his life in the shower or on the counter having sex, he found a small studio in downtown Long Beach.

By the time he'd met Evie, he was living in a one-bedroom apartment on a quiet residential street with a balcony that overlooked a small green courtyard. He had a double bed then. In the king-sized bed he now shared with Evie he'd wondered how on earth they'd slept so comfortably in that small bed. Evie pressed into his chest and there she'd remain all night snuggled into him. Her body against his, a perfect fit.

Unpacking his suitcase, Colm stopped, looking up from the bottom drawer to the white vase of pink flowers atop the dresser. It had never made sense to him to buy something that would just die, so he never had. Evie loved flowers and didn't seem to care, though. She'd buy flowers at the market for herself.

That was Evie. If she wanted something, she'd get it. If there was a dopey rom-com she wanted to see, she'd go alone or with a friend. If there was a party she wanted to go to, she'd go by herself. Evie didn't need him to get it or take her, but she wanted him to.

At least, she used to want me. Colm sighed, staring at the mocking flowers.

His phone buzzed from his pocket. It was a message from Evie in response to his message two hours ago after he'd arrived in Costa Rica. It was nine a.m. in Costa Rica so it was only eight a.m. in Long Beach. She'd likely just woken and was slipping on sweatpants and flip-flops to take Queen Elizabeth out before starting her day. He picked up the phone.

My Little Chatterbox: Ok.

Ok? That was not Evie. Even when she was upset with him, there'd be a multiple word response. Evie was not a one-word-answer person, not even on text. She tossed her words about like candy from a parade float. They were a gift for everyone. His eyes willed the little ellipsis to appear indicating there would be more.

Nothing came. Maybe Queen Elizabeth was rushing her out the door to pee. Maybe Evie dropped her phone. Maybe she'd stopped to chat with one of the neighbors as she'd left with Queen Elizabeth.

Maybe it's me?

Shaking away the doubt, he picked up the phone and texted.

Colm: Señora Garcia Ramirez and her family seem very nice. They're going to have a welcome dinner for me tonight. Do you want to video chat tomorrow evening?

My Little Chatterbox: Ok.

OK? He never hated a word so much.

CHAPTER SIX

In The Goodbye- Evie
Present - Two Days Later

Lucy shuffled into the postage stamp-sized office carrying a box of donuts. "My diet is over," she huffed, plopping the pink box onto the credenza in the corner of the Social Work Administration reception area.

"Oh no! But you've been doing so well since you started on that keto diet last Thursday," Evie encouraged her always diet-beleaguered secretary.

Diets weren't something Evie subscribed to, but Lucy was on a new one each week. Mom had been a dietician, so Evie grew up with the balanced diet and exercise routine stamped into her DNA. Even so, she never met a bakery she didn't want to visit. Colm teased her that the only criteria they needed for any vacation spot was, "Is there a bakery?"

Last summer they'd traveled to Vancouver, British Columbia for a week at the end of June. While some couples go wine tasting, they went bakery hopping. Colm researched the four must-go-to bakeries in the city. At each place he ordered their most popular pastry and her favorite cookie, chocolate chip.

They always had good vacations. This summer, though, there wouldn't be a trip together.

Because Colm is helping people. Selfish much?!

Frowning, Evie took a double chocolate donut from the box. "We can split a donut if you like, so it's not a complete fall off the wagon," she offered, holding the donut up to Lucy.

"I'm not falling off the wagon. I'm diving head-first into at least three donuts." Lucy grabbed a bear claw and bit into it. "How's Colm doing in Costa Rica?" she asked as she chewed.

"Good. We video chatted last night. The family he's staying with seem nice." Evie took a bite to avoid another quick question from Lucy.

Last night's video chat was like strangers on a stuck elevator. The conversation was laced with small talk, punctuated with long pauses of silence and stilted discussion. They weren't them. They hadn't been for a while.

"Good morning, Ms. Johnson," Dr. Keeney said, stopping Evie in the hall as she walked back from the department meeting.

Wyatt—or Dr. Kurtzman as she called him at the hospital—stood beside their chief of staff, whose bad toupee sat askew atop his head. Evie fiddled with her butterfly necklace debating about which was less polite—to point out someone was wearing a toupee, or to not let them know it was a little crooked?

Dr. Keeney gestured to Wyatt. "Ms. Johnson, I believe you met Dr. Kurtzman during Dr. Peterson's wedding over the weekend."

"Yes, Dr. Kurtzman, nice to see you again." Evie shook his hand and a micro-jolt of something pulsed through her. Taking her hand away, she discreetly brushed it against her maroon pencil skirt as if trying to cleanse her hand of whatever that was.

"Lovely to see you again Evie. Please, call me Wyatt." There was a strange mix of bashful confidence in his eyes.

"I was just giving Dr. Kurtzman a tour. He starts officially with us as our deputy chief of internal medicine next week," Dr. Keeney explained, looking at his phone with furrowed brows. "Blast, they need me in the OR."

"That's alright Keeney, I can just wander about on my own," Wyatt assured.

"I can finish your tour. I have some time now; it wouldn't be a problem. I can show Wyatt all the hidden corners for naps," Evie suggested with a giggle.

"Ha!" Dr. Keeney dropped his phone into his lab coat pocket. "Thank you, Ms. Johnson. We can always count on you to help out. Wyatt you're in excellent hands."

As Dr. Keeney moved down the hall, Wyatt bent close to Evie's ear, his minty breath almost a whispered kiss against her skin. "Do you think someone will tell him his toupee is lopsided?"

"Oh, my goodness!" This was the first time she'd truly laughed since Colm left. "I'm so torn between telling him or not."

"I can't imagine he doesn't know."

"I've sometimes wondered if it's his own personal social experiment to see what people will do. You know, like that John Quiñones show *What Would You Do?*" she laughed.

Evie wouldn't lie to herself that Wyatt wasn't attractive.

The closely cropped dark hair, ashen eyes, and well-defined form hugged by his black suit was straight out of central casting for sexy doctor on a medical drama, but she didn't have wandering eyes. Her eyes were only for Colm. Even if right now they were dry from the excessive tears she'd shed since Saturday and narrowed in frustration with the extra stiff responses he'd given during their video chat last night.

Still, she could appreciate Wyatt's good looks and open personality. They'd gotten along famously at the wedding. He melded with their little group like he'd always belonged. He'd understood all the inside jokes cultivated over years of working together. In fact, several new ones had sprung up during the wedding that he was now part of.

"Come, let me buy you a coffee in the cafeteria and you can show me those nap spots for my future all-nighters." Wyatt's lips tugged up.

"Make it a latte at the coffee cart near the giftshop and you have a deal."

"See? You're already a better tour guide than Keeney." He winked.

Evie twirled a long dark lock that hung loose past her shoulders. "And my hair is real, too."

Wyatt's eyes sparked and seemed to focus on her fingers. Cheeks flaming from the heat of his gaze, she dropped the hair and let her hand fall to her side.

"Lead the way Evie, and I'll follow," he said, gesturing to the elevator at the end of the hall.

For a moment she hesitated. The way his eyes lit when he looked at her flashed a warning sign of danger. Perhaps she should excuse herself, maybe there could be a meeting she'd forgotten about? Fumbling with her necklace, she considered her choices. Listen to those warning bells or be rude?

"Follow me," she said, leading them toward the elevator.

CHAPTER SEVEN

In The Hello - Colm
His First Mistake - Five Years Ago

"You didn't kiss her? What the actual fuck man?" Jonathan gaped, beer bottle halfway to his mouth as he and Colm sat on his couch.

"It was…I don't know." Colm pushed the jumbled words back down with a swig of his beer.

The date with Evie had been perfect. There were so many times he wanted to kiss her. When she skipped up to him in front of Mama Gurga's in that short dress that somehow danced a perfect tango of seductive sweetness. When she chatted with their server Bastian about his name being the character from one of her favorite childhood movies, *The Never Ending Story*. When she sang the words along with the instrumental version of "To Make You Feel my Love" while they shared stuffed mushrooms. When she cut the last nibble of cheesecake in half, that he'd pushed over to her, insisting "Splitzies!"

There were so many times he'd wanted to kiss her, but

none so much as when they'd stood in front of her car. He'd kept his hands in his pockets, not trusting them to not touch her if they were free. There was a soft Santa Ana breeze pushing a piece of her hair across her cheeks. His fingers itched to sweep that strand behind her ear.

How he wanted to be a man of words. Even more so, a man of action. He'd wanted to move two steps forward and eliminate the space between them, his hands on her waist pulling her close. His lips covering hers slowly sipping up her kisses. Evie had lips that should be savored like an eight-course meal, each kiss more decadent than the last. But he didn't do any of that.

"Fuckhat! You shook her hand? It was a date, not a job interview," Jonathan said, aghast.

He buried his face in his hands. "I don't know. I just kept thinking what if she didn't have a good time? What if I kissed her wrong? What if she didn't want to be kissed? When should I kiss her? How should I kiss her?" He leaned his head back, trying not to think of how many girls Jonathan had kissed with zero hesitation on this very couch.

"You are too much in your head. If a woman doesn't want to be kissed, she'll tell you. Or just ask if you can kiss her, and if she says yes, do it. If she says no, and you don't want another gal pal in your life, then pay the check and tell her it was nice knowing her." Jonathan tipped his beer towards Colm like a laser pointer he'd use in one of his freshman lectures.

"Easy for you to say."

Jonathan nudged Colm's knee, pulling his attention to him. "Hey buddy. If you like Evie, then you need to rectify this kiss situation pronto or else you'll be relegated to the Friend Zone watching other men slip her some tongue."

Colm punched him in the arm. "Shut up."

"Dude." Jonathan winced, rubbing his bicep. "You can

punch me, but I'm not the one that screwed the pooch here, you are."

"You're right," he sighed in defeat, putting his beer down.

"Of course, I'm right. I always am," Jonathan said magnanimously. "If you want my opinion—and you do, because this is just one of the many areas that I am an expert in—when you pick her up for date number two, plant one on her as soon as she opens the door. Then, if it's bad, or she didn't want to be kissed, you'll save fifty dollars on dinner and can come drink beer with me instead."

God, he knew this. He'd had girlfriends in the past. Evie wouldn't be the first woman he kissed. Why was he so fucking nervous? But something told him the first kiss with Evie would be like that pumpkin cheesecake...world changing.

CHAPTER EIGHT

In The Goodbye - Evie
Present - Seven Days After The Wedding

Evie inhaled a steadying breath as her phone rang. It was Colm for their scheduled weekly video chat. They'd chosen Saturday nights because it would be like their own virtual date night. Their last video call, the check-in on Monday night, had been awkward. She wanted to make it different, to somehow shake the stank of whatever had been souring the once sweet aroma of their relationship.

That's what she kept telling herself as she got ready for the call. If this was their date night, then she'd treat it as such. Showered, moisturized, lips painted in shiny red lipstick, and hair blown out, she slipped into the low-cut red dress she'd bought four years ago for their first anniversary getaway to Santa Barbara. Cleavage-heavy dresses weren't her go-to, but Josephine talked her into it, saying the girls needed to come out to play.

That night, Colm pressed her up against the wall of their hotel room, lathering her exposed collarbone and cleavage with hot kisses. He inched up her skirt and slid her panties down. Falling to his knees, he looked up at her as if she was a goddess stepped fresh off Mount Olympus. With his strong hands he rested her legs on his shoulders pressing her tight to the wall as he worshiped at the altar of her core until she cried out his name with climax.

The memory heated Evie's blood as she answered the call. "Evening, sailor."

"Evening," he said a little unsure, one eyebrow cocked at her sultry tone.

"Fancy meeting you here," she purred, her fingers flirting with the edge of the satin fabric, calling attention to the thin border between dress and breast. It felt a little Jessica Rabbit, but maybe they needed that.

"Did you have a good week?" Colm said, clearing his throat.

"Yep…you?" she asked seductively, sliding her finger up her chest to her collarbone in a slow swipe knowing it was one of his favorite places to kiss.

"Good," he replied.

Evie bit her lip. Maybe she'd need to be less subtle.

"Sooo…." She batted her eyes, "…this is date night. If I was there with you, what would you want to do?"

"I don't know…there's a good bakery downtown. You'd like it, but it's already closed. There're nice places to hike. Maybe that, but again it's late. I don't know. I haven't really thought about it."

Evie's fingers ceased their movement, dropping to her lap. An embarrassed pink replaced the heated blush on her cheeks, and disappointment threatened to swallow her. Twisting on the bed where she sat, she scooped up her University of Missouri sweatshirt and pulled it on over her dress.

"Cold?" Colm asked.

"Yes. It's cold in here." A firm line tightened on her face.

"Is the AC acting up again? I can email the landlord."

"No. It's fine." She blew out a long breath. "So, tell me about the school."

If he wasn't thinking about her, then she'd pelt him with questions. Maybe if he thought about her questions, he'd think about her.

CHAPTER NINE

In The Hello - Colm
The First Second Chance – Five Years Ago

I t was ten minutes before he was supposed to pick Evie up. Colm sat in his car debating whether to go up early or wait. He didn't want to appear too eager, but he was. He didn't want her to feel rushed, even though he was in a hurry to see her. He didn't want to shorten her time to get ready, even though he knew she was already perfect.

"Fuck it," he said, pulling his keys out of the ignition and jumping out of his Prius.

There'd be no more waiting. It was time to fix this before he was banished to the shadowlands of the Friend Zone. All week he'd dreamed of Evie's lips against his while she made the same sexy moans that escaped when she ate that pumpkin cheesecake.

Colm took the stairs to her apartment two at a time. A tad winded by the anxious excitement surging through him, he knocked. "May I kiss you?" he blurted as the door swung open.

Evie blinked at him; her mouth open in mid-greeting.

His heart sank to his feet. He'd waited too long. It was over. *I am a fuckhat.*

Evie's face erupted in a giant smile. "Yes."

"Yes?"

"YES!"

Oh god, did her smile get bigger? He stepped closer and brushed a wayward dark lock behind her ear. God, she was so soft. This must be what blankets felt like in heaven. Leaning in, his breath pressed a promised kiss as he said, "I'm going to kiss you now."

"Ok."

Those two letters were his new favorite word. Colm captured her silken smile in a slow kiss.

Evie's hands reached up to encircle his neck, their lips moved together like a couple holding hands strolling along the seashore. This is how Evie should be kissed. Not a crashing together like in rom-coms with feverish make out sessions, but savoring sips of her heart-shaped mouth.

A throaty "Mumm" slipped from her as he teased her mouth open allowing their tongues to find each other in a languid first dance.

"Wow," Evie said breathlessly.

His fingers weaved into her long hair. That hair was as silky as he'd imagined. Now that he'd kissed and touched Evie, he knew he'd never want to stop.

"A good wow or…"

"Very good," she interrupted. "Like that was *The Notebook* of kisses."

"*The Notebook?*"

"It's only the most romantic movie of all time. If you Netflix and chill with *The Notebook* you are guaranteed the chill"—she made air quotes with her fingers—"portion commencing by the kissing in the rain scene."

"Are you saying my kissing makes you want to *chill?*" Colm's lips lifted with devilish daring.

All of Jonathan's swagger pulsed through him. Looking at the crimson invading Evie's complexion and listening to the little hitch in her breath transformed him to Alexander the Great. Instead of ancient city states, he captured Evie's heart.

"I'm going to ignore that you just totally asked me if I wanted to have sex on our second date, because that kiss was epic. Like, I'll tell my grandchildren about it someday."

"*Our* grandchildren." The words broke away from that lump in his throat where they usually hid.

"Our grandchildren," she repeated.

Fuck Alexander the Great, he was Colm the Magnificent. Never had he felt so sure of himself as he did in front of Evie, her blue eyes a little starry, gazing back at him.

"Should we head out?"

He bent and placed a lingering kiss, tasting her sweetness one more time. "*Now* we can head out."

It was a beautiful Saturday afternoon as Colm pulled onto the Cal State Long Beach campus. But today he wouldn't remember the beautiful weather. The blue he'd remember would be Evie's adoring eyes as she looked at him from the passenger seat where she sang along to the radio. The sunshine he'd remember would be the brilliance of her smile as she lit up when a favorite song played. It had already been a perfect date and they hadn't done anything besides kiss at her door and ride in his car.

"I've never been to the Japanese Garden before. I've heard

about it, but I thought it was only for students and faculty at the college."

"Nope. You'd be surprised how few students take advantage of it. I used to go there to read when I was a student here," he explained, parking the car.

"Oh, Co-ed Colm being all studious at the Japanese Garden. Hmmm…" She tapped her finger on her chin in consideration. "I wonder if you were a sit-on-a-bench, lounge-under-a-tree, or perch-on-a-rock reader."

"Do you want me to tell you?"

"No…yes…no."

He laughed at the contorting of her face as she tried to decide until her smile blasted him with ah-ha.

"I have an idea! Let me guess. While we're walking, I'll figure out the spot that screams Colm."

"Ok. Hold on," he said, popping out of the car and running to her side to open her door.

"Ready?" He smiled, holding his hand out.

"Yes." Evie's fingers threaded with his.

This date would be perfect. Maybe not for some women, but for the one who he hoped to soon call "His Evie." During their first date she gushed about how much she loved flowers and plants. Her small balcony and apartment were filled with fresh cut flowers purchased at the market and potted plants.

"Colm," she whisper-squealed.

A large koi pond outlined by lush bushes of pink roses and cherry blossom trees in bloom swaying in the warm breeze greeted them.

"This place is so beautiful."

What he wanted to say was 'not as beautiful as you', but instead he said, "This is just the entrance."

As they wandered the pebbled gravel path looping through the garden, Evie would bend to inhale flowery scents deeply or read aloud the small plaques explaining the different plant species. A quarter of the way into the garden she plopped on a small patch of grass beneath shady branches of a large tree tapping her chin thoughtfully before jumping up and proclaiming, "Nope, not this one."

"What are you doing?"

"Trying to figure out your reading spot, remember?" She took his hand, pulling him along. "I also need to figure out what I'll claim for my prize if…*when* I win."

"Prize?"

"There always needs to be a prize. When I was a kid, I used to play board games with my papa. He'd give me prizes for winning. Good prizes, like Snickers."

"Did you spend a lot of time with him as a kid?" he asked, as she dragged them up a small hill towards a large boulder surrounded by giant palm leaf plants overlooking the garden.

Evie released his hand, surveying the rock before climbing onto it. "Yeah. My parents separated for the first time when I was six, so we moved in with papa 'til my parents got back together three months later. Then when dad left for the second time, this time for good, we lived with papa 'til I was thirteen."

"Why just 'til thirteen?" He held Evie's waist while she shifted and settled herself on top of the stone.

"He died." There was a tiny crack in her cheerful tone.

"You were close to him." It was a question but came out like a statement.

"Yeah."

Colm climbed onto the boulder, settling beside her. "Tell me about him."

"You mentioned wanting to become a teacher to give your students someone that understood them. Someone that got them." Her fingers grasped at her necklace holding it as if for strength. "When I was younger, papa was that for me. He was the one person that never said, 'Be quiet, Evie.' Instead, he would say, 'What do you think, Evie?' He'd sit for hours listening to me ramble. With him I never felt like I had to be anybody but me. I could say anything, and he'd still love me."

"Did he give you that necklace?"

Evie held tight to the butterfly pendant like she was holding her kind papa's hand. "For my thirteenth birthday. It was the last thing he gave me. He said that it represented the woman I was becoming, that just like the caterpillar I'd emerge from the cocoon of awkward adolescence like a beautiful butterfly. It was so cheesy, but that was papa. When I'd tell him he was a cheeseball he'd joke, 'But I'm a gouda papa,'" she made a sad laugh.

Colm's fingers tangled with Evie's. "He was right. You are beautiful in so many ways."

Their gazes interlocked as they sat there, their eyes saying all the words not spoken. Colm's telling Evie that she was that butterfly, gifting the world with her beauty and fluttering from lonely flower to lonely flower, kissing them softly with her presence. In Evie's eyes, he thought he saw gratitude for listening and something else that he couldn't quite interpret. He was still learning the language of her eyes. One day, he wanted to be fluent.

"Are you close to your grandparents?" she asked.

"Not particularly. I mainly see them on the holidays. They live in Riverside. They're not Snickers-prize grandparents. They're my mom's parents. My father's parents died before I was born."

Evie's smile eclipsed, but not with pity, with regret. As if she mourned Colm's grandparents not knowing him.

"How about your mom?" Her thumb danced along his skin.

"She's good. We're close. I have dinner with her once a week and we talk every few days. She's in Fullerton."

"It was just you and her after your dad left?"

"Yeah. We lived in a two-bed apartment near downtown. Mom still lives in the same apartment. She works at Cal State Fullerton as a librarian. When I was a kid, she worked there and part time at a bookstore. I spent a lot of time at the library or bookstore after school and on school breaks."

A gleeful expression etched on Evie's face. "Oh, my word! Is your bedroom the exact same? Like a museum with your high school posters and a stuffed bunny rabbit from when you were a tiny little Colm on the bed? How much is admission? Do I get a discount?"

"No, it's not a museum" he laughed.

Evie studied him intently. "Ok, but I bet you had a stuffed bunny? No wait, a teddy bear…no…stuffed dog. You had a stuffed dog with floppy ears, and I bet your mom still has it in your old room?"

"His name is Flopsy. I've had him forever. He sits on a bookshelf in my old room, that's now the guest room. Some of my old books from high school and some framed photos of me as a kid are on the same shelf."

"What books?" Evie asked, the warm breeze making a single brunette strand waltz in the wind.

Smiling, Colm brushed the runaway piece of hair back, remembering he no longer needed to fight those urges, the new knowledge intoxicating in its freedom. He could kiss Evie. He could touch her. He could tell her about the stuffed dog that he would still duck in to look at each time he visited his mom. As if it were an old friend and he was just popping in to say hello.

"Books on countries, animals, and science. I especially like books about different parts of the world. Places I'd like to travel or just places I want to learn about. I still read a lot of travel books."

"No R.L. Stine or C.S. Lewis?"

"Nah." Colm shook his head. "I'm more a nonfiction reader. I don't really like make-believe. I can't enjoy something that doesn't seem real. You?"

"Oh, I love make-believe. Give me all the 'Once Upon a Times' and 'Happily Ever Afters'!" Those blue eyes sparked with mirth.

"So, no real world stuff for you?"

"At the hospital we get a lot of real world. Almost too much sadness sometimes, so it's nice to fill my free time with the happy. With stories that don't end with someone arrested, someone dying, or someone being taken away," she said, her gaze sweeping across the garden.

"Yeah." His tone was sober. "I should have thought about that. Our school social worker only gets called if there's an issue. I'd imagine it's the same way at the hospital."

Evie sighed. "It is, and I'm not complaining. I knew what I was signing up for. It's why I became a social worker. People think social workers are the huggers of the hospital. They think that's all we do, but when the doctor leaves the room after examining an abused child, telling someone their loved one died, or discharging someone without a place to live, I'm the one that walks into the room to help pick up the pieces. To hear the stories. To dry the tears. To solve the problems."

"I think the stronger person is the one that stays in the room," he said, lifting their threaded fingers to his lips and pressing an appreciative kiss.

"This is it, isn't it?"

Colm knew she was asking if this was the spot that he'd sit to read while a student, but for him that question spoke of so much more.

"It is," he paused, his eyes joining Evie's to take in the

garden covered in leafy green plants with vibrant pink, red, yellow, and white roses.

"I knew it! As soon as I saw this boulder. It's the perfect Colm spot. You can see everything, but it's far enough away to be your own little quiet corner of the world. Your part of things, but undisturbed."

"Yup." It was such a small response for such a big thing.

This is what Jonathan and his mom didn't get. There was a desperation to be part of things…to belong. However, something always tripped him up each time. Himself. Here, he could still feel a part of things. If he didn't belong to the world he could still feel as if he played some role. Even if it meant just being its observer from afar.

"I know what I want for my prize," Evie announced, her big smile returning.

"A Snickers?"

"Nope…*this*." She leaned in, her mouth finding his.

Pulling her close, his hands splayed on the small of her back as he deepened their kiss. A pleading whimper slipped from Evie while his tongue twisted with hers.

"Wow," She panted, their faces inches apart. "I take it back, *that's The Notebook* of kisses."

"Well, I have to give you lots of stories for the grand-kids," he murmured, moving his hand to twirl a tendril of her hair around his finger.

"Our grandkids," she winked.

"Our grandkids." If this was *her* prize, why did he feel like he was the one winning?

CHAPTER TEN

In The Goodbye - Evie
Present - Ten Days After The Wedding

Evie's eyes bounced between the text thread with Colm and his Instagram. His feed was littered with photos of the sunrise from the backyard of the Garcia Ramirez's home, a beautiful white brick church in downtown San Ramón, and the outside of the school he was working at. The difference between the communication directly between them versus all that Colm shared with the world of Instagram was stark.

An uneasiness swam in Evie's belly as she scrolled through weeks of *Be home late*s, *Should I pick up takeout*s, *Need anything at the store*s, and *OK*s messaged between them. There was a time that their thread was consumed by funny thoughts, interesting things they'd seen or heard, flirty emojis, *Miss you*s and *Love you*s. Digging back as far as thirty days ago, there wasn't a single *I love you,* or even a quick *Love ya* message. At what point had they stop texting it? At what point had their texting gone from true communication to the mere logistical coordination of their lives?

Sighing, Evie placed her phone down on the cafeteria table. She didn't want to look at it. Although not looking at it didn't steal away the knowledge that something had shifted.

Picking up her phone she typed *What's your favorite pastry from the bakery in San Ramón?* Then she deleted it.

Evie closed her eyes and put her phone down. Was she really about to ask Colm a food question in an effort to save their relationship? The thought was sobering. Did their relationship need saving? This was all too much to think about in the middle of the bustle of the crowded hospital cafeteria over a wilted chicken fajita salad.

"May I join you?"

"Wyatt, hey." Evie looked up, then around to the sparse seating options.

Most of the big tables were filled, but the seat across from her at the small two-person table tucked against the floor to ceiling windows overlooking the courtyard was free. The only thing occupying the space was her phone, sitting on the table in front of the empty chair, mocking her.

Scooping the phone up, she nodded. "Sure."

Wyatt slipped into the chair plopping his tray of sushi on the table. "Thanks."

"Cafeteria sushi? You're a brave man," she teasingly warned.

"Well, I figured I work in a hospital so it may be worth the risk."

"You know there is an *amazing* sushi place down the street. Their California roll is so yummy. Josephine, Leo, and I try to go there at least once a month for lunch."

His lips quirked. "I'm aware. It's in the *Guide to Long Beach* you emailed me after the tour."

Evie flushed with embarrassment. "Oh yeah. Sorry. I may have been a little overzealous. When I moved here eight years ago, I had no idea what was good or where to go for anything. I would have loved a guidebook, so I created one. It may be a little overkill, though."

He waved her concern away with his hands. "Nah, it was sweet. This is the third city I've lived in since medical school, and I would have loved something like this. I mean it's thorough. You have it indexed in a PDF document. Impressive. I tried one of your recommendations for best French toast on Sunday."

"Oh, Crema Café?"

"Delicious!"

"So, three cities? Where have you been?" she asked, sipping her iced tea.

"Medical school was in L.A. Then I did my residency in Chicago. The last few years I've been working at General in San Francisco," he explained.

"I know you were at UCLA with Josephine, but did you grow up in Los Angeles?"

"Nope. I grow up in San Diego. My family is still down there. That's part of why I took this position. Home is a short two-hour drive. Close enough to visit on weekends and do holidays, but far enough where my mom won't show up unannounced every day. Although…" he paused, face scrunched, "…I wouldn't be shocked if she did."

"Are you close with your family?" Evie shifted in the chair, crossing and uncrossing her legs.

"Yeah. It's mom, dad, and my younger brother Michael, who lives twenty minutes from them. He's an optometrist like my mom."

"Wow, a whole family of doctors." Her lips curved into an impressed smile.

"Nah. Dad is an accountant. He and mom are retired

now. Michael took over her practice two years ago. Now that I'm living here, I'll be able to go down a few times a month for family dinners. Mom is using her retirement to go through the hundreds of cookbooks we've bought her for gifts over the years," he chuckled.

A tightness formed in her throat as Wyatt spoke and a jitteriness nipped at her nerves.

"Have you tried the happy hour places on my list?" Her question was abrupt, but the compulsion to switch the topic overpowered her good manners.

His forehead crinkled. "Umm…yes…well no. I noticed the happy hour section in your guidebook but haven't gone yet."

"Oh, you should get on that. The happy hour scene in Long Beach is epic. I mean I only have Kansas City and Columbia, Missouri to compare it to, but it's good. Wait— that's not true. I've done happy hour in Fullerton with Colm when we've gone to see his mom. Still, Long Beach is epic," she sputtered.

"Colm's the boyfriend, right?"

"Yes." She grabbed her plastic fork and poked at her salad.

"The one in Costa Rica for sixty days?"

Evie was surprised he remembered that level of detail from the wedding reception. When they'd sat at the table, she'd mentioned Colm a few times.

Ok, it may have been more than a few times. During dinner she'd mentioned that she ordered the vegetarian meal out of habit, because Colm was vegetarian and often finished what she didn't eat. When Martin was drinking beer instead of joining the rest of the table with champagne, she laughed that if Colm was there, he'd be drinking beer too. As the cake was served, she mentioned that Colm would never eat his piece, but would take it home for her to have a second piece later. So yeah, there had been a lot of Colm factoids shared.

"How's he doing in Costa Rica?"

"Good. He's been enjoying jogging in the hills above the city each morning before heading to the school," she replied with a firm smile, thinking of Colm's social media.

Thank goodness he posted there or else the only thing she'd know about his time in Costa Rica was that it was *fine* and *ok*. Despite her questions, there hadn't been a lot of details, nor any questions about how she was doing besides the standard *hope you had a good day*. That wasn't even a question. It was like how she'd come home from work and he'd say, "Did you have a good day?" It was a question, but not one that wanted an answer beyond yes or no. If she'd answered no, it may have forced him into further questions, but Evie always answered yes. A smile and a yes was how she faced the world.

"You must miss him. How are you doing?"

She blinked. "Yes, I miss him…But this is such a good thing he's doing. I'm so proud of him. Colm has such a big heart. Almost too big sometimes. He's doing such good work there."

"From everything you said at the wedding, he seems like a great guy."

"He is," she said, her tone a little defensive.

"Agreed. He's with you, so he must be pretty special."

Goosebumps bloomed along Evie's arms with the heat of his words and stare.

"Back to my question, how are you doing? I know you're proud, but it still must be tough to be separated, even for a good reason."

"I miss him, but it's fine. Only fifty more days," she said through a forced smile.

"Ok," he paused, seeming to examine her before continuing. "How about this happy hour? Should we get the gang from the wedding together next week? I'd be down to check out the place where you can make s'mores. Alcohol and open flames—sounds terribly fun and dangerous. Perfect for healthcare workers."

"How much of my guidebook have you read?" Evie laughed.

CHAPTER ELEVEN

In The Goodbye - Colm
Present - Two Days Later

The distant aroma of cinnamon and sugar danced with the thick humid air as Colm and Antonio strolled towards Dulce Vida, the small bakery downtown. It had become part of his daily routine in San Ramón.

Colm woke at five a.m. each morning to jog or hike. By the time he returned, Sylvia had a spread of fresh fruit and gallo pinto on the table. After breakfast, he'd shower and dress. Then they'd head to the school until two-thirty p.m. Back at the house, he'd rinse off and change, then walk to the bakery with Antonio to pick up a few mid-afternoon pastries. Tension eased through him with each activity checked off the to-do list stored on his phone.

"Sylvia says you are a huge help at the school," Antonio said, breaking the companionable silence while they walked.

Colm was enjoying getting to know Antonio. He and Sylvia were about five or six years younger than his mom. Sylvia was a colleague but there was something maternal in her interactions with Colm and the other staff, even the ones her age. Everyone went to her for advice or encouraging words. And Antonio had the matching fatherly vibe. With his warm mustached smile, Colm could picture Antonio calling young men *son*, though he'd not yet experienced that. Both Sylvia and Antonio were like the steadfast parents in early nineties' sitcoms. He half-expected music to play any time they'd talk or give advice.

The parental vibe was foreign to Colm. Mom was…well, mom. She was kind, loving, and warm, but she wasn't the stoic maternal figure bestowing advice with homemade cookies. And dad…was the man that left.

"I'm happy to be of service," Colm said, wiping his brow.

"I've noticed. Ricardo says you've been helping him with his English. Teaching him the American slang words. Thank you for that."

"Of course."

Most nights, Colm spent watching TV with Ricardo. A lot of the shows they'd watch were Spanish-dubbed American shows. Some of the jokes translated well, others didn't. Colm would explain them to Ricardo.

It made him smile a bit, reminding him of translating things for Evie. If someone spoke Spanish in a movie or TV show, she'd turn to him instead of reading the subtitles. She did it so much that if he knew there'd be a potential for Spanish speaking, he'd pull her in extra close to whisper the translation in her ear and watch that smile of hers pop. That is, until about three months ago. The last time they were watching a movie where Spanish was spoken, Colm opened his mouth to translate and Evie shrugged, saying she could read the subtitles herself.

They reached the door of the bakery, and the sugary sweet scent triggered memories of bakeries past. Colm hadn't spent a lot of time in bakeries until Evie. If there was one vice she had—besides her predilection for bad reality TV—it was baked goods.

"Sylvia has such a sweet tooth," Antonio said, taking the bag of pastries from the cashier. "Does your Evie?"

Colm nodded looking around the bakery at the assortment of cookies, sweet breads, and tiny pastries that he didn't know the name of. *Evie would know.*

"Evie loves a bakery."

"They say sweethearts have sweet tooths," Antonio chuckled, leading Colm outside.

"Evie has the sweetest heart." The words came so quick that he wasn't sure he had said them aloud until Antonio's hand rested on his shoulder.

It was a paternal gesture. Something Colm had never felt. Even before dad left, he wasn't paternal. The most prevalent memory of dad was of his back as he left time and time again.

"Evie sounds very special. You've mentioned her a bunch."

"I have?" He rubbed the back of his head.

"Yes. When you saw the garden in the backyard you talked about her potted plants and how much she'd love our little garden. When you and Ricardo were watching a movie the other night you said you had seen it with Evie. Just little things here and there. You sprinkle her in like someone would toss salt onto food to add some flavor."

"She's a big part of my life."

"Colm, the women we love aren't part of our life—they *are* our life," Antonio corrected, his lips quirked up in a warm smile. "I knew that when Sylvia had Ricardo. We almost lost her in labor. The idea of losing her…" His words halted; his face twisted with pain. "…it was too much. I knew I had my children to worry about, but if I had lost her,

I'd only have half a heart. I would be half a man without her."

There was a stinging pang in Colm's chest as the image of this man in a plastic hospital chair, his face buried in praying hands, flooded his imagination. The zip of the closing and opening of privacy curtains loud, the vision vivid. Colm walked silently beside Antonio, whose face washed in relief with each forward step as if remembering Sylvia was there with him. That he hadn't lost her that day.

"I'm sorry you almost lost her."

"Nothing to be sorry for. I kept my Sylvia. I kept my whole heart." He patted Colm's back as they walked down the winding street towards the house.

"Thank you for sharing that with me." His voice quiet.

"You're welcome, my friend. I tell you not to make you sad, but as one man in love with his sweetheart to another. Cherish her because there may be a day she is gone. I never knew that until I almost lost Sylvia. Therefore, I go to the bakery daily. So much of what I do is done to show and tell her how much I love her."

"You're a good man," Colm said, thinking of all the ways he'd seen Antonio cherish the people he loved since arriving. How he'd save the last piece of mango each morning for Ricardo, knowing it was his son's favorite. How he had a special bottle of wine for his daughter Letitia and her husband at dinner. How he'd kiss Sylvia's cheek when he got up from the table to grab more coffee—and kiss it again as he sat back down.

"What an honored compliment coming from such a good man like you."

Colm just shrugged at Antonio's words. *Was he a good man?* There had been so few models of that in his life. Dad was *not* a good man. Grandfather Bill was more ornery than good. His mom's brothers, Daniel, Jack, and Bill Jr. were okay guys, but none he would call good men.

Colm wanted to be a good man but feared that he wasn't. That he was like his father.

The look in Evie's eyes when he left for the airport seemed to signal that his fear may be valid.

CHAPTER TWELVE

In The Hello - Evie
Four Years and Eleven Months Ago – The First Meatloaf

"So, what time will Colm be there?" Evie's mom asked, her blue eyes twinkling with giddiness on the phone screen.

"Seven." Heated pink invaded Evie's cheeks.

It had been a month since they'd met. After their second date at the Japanese Garden, they'd seen each other twice a week, texted daily, and spoke on the phone at least three times a week. Things had accelerated, yet still maintained an appropriate trajectory. Tonight would be the first night they'd stay in for a date.

"Evie, he's going to love it. This is so sweet of you to make him vegetarian meatloaf. Colm must be a very special boy."

"He's not a boy, he's a man," she guffawed, pushing the pan into the oven before turning the timer on.

"Oooohhhh, a *man*," Mom made a high-pitched squeal.

"Mom!" she laughed, covering her face with a corgi-shaped oven mitt.

There was something about talking to mom about boys —*men*—that made her feel like she was in high school again, sitting on the couch with a bowl of popcorn between them and a Sandra Bullock movie on.

"So, is tonight *the* night?"

"Mom!"

As much as she talked to her mom, there were still lines that shouldn't be crossed. Sex was a *giant* no-fly zone.

"Don't play coy young lady. You're twenty-six. I'm aware you're sexually active. Do you think tonight is the night? And if so, are you prepared? Never depend on the man to bring protection. That's how your Aunt Linda ended up with your cousin Jeffery."

Evie untied her cartoon corgi apron and hung it on the hook in the kitchen. "I'm not sure if tonight is the night, but yes, I'm prepared."

In the month of dating, there had been lots of kisses and two hot PG-13 makeout sessions. The latest one in his car Tuesday night after their mini-golf date. What started as a slow kiss ended up with Evie straddling him in the driver's seat, his hands cupping her behind over her jeans. Feeling his enthusiasm beneath her and her own temperature rising, she almost invited him up. But moments before she could open her mouth, he'd placed his head against hers, sighing and saying they should stop.

Colm had been a perfect gentleman, minus the butt grabbing. She didn't mind the butt grabbing, though. *More butt grabbing, please.* His hands never wandered beneath skirts or blouses. While she appreciated it, there was a quiet tension building in her to feel his fingers and mouth roam over her body. Twice in the last two weeks after getting off the phone with him, his deep, low voice still lingering in her ears, she pretended her fingers trailing down her body to that sensitive button were his. This she did *not* share with mom.

"Good girl." Mom snapped her fingers, looking proud, like Evie had gotten a promotion or saved puppies from a burning building, not bought condoms to maybe have sex. "Now, should I refer to him as your boyfriend, or is he still the boy—excuse me, *man*—you are seeing?"

"We haven't discussed labels yet. So, I guess he's still the man I am seeing but I know he's not seeing anyone else nor am I. I'd like him to be my boyfriend, though."

"Well, slip into his DMs or send one of those 'In a Relationship' requests on Facebook," Mom suggested with a huff of laughter.

"Mom, slipping into someone's DMs doesn't mean what you think it means."

"Either way, take him out for a test drive tonight and then have the talk." Mom combed her manicured fingers through her short dark hair.

"For a *test* drive?!"

"Sweetheart don't be obtuse. You've been salivating over this boy-next-door version of Thor, God of Thunder, for weeks."

"There's been no salivating," she scoffed with mild indignation.

"Baby girl, I believe you referred to him as 'yummy with a spoon.' Just jump in. You're too cautious sometimes."

"Hey, I approached *him* at the coffee shop, remember? Would someone too cautious do that?" she protested.

"True. That was a big step for you. You tend to wait for the boy—*man*—to approach you. I know things with your dad and papa…"

"Mom," Evie interrupted, her voice pleading. The last thing she wanted to do was unbandage old wounds an hour before a date.

An apologetic smile washed over Mom's face. "Sorry honey. We won't go there, but I know you like him a lot. I'm hopeful when Terrance and I fly in over the holidays that I get to meet this young man of yours."

"Me too, Mom." Evie glanced at the apple clock in the kitchen.

"I'll let you go finish getting ready," Mom said, almost reading her mind, which was racing with all that still needed to be done before he arrived. "I love you, honey."

"I love you, Mom. Tell Terrance I said hello."

At six-fifty p.m. on the dot Evie stood in a pink tea length A-line dress, her dark hair in fat curls hanging loose. A delicate sexy confidence washed over her in the outfit as if channeling her inner Audrey Hepburn or some other equally fabulous fashion icon from the late fifties and early sixties. A lot of her dresses had a vintage nod. The styles were flattering to her figure and a little whimsical. There was something fun about a skirt that you could twirl in. No matter how old she got, she hoped she'd never lose the desire to twirl in a pretty dress.

At large smile bloomed on her face with the knock at the door. He was ten minutes early, just as she knew he would be. Over the last four weeks, she'd sketched who Colm was. He was always early, just as she was. At restaurants he preferred a quiet table tucked in the corner. When they walked, he'd always be on the street side, to be a human wall between her and potential danger. He'd order one beer and nurse it throughout dinner, never having more than one. When he was thinking he'd often snap his fingers three to four times before speaking. After the Japanese Garden he always held her hand when they walked, pulling their inter-twined fingers to his lips when she said something he liked, which was a lot.

"Hello," she greeted, beaming.

"Hi." Colm grinned with boyish charm, his eyes meeting hers. He didn't always look at her when he spoke, but when he did she could read volumes in his eyes. "I brought you these."

Colm handed her a bag with *Pietris* printed in black script on the front. It was one of her favorite Greek bakeries in Belmont Shore. They'd gone there two Sundays ago for brunch.

"Thanks." Evie opened the bag and pulled out two plastic containers. "Is this pumpkin mousse?" She squeaked with glee.

"I figured since you were cooking, I could bring dessert."

"Very sweet." She raised to her tiptoes to give him a thank-you kiss.

Yep, I'm going to have sex with him tonight. It was decided. All it took was some pumpkin mousse.

"Is this vegetarian meatloaf?" He asked, his eyes wide as Evie placed the platter of Teriyaki-glazed veggie loaf on the table.

"Yep. There's mashed sweet potatoes with candied pecans. I put a little Cayenne pepper in it so there's a sweet and spicy balance. There are green beans, boring but yummy, plus they're good for you. Oh, and homemade biscuits. They're my mom's recipe. Let me grab them from the oven. I kept them in there to stay warm." She bounced, skipping back to the kitchen.

"This is all homemade? You did this for me?" Colm awed as Evie returned with the plate of buttery biscuits and added them to the rainbow of flavorful food on the table.

"Yes." She raised her hands. "Wait." Evie trotted towards

the fridge, returning with two cold bottles, placing one in front of Colm. "Oktoberfest for you, and Pumpkin Cider for me," she announced, placing the second bottle in front of her plate before sitting down.

He rose and walked over to her chair, dipping to capture her bottom lip in a savoring kiss. Each one slow, gentle, and exploring, as if he were drinking an expensive wine, luxuriating in each taste of her. These kisses were addicting, something she could get drunk from.

"Thank you," he said, his hands caressing her now rosy cheeks.

"It wasn't any trouble."

"That's just one of the things that I like about you." His fingers skimmed across her lips as his eyes studied her. "Things that are a big deal for others to do is just how you operate. It's like how you bought drinks for that old man and me the day we met. And how three times in the last two weeks you've baked cupcakes for someone's birthday at the hospital. How you text me encouraging messages during the day. You're authentically sweet and don't realize how special that makes you."

A lightheadedness set in. This may be the longest extended eye contact with him in the last four weeks. She wanted to melt into it, sinking into the sensation of admiration that sparked in his eyes as he drank her in.

"We should eat before it gets cold," she whispered, her heart racing.

"Ok." Colm's fingers danced over her cheeks before he returned to his seat.

The dinner was a success. Evie wanted to fist bump herself. They'd chatted about Jonathan's newest girlfriend, whom Colm would meet at lunch tomorrow. Colm and Evie hadn't done the "meet the friends" thing yet. Evie reserved that for a boyfriend, but since moving to Long Beach there'd been no boyfriends, so nobody to introduce. Colm mainly spoke of Jonathan and his mother, and Evie had not met either of them yet.

"This is great. I can't remember my last home cooked meal," he said, biting into a second piece of veggie loaf.

"I thought you did dinner with your mom weekly. She doesn't cook?" Evie asked, sipping her cider.

"Mom was never a cook. Not like this. We did a lot of takeout and premade foods growing up. When we meet now, it's generally at this diner down the street from her place that we've gone to since I was a kid or ordering pizza at the house."

"It's funny, when I was a kid, I would've loved that. Mom insisted on cooking everything. Pizza night was even home-made. It's how I learned to cook."

"Homemade pizza?"

"With dough from scratch," Evie bragged, lightly waggling her brows.

"Perhaps the next dinner date," He grinned. "I think we can agree that all cooking dates will be your purview, unless you want some killer boxed mac and cheese."

"Never underestimate some good boxed mac and cheese. When I was little, Papa would make it with cut up hotdogs for lunch. Mom would get so annoyed, saying there was no nutritional value, but it was the best. I loved when mom was gone on a Saturday, or there was no school, because he'd make it for me. He was retired, so even when we didn't live with him, he'd watch me if my parents were gone."

"If you don't mind veggie hot dogs, I can make you boxed mac and cheese with hot dogs for our next date. I can't promise the same caliber of a meal, but I'd like to make that for you…if that's okay," he offered.

"I'd like that. A lot." A fluttering warmth spread from her belly. Papa would have liked Colm.

"When I was little, my dad and I had a secret meal like that. When he was around and had to make dinner because mom was working, he'd make grilled cheese and Spaghetti O's. Same thing, he'd say 'Tell your mom I made you eat broccoli.' As much takeout and premade meals as we had, mom always made sure they were healthy with lots of vegetables."

"Do you ever see your dad?" She winced, wishing she could wrangle the words back in like escaped pigs from a pen.

He leaned back, exhaling and looking above her head. "No. When I was ten, he left. He was in the kitchen drinking coffee when I left for school in the morning, and when I came home…he was gone. I never saw him again."

"No phone calls? No birthday cards? No visits?" Outrage dripped from each question.

"Nothing. He was just gone."

"I'm sorry," she murmured.

"It wasn't your fault." His tone was flat, but his eyes reassuring as they turned to her.

"I know. I'm sorry I asked. I shouldn't pry like that. I was just curious and…" she trailed off, her eyes falling to her plate of half-eaten food.

"I like that you ask me things. Most people don't. Please don't ever apologize for asking and please don't ever stop asking me questions."

"Ok." She blushed. "I haven't seen my dad in eight years. He was in and out of my life since my parents divorced. There'd be the occasional Saturday lunch or school concert he'd attend. The last time I saw him was the day after my high school graduation. He came by the house with a box of chocolates to apologize for missing the ceremony."

"He *what*?" Colm's eyes flared.

"He said he got the dates mixed up. I believed him and

accepted his apology. We drove from Westin to Kansas City to go to Jack's Stack, my favorite BBQ place. We ordered too much food and laughed the entire time. Dad had this way of making me forget about the missed dates and forgotten birthdays when we were together. Like I was just his little girl and I felt special. It was a good day."

"That was eight years ago. Was that the last time you saw him?"

"Yes," she sighed. "We made plans to drive to Columbia, where I'd be going to undergrad, the following weekend. Dad wanted to see the campus. He never showed. He called two weeks later saying he had forgotten. There were random calls and emails promising get-togethers that never happened. He texts from time to time. He still thinks I live in Kansas City, despite me telling him I moved."

Like a passing ray of sunshine, for a moment Evie would feel special basking in her dad's attention, but in the shade of his abandonment, the sense of being "not special" chilled her.

"Ugh," Evie cringed. "I shouldn't have just emotionally vomited all over you like that. You told me about your dad and now here I am blathering about mine like this is the Terrible Father Olympics. Sorry."

"I like it when you blather," Colm smirked.

"Well, thank goodness for that because I am a champion chatterbox," she laughed. "Our dads stink, but our moms are amazing. We're lucky compared to a lot of people. Your mom sounds wonderful."

"She thinks *you* sound wonderful."

"Colm Gallagher, have you told your mom about me?" she teased, placing her hand on her heart.

"Yes…and I assume you've told your mom about me." His right brow arched.

"She's hoping to meet you when she and her boyfriend come to visit over the holidays."

"That could be arranged—*if* you're open to having dinner with me and my mom next Sunday."

"That could be arranged." The Cheshire cat had nothing on the smile painted on Evie's face. They hadn't had the talk yet, but all of this reeked of boyfriend/girlfriend territory.

Adele streamed from Evie's phone as she scooped leftovers into Tupperware while Colm rinsed and loaded dishes into the dishwasher.

Clearly his mama raised him right. *Who said good men needed fathers?* Despite Colm's terrible example of how to be a man, he'd grown up to be the best. True it had only been a month, but Evie knew it in her bones. This was a good man.

The dishwasher hummed as Evie wiped the counter, the last Tupperware stacked in the fridge. A contented smile on her face.

Colm's arms wrapped around her middle. "Thank you for dinner," he whispered.

The heat of his breath ignited goosebumps across her body. She spun, looping her arms around the nape of his neck and giving him the sultriest stare she could muster. It was time to channel her inner Jessica Rabbit and take this from PG-13 to NC-17.

"You're welcome," she purred, raising to press her lips against his.

With a slow lick she ran her tongue along the seam of his mouth until he opened with a groan. Colm's hands tightened at her waist, and he pressed hard against her as their tongues tangled and liquid desire pooled between her legs. He lifted her onto the counter and his hands moved down the cotton fabric of her dress to the hem.

He pulled out of their kiss, his fingers grazing her bare legs beneath her skirt as if dipping a toe into water before venturing deeper. "Is this okay?" he asked.

Evie could barely breathe. "Yes."

With permission granted, his hands slid up her thighs as he nipped at her collarbone. She leaned back giving him greater access and moaning with pleasure as his fingers moved to her inner thighs.

"Bedroom." It was supposed to be a question, but her sultry voice commanded.

He growled, hoisting her into his arms and she wrapped around him like a horny koala, laughing as he carried her to her room and placed her on the bed.

Colm proceeded as if he had a map of where and how to touch her. "Evie, please tell me if you like—or don't like—what I'm doing. Tell me what you want."

She liked everything and wanted more. A need pulsed in her core, not just from his kisses and touch, but because of the way his focus was on her…only her.

"You want me to talk during sex?"

"Yes. I like my little chatterbox and I want to make her happy." He raised her skirt, his fingers grazing the satin of her underwear. "You like when I touch you here?"

"Yes."

"How about here?" His finger slipped beneath her underwear, gliding along her slick center.

"Colm…" she begged, her body greedy and wanting more.

He moved off, and with a wicked glint in his eyes, stood at the edge of the bed and dragged her hips toward the edge. She giggled as he yanked her panties off, bending her legs and holding them up while he lowered himself to the floor between them.

His hot breath caressed her nakedness. Her pelvic muscles convulsed with anticipation as he kissed her inner thighs, teasing what was to come. She bit her lower lip, fighting to keep her hungry hips from pressing against his mouth.

"Please…" she whined.

In response to her plea, Colm licked down her center, finding that bundle of nerves and rolling it with his slick tongue. Waves of pleasure crashed with each lick and suck. First gently, then more vigorously. Chasing her climax, she ground her core against his mouth. Her fingers tugged at his hair, and he sucked harder, slipping a finger inside her, tipping her to release. Evie cried out and her thighs seized Colm's head as she shook with orgasm.

"Oh my goodness," she finally said, trying to catch her breath.

"Did you just say *Oh my goodness*?" Colm chuckled.

The combination of this man's face looking up at her from between her legs with a question mark of a smile and pure self-congratulation in his eyes was too adorable. Evie couldn't help but grin.

"Yes, I did," she smirked. "Now, take your pants off so I can make *you* say oh my goodness!"

Sex kitten Evie was coming out to play and kitty had claws to dig into Colm's back as he fucked her. Even thinking the word *fucked* rang brazen for Evie, but she wanted to be brazen.

"I can't. I don't have a condom. I didn't plan on this tonight. I'm enjoying taking care of you though. We could just do that." Earnest eyes looked up at her as his fingers danced along her bare legs.

A big grin spread on her face. "I have condoms." she slipped off the bed and walked to the bedstand.

Opening the drawer, she pulled out two unopened boxes, one regular-sized and one magnum. Something told her with his Viking-like build the magnums would be needed, but she didn't want to assume and embarrass him, so she got both.

"Did you just buy these?" Colm asked, studying the sealed box of magnums.

"I wanted to be prepared."

"Evie Johnson, did you plan to seduce me with vegetarian meatloaf?"

"Maybe," she purred, her fingers running down the smooth fabric of his green polo shirt.

"Do you want to disrobe yourself or shall I?"

With a bat of her eyes, Evie shimmied out of her dress. Her bra joined it on the floor. She had no idea where her panties had been flung to.

Naked, she stood in front of him, allowing his eyes to drink in every curve. That needy sensation between her thighs resurfaced as she watched him lick his lips, his eyes shaded dark with desire.

Colm placed the box of condoms on the bedstand and pulled off his shirt, revealing the sculpted physique that Evie suspected hid under his unassuming-nice-guy uniform. Unbuckling his belt, he unbuttoned his jeans and pushed them off. The evidence of his arousal bulged from his blue boxer briefs.

Evie gulped. Her eyes locked on the bulge.

Definitely the magnums.

"We'll go slow. I know it's…"

For once Evie was speechless.

She suspected it was big when feeling his growing excitement during their more intense make-out sessions. But suspicion was one thing, the truth standing at attention in front of her was quite another.

Colm cleared his throat, "We don't have to. I'm okay with just fooling around, holding you, or we can put our clothes back on and go eat pumpkin mousse and watch a movie. Whatever you want."

"What do you want?" she asked, shifting on her feet.

"I want to make you happy."

The earnest raw emotion in his voice blended with his

naked vulnerability melting any apprehension in Evie. It wasn't a ploy to pretend to be the nice guy. He really was the genuine article.

"I want to do this."

He nodded, pulling her close and kissing her, his hands glided down her curves and sliding between her legs. With languid circular strokes, his fingers caressed her throbbing clit.

The scorching heat of his mouth moved between each breast covering her taut nipples in a mixture of delicious rough sucks, playful nips, and soothing tongue caresses. His fingers and mouth moved with deft focus and her body trembled and arched in response until a tingle spread from her center through her limbs as she came again.

"You're going to ruin me for other men," Evie whimpered as the aftershocks of pleasure subsided.

"That's my plan."

He stepped back, grabbing the box of condoms. Evie sat on the edge of the bed watching him unwrap and roll on the condom.

"I think you should be on top," he said climbing onto the bed, his fingers skating across Evie's bare shoulders. "If that's okay. I don't trust myself to not get too excited and I don't want to hurt you." The gentleness in his touch countered the ravenousness in his eyes.

"Lie back." Evie pushed him down, the low, sexy quality of her voice almost unrecognizable to her own ears as she straddled him.

Colm groaned, his eyes lifted to the ceiling as she lowered herself onto him, slowly at first, then sinking further. "You feel so…good." His hands on her hips guided her in a slow rocking motion.

Delicious tension tightened between her legs with each deepening pump. His breath ragged. Uncontrolled hunger flashed in his eyes. As if a goddess gazing down on adoring eyes she watched the God of Thunder look-a-like fall apart beneath her.

His fingers bit into her hips, coaxing her faster, their thrusts colliding in a mutual chase of pleasure. A string of unintelligible swear words and praises flew out of his mouth.

"Oh dear," she cried out as he slipped his fingers between them and stroked her just where she needed it.

"Come for me, baby," he commanded with a growl.

The pressure coiled tighter and tighter until…

"Colm…" she gasped and threw her head back, drowning a wave after wave of satisfaction.

He joined her with a grunted "Fuck, Evie."

Their naked, sweaty limbs intertwined in a sated snuggle as they came down from their mutual bliss. It had been very good sex—the best sex she'd ever had. Colm's sweat-kissed face shined with satisfaction.

"I'm going to use the restroom," he said.

Evie sat up and watched him walk away. She pulled her legs to her chin, listening to the muffled sound of the water running.

He returned holding a wet washcloth in one hand and a dry towel in the other. "Lay back," he murmured.

With an unsure nod, she did as she was told, and he used the warm wet cloth to clean her with gentle passes across her lower belly and inner thighs.

"This is sweet. I don't think anyone has ever cleaned me up after sex."

"I'm full service." A self-impressed smirk lit his features as he threaded his fingers into her sex-rumpled locks.

"You are." Her cheeks heated.

Why was she blushing? She was naked. The man had been inside her. He'd tasted her. After it all he wiped away the proof of what he'd done to her. In what world should she be bashful with this man?

"Can I sleep here tonight?" he asked.

"Yes." Evie grinned.

"I love that." His fingers traced the outline of her smile. "You smile with your whole face. It's like an explosion of happiness."

"You make me happy."

"I hope I always do."

"Do you want to eat pumpkin mousse and then cuddle?"

"On one condition. Tomorrow, you join me for lunch with Jonathan."

"To meet his new girlfriend and him?" Evie's head cocked to the right.

"Well, if I'm meeting his new girlfriend, I want him to meet mine." He winked.

"Girlfriend?"

"I should probably ask properly." Colm tucked Evie into his chest. "Evie Johnson, will you be my girlfriend?"

She sighed, pretending to consider her response with a tap of her chin. "I guess."

"You guess?" He tickled her until she admitted defeat.

"Ok! Truce," she giggled. "I'm your girlfriend."

"My little chatterbox," he said, kissing her.

CHAPTER THIRTEEN

In The Goodbye - Colm
Present - Thirteen Days After The Wedding

Colm folded himself onto the child-sized chair while students giggled and chattered over their art projects. He sat a few feet away from the group because his knees were too big to fit beneath the table. That's why he'd chosen to teach seventh and eighth graders. He fit in that furniture.

While at El Pequeño Corazón, he'd spend the afternoons in Sylvia's classroom. Most of the morning was spent with Miguel Rivera Pabon, the school administrator, and Sarah Clark, a fellow special ed teacher from San Francisco. He and Sarah worked with Miguel developing classroom curriculum and special education training for teachers. The last hour of the day, he'd sneak into Sylvia's class full of six- and seven-year-olds, soaking up some classroom time.

"Everyone, please, join me on the rug," Sylvia announced in Spanish, clapping her hands.

The students were drawing pictures inspired by the book

read during story time. Each student would need to present their picture aloud to the class.

"Who wants to share first?" Sylvia asked the class with a warm smile.

Several hands shot up in excitement, while others hid behind their construction paper. Sylvia pointed to a little girl with black curly hair, who popped up from the rug and skipped to the front.

If only I had her confidence. His belly fluttered at the memories of such assignments when he was a kid. The only way he'd get through them was the script clutched in his hand the entire time. As long as he stuck to the script it would all be okay.

"Queso," Sarah chirped, holding up her phone to take a picture.

He glowered. Sarah, his personal paparazzi, loved snapping candids of him. She thought it was *hilarious.*

Sarah laughed, holding up the picture of his stiff body scrunched into the chair. "Classic. I'm going to post this with the caption *Gigantor.*"

"Very funny," he grumbled, rising to stand beside her.

"Oh, don't worry. I'll tag you in it," Sarah said, tapping on her cell.

"Thanks."

"I do so love your sunshine and rainbows personality," she quipped.

"Clearly, as you harass me daily."

"What can I say, I enjoy grumpy people. It's like hanging with Oscar the Grouch."

"I'm not grumpy."

"Oh, you've been extra grumpy this week. What? Are we missing the girlfriend?" she teased, elongating the word girlfriend.

"Nope. Just annoyed with these photo shoots you spring

on me. Can you find a new subject to harass?" He rolled his eyes, but there was a warm smile.

The photos catching him in embarrassing positions aside, she'd been nice to talk to during his trip. Outside of Sylvia, Antonio, and Ricardo, Sarah was the only friend he'd made since arriving. They'd checked out a few restaurants in town, some hiking trails outside the city, and were planning a trip to some coffee plantations next week.

"Nope?" She gaped, her hand on her heart in mock dismay. "Best not tell the girlfriend you don't miss her."

"I miss her." Colm scowled.

"You just said you didn't."

"No, I didn't."

"I'm going to stand here fighting the urge to take a picture of the moment your expression changes from defensive to dismayed realization as you replay our verbal exchange."

Colm stood quiet, knowing that he was indeed doing just what Sarah had said. He had said no, but he didn't mean it. There were few moments since arriving in San Ramón that didn't make him think of Evie. How could you miss someone if they seemed to haunt every thought? Even sitting there watching the children's art projects conjured Evie. The sky colored in blue marker made him think of her eyes. The rainbow butterfly with uneven wings drawn on white construction paper made him think of her necklace. The cheerful chattering of working children made him think of Evie's sputtering as she did something.

But those were only thoughts. Memories of Evie. She wasn't here. His only connection to her from afar was the phone in his pocket, full of one-word or single sentence text message responses or those awkward video chats. There was part of him that wanted to blame the adjustment of being apart.

It's not the physical distance. Colm sighed, knowing that the distance between who they'd been and who they were had been there even when he'd sat inches away from Evie on the couch.

"Hey." Sarah nudged her shoulder against his. "I wasn't trying to make you feel bad. I know you miss your girlfriend. You've mentioned her enough to show me you miss her."

"I do miss her," he whispered.

"Want to hit up El Gato Azul for drinks tonight? I'm a good listener," she offered.

"I'm not a big drinker."

"You're also not a big talker."

He narrowed his eyes at her.

With a cheeky smile she patted his cheeks. "It's totally fine. You don't have to talk or drink. I can drink beer while you scowl or play wingman helping me find someone to flirt with."

"You just want me to go to help translate with potential hookups."

"Perhaps." Sarah clucked her tongue. "While you have someone stoking the home fires, I am as single as a lost sock just looking for my match."

"Are you the left or right sock?"

Sarah waved her hands down her body. "Naturally the left. So, we need to find me *my* Mr. Right sock. As a Mr. Right sock in a committed relationship you're morally obligated to aid my search for either lasting love or just a summer wham-bam-thank-you-sir romance whose memory will keep me warm in the long, lonely San Fran winters."

"It's a wonder you're still single."

"Ha!" she barked. "It's a wonder you're *not.*"

"That it is," he sighed.

"The girlfriend must be really special to put up with

you." She hip checked him as they strolled out of the classroom.

"She is." The words barely a whisper. Maybe what'd changed wasn't them, but maybe she finally realized he wasn't her Mr. Right sock.

CHAPTER FOURTEEN

In The Goodbye - Evie
Present - The Next Day

I'm carrying Queen Elizabeth's poop in a bag. That thought never got old as Evie scooped up the corgi's mess from the grass. Cleaning up after a dog was always humbling, but even more so when it was Queen Elizabeth. Just like her namesake, the caramel-patched white corgi had an air of regal refinement. The haughty glint in the corgi's dark eyes was why Evie easily settled on naming her for the British monarch. Colm had wanted to call her Angela.

"Angela?" Evie scoffed.

"I don't know. She looks like an Angela," Colm shrugged.

"Let's ask her," Evie suggested, looking down at the puppy wearing her red bow.

"Okay. How does Angela sound to you, girl?" Colm asked.

The corgi opened her mouth in a dramatic yawn as if on cue.

"Queen Elizabeth," Evie cooed.

The corgi scampered over to Evie excitedly, begging to be held. She scooped her into her arms, smiling victoriously.

"Queen Elizabeth it is," he sighed with resignation, leaning close to scratch the puppy's ears, earning him a wet lick on his face. "I've just been tongue kissed by Queen Elizabeth."

The memory warmed Evie, but at the same time left her chilled. The poop bag tossed into the waste bin, she walked towards the townhouse with Queen Elizabeth in tow. Tonight was date night, and she was determined to make it better than last week.

This time she'd nix the sex kitten outfit and not attempt phone sex. What had she been thinking? Colm wasn't a phone sex type of guy. She wasn't a phone sex type of girl. They weren't even into sexting. The steamiest their texts got were Evie messaging that she wanted to *smooch* him.

Instead, she would do what she did best: question and talk. Try to draw him out. Being in a different country had to be tough for a man who needed time to process the seasonal changes at their favorite local coffeeshop, let alone a whole new culture. The last thing he needed was a needy girl-friend having a hissy fit. She had realized that during last night's happy hour.

Josephine had returned from her honeymoon, so Evie coordinated a combo welcome to town and welcome home happy hour for both Wyatt and her at Fire Ball, a bar down-town featuring several fire pits on their outdoor patio where customers could make s'mores.

"I don't think I've roasted a marshmallow since I was in Boy Scouts," Wyatt laughed, lifting up his roasting stick with a blazing marshmallow.

"Clearly," Josephine deadpanned, arching a blonde eyebrow.

"Of course, you were a Boy Scout," Martin scoffed.

"I hope you're better with patients than marshmallows," Leo muttered as Wyatt blew out the flames.

"Oh, leave poor Wyatt alone," Evie scolded with a smile, handing Wyatt a fresh one. "Here, maybe not so close to the fire this time. If you hold it above and turn it slowly it will get perfectly golden."

"Thanks." Wyatt's eyes met hers.

A charge tingled through her at the eye contact and she quickly averted her gaze.

"What a Girl Scout you are!" Josephine elbowed Evie. "I bet you had a s'more badge."

"Do they have those?" Mandala asked, biting into one of the Evie-made s'mores piled on a metal tray balanced on the edge of the stone firepit. "If they do, Evie gets them all! Delectable."

Martin crunched into one of the s'mores, and the marshmallow and chocolate goo oozed out of the sides. "Agreed! Worth what it will do to my abs."

"You have abs?" Josephine jested.

Martin frowned, but Leo patted his squishy middle and gave him an appreciative kiss.

"You just have to be patient," Evie explained.

"I'm not very good at that. I tend to rush things," Wyatt said, mimicking Evie's motion with the roasting stick.

"Our little Evie is nothing but patient," Martin praised.

"She does tolerate you," Josephine snarked with a grin.

"Speaking of tolerating things, how's Colm doing in Costa Rica? That must be hard, to be away for so long," Mandala asked, finishing the last sips of her cocktail.

"Good," Evie said, noticing Wyatt shoot her a suspicious look.

He'd been doing that the last few days, when Colm's name came up or someone asked Evie how she was doing and she said fine. Evie shifted foot-to-foot, moving her stare back to Mandala.

"I can't believe he deserted you on his summer break." Josephine huffed, picking up her now-empty martini glass and frowning in annoyance as if saying "How dare you be empty."

"He didn't dessert Evie, he is helping children," Leo defended.

"Well…"

"Looks like most of you are out of drinks. Let me go get everyone another round." Evie offered, cutting Josephine off before she finished. It was totally an excuse to slip away from the questions about Colm, Josephine's accusation, and the looks Wyatt was throwing her way.

"I'll help," Wyatt said, handing the metal roasting stick to Leo.

"Such a Boy Scout." Leo's forehead puckered.

As she turned, Wyatt's palm rested on her lower back guiding her through the crowded patio towards the bar inside. She should pull away from his touch. Leo and Martin would sometimes do this with Evie when they were in crowded places. It was a protective gesture from a friend, but with Wyatt it was different. When he stopped to hold the door for her, she sped up leaving him trailing behind.

"Evie!" Jonathan's deep voice stopped her mid-step.

"Jonathan?" She turned.

Jonathan stood at a high-top with a woman with caramel hair and a figure Evie would kill for—tiny waist, long legs, and ample curves. Every few weeks there'd be a new lady in Jonathan's life. He wasn't a player in the traditional sense of the word, but definitely a serial dater. Jonathan never dated more than one woman at a time, but there were a lot in consecutive order.

"How are you?" He stepped towards her, giving her a hug. "I just messaged Colm. How funny to run into you!"

"You know Long Beach, it's a small city."

"Yep. Oh, this is my friend, Willa Sanchez," he said nodding to the woman at his table. "Willa, this is my friend Colm's girlfriend, Evie."

"Nice to meet you." Willa smiled and reached out her hand.

"You, too."

"And who's this?" Jonathan tipped his beer towards Wyatt.

"Who?" She turned to look at Wyatt, realizing she'd totally forgotten about him. "This is Wyatt Kurtzman. He's a new doctor at the hospital. We're here with a bunch of people from work, welcoming Josephine and Mandala back from their honeymoon and Wyatt to Long Beach. He just moved here from San Fran. This is his first Long Beach happy hour," Evie sputtered, tugging at her necklace.

Jonathan's questioning gaze shifted between Evie and Wyatt.

"Oh, the LBC has a tight happy hour scene," Willa cheered.

"I'm gathering." Wyatt flashed a charming grin. "Evie provided me a personal 'Welcome to Long Beach' guidebook. There's at least three pages out of the twenty dedicated to happy hour." He chuckled.

"Yes queen! I love that. I may need to see this. My besties and I do brunch almost weekly." Willa snapped her fingers.

"Yeah." Wyatt placed his hand on Evie's shoulder. "It's thorough. Evie's been so sweet and helpful."

"Yup. That's *our* Evie." Jonathan narrowed his hazel eyes at Wyatt.

"Oh wait. I'm putting it together now. Evie, your

boyfriend is the one building the school in Costa Rica, right?" Willa's eyes grew wide.

"He's working with a school down there. It's already built."

"I may have been a little unclear on the details," Jonathan said, running his fingers through his sandy hair.

"Building or helping, that's really great. He sounds like a sweetheart of a man. Although it sounds like you're a sweetheart too." Willa tipped her drink in salute to Evie.

Ugh. Colm deserves so much better. Her fingers clung to her butterfly pendant. While he's thousands of miles away in a new country with different customs and language helping children, she was at a bar with McDreamy's palm on her lower back.

Jonathan bent close whispering, "I've only texted Colm a few times, but I know he misses you."

"Did he say that?" She glanced at Wyatt and Willa, who were chattering about different brunch spots.

"No, but I know he does."

"Ok." She shrugged.

Jonathan studied her. "Just because he doesn't say it, doesn't mean he doesn't feel it. You know Colm better than anyone. So much is trapped inside him just waiting for his little chatterbox to pull it out with her mad verbal skills."

Evie sighed at Jonathan's use of Colm's endearment for her. Colm had a lot of sweet and silly things he affectionately called Evie—baby, sweet girl, chit-chat monster, and lovely girl. The most frequently used one was chatterbox. Always said lovingly sweet and with admiration.

"It's an adjustment to be down there for him. You know how much he loves any change. He'll never say it, but he needs you." Jonathan cleared his throat.

Evie left happy hour resolved to be there for Colm. Jonathan's comments were a wake-up call. Sulking from afar did nothing for Colm, nor her. She would have to swallow her mixture of hurt, self-doubt, and frustration. She'd be Colm's little chatterbox peppering him with questions to pull out the words trapped in his throat as she pushed down all the worries that roamed inside her.

Letting the memory of last night fade, she sat on the couch, her iPad in hand, waiting for Colm to call. As she waited, she scrolled through his social media posts since Wednesday. His feed dominated by pictures tagged from someone named @SClarkSF83.

There were several pictures of Colm in child-sized furniture. One with a grimace, cheeks smudged with glitter. One of him teeter-tottering with five children on the other side anchoring him down. There were a few with a stunning woman with flawless skin, a mane of lush black curls, breathtaking smile, and eyes like pools of milk chocolate.

It was @SClarkSF83. Sarah Clark. They were smiling in several selfies at different restaurants and hiking trails.

"Who are you, Sarah?" Evie asked aloud.

Queen Elizabeth's head popped up as if warning Evie not to do it, but the temptation was too great. Evie fell into the rabbit hole of Sarah's social media.

Bad idea, Evie. She exhaled a sharp breath, swiping through Sarah's Instagram.

Sarah, a teacher like Colm, was his age and from the Bay Area. When she wasn't volunteering with the Wounded Warriors Foundation or at the Ronald McDonald House, she was spending her school breaks traveling around the world, working with schools and organizations.

She's perfect! A throbbing ache slithered into Evie's belly and she clicked out of Instagram. Eyes shut, she breathed in for one and out for two, repeating until the video chat notification rang.

"Hello," Colm said, his face filling the iPad.

"Hi." Her tone clipped.

The images of Colm taken by and with Sarah pushed slivers of anger into her, even though there was nothing to worry about. Colm was loyal as a golden retriever. He would never stray.

"Did you have a good week?" He asked.

"Yeah." She blew out a long breath. "You?"

"Yup."

There was an extra-long silence as they sat staring at each other.

Nope. This wasn't what Evie wanted at all. Why was she letting this Sarah trip her up? The plan was to pepper him with questions. Use her natural chatterbox skills to get them talking and past this weirdness.

Inhaling a steadying breath, she recalibrated. "So, I saw on social media you've been hitting some spots around town. Where have you been going?"

"Oh, a few spots. They're tagged on Instagram."

"I saw you went hiking. Where'd you go?" Evie pushed on, gripping the side of her yoga pants.

"It was on Instagram," Colm offered.

"Umm…" Evie closed her eyes reminding herself to not be *that* girlfriend. "…I've seen postings with Sarah. She looks fun. What things have you been doing with her?"

"It's all posted on social media."

"Well, maybe I should just do date night with your social media, then." The words were out of her mouth before her brain could stop them.

"Excuse me?" Colm asked, a slight twinge of incredulity in his voice.

Evie winced. "I'm sorry. I didn't mean that. I'm sorry. I'm just tired. I apologize."

"I saw you were out late last night at the bar with your friends," he said, his forehead creased with slight annoyance.

"I wasn't out *that* late." Evie gripped her necklace.

There was another long pause. Colm's eyes moved around as they sat in the thick silence, the quiet surrounding them like a scratchy blanket.

"Jonathan said he saw you there with some guy named Waylon?"

"Wyatt," she corrected with a huff of breath. "He's not *some* guy. He's a new doctor at the hospital and friends with Josephine from medical school. It was a happy hour welcoming him to Long Beach and welcoming Josephine and Mandala back from their honeymoon."

"Looked like you had fun." His tone wobbled between soft and annoyed.

"It was." Her's stern.

"Good." His flat.

There was more silence punctuated by avoided eye contact. This was not going to plan at all.

Queen Elizabeth shuffled over and sniffed at the lavender lotion on Evie's legs. She scooped the corgi up in a last ditch effort to fix what she feared she'd already broken.

Cradling Queen Elizabeth in her lap like a baby she sweetened her tone, oozing in as much honey as she could as she spoke. "Look who's joined us. Say hello to daddy, Queen Elizabeth."

"Hello, Queen Elizabeth." There was a small smile.

"She got a bath this week because someone got flour all over her when mommy was baking," Evie cooed through a fake smile.

"I saw the picture of the cupcakes on Instagram."

"Oh, I hadn't realized you saw it. You didn't comment or like the post," she said, settling Queen Elizabeth beside her on the couch.

"I always look at them."

"You never comment or mention."

He just shrugged in response.

There were endless back and forth comments between Colm and Sarah below each picture on Instagram. This Sarah that was a friend he'd met two weeks ago appeared more the girlfriend than Evie. At least to the two hundred and fifty followers of Colm Gallagher.

I'm losing him. Evie's eyes dropped close as that stinging truth settled.

"You seem tired," Colm said breaking the long stretch of silence.

"Yeah." She *was* tired. *So tired.*

"Why don't we call this a night, and you get some sleep, baby," Colm suggested.

"Ok."

"Goodnight."

"Ok."

"I love you."

"Ok." Evie hung up.

CHAPTER FIFTEEN

In The Hello - Colm
Four Years and Nine Months Ago - The First Birthday

"Thirty-one is just another year. It's not even a milestone birthday," Colm muttered, buttoning his shirt.

"It is *a* big deal, my baby man," Mom protested, her sing-song voice hummed from the cell phone on the dresser.

Colm rolled his eyes.

"I'm glad Evie is taking you out tonight. I'm sorry I have to worky poo," she said.

"It's okay mom. It's not a big deal."

"My baby man, all birthdays are a big deal."

"Mom, please stop calling me baby man," he grumbled, unnecessarily smoothing down his shirt and examining himself in the full-length mirror to ensure there were no rogue wrinkles..

"Well, you won't let me call you baby boy anymore."

"How about no more baby-related nicknames?"

"Nope," she said popping the P. "I went through thirty-two hours of labor; I've earned the right to call you baby."

"Fine," he groaned in defeat.

"Please, tell Evie I said hello. I like her so much. I'm so excited to have Thanksgiving with her."

He smiled as his mom went on about Thanksgiving. While mom wasn't a from-scratch chef like Evie, Thanksgiving was the one exception. She'd spend the entire day cooking a turkey and making homemade mashed potatoes. Everything else was from boxes or pre-packaged, but mom would brag all day about the turkey and mashed potatoes. Since he became vegetarian, she would make a small turkey breast for herself while he would eat the non-meat sides.

Evie had come along to several Sunday dinners with his mom since he introduced them two months ago. The way they got on, giggling like old friends gushing about the same books and TV shows, set an almost permanent smile on his face each time they went.

"So, do you think Evie is the one?"

The one? Colm gaped at the phone. Had she really just asked that?

A rhythmic knock at his door saved him from having to answer. "Mom, Evie's here so I need to go. Bye," he said, ending the call.

"Happy Birthday to you, cha-cha-cha. Happy Birthday to you, cha-cha-cha. Happy birthday to you…" Evie sang, shimmying her hips as Colm opened the door.

"You silly little chatterbox," he chuckled.

Evie beamed. She was the perfect vision of his dream-girl-next-door in her short plaid dress with flowy skirt, a matching plaid headband in her long loose strands. A bakery box, sparkly gift bag, and reusable shopping bag covered in corgis adorned her arms.

How is this adorable creature with me?

"Happy birthday, baby." She pressed her big smile against his before she skipped into the apartment.

I love it when she calls me baby. There was nothing diminutive about the term of endearment when it slipped from Evie's lips.

"Thank you," he said, unable to hold back a grin. Thirty-one wasn't a big deal, but every first with Evie felt like a big deal. "Can I take something?" He gestured at the items in her hands.

"Nope." She kissed him. "You're the birthday boy. The only work you'll do is open gifts and digest cake."

Colm followed her to the small two-person dining table pressed up against the window. She put the box down in the middle of the table, placed the gift bag beside it, and sat the corgi grocery bag on the chair.

"This really isn't necessary," he insisted.

"Colm." She swatted him. "It's always necessary to celebrate the people we love."

"Wait...love?" The thump, thump of his heart roared.

There'd been lots of "I love spending time with you," or "I love this," but there hadn't been an official I love *you* yet.

Hiding her face behind her hands, she squeaked, "Did I just say that out loud?"

"Yep." The smile on his face was uncontainable.

"Colm, wait," she said, covering his mouth with her hand. "Don't say anything. I didn't want to say this accidentally. I wanted to wait for the right time. I almost said it on Halloween when you showed up to help me pass out candy with an index card taped to your shirt with 'Jonathan' written on it saying that was your costume. It was so adorable. My heart almost exploded with love for you. Then you handed me a bag of Peanut M&Ms, saying I didn't have to share...I knew. I love you, Colm Gallagher. I love you and I don't want you to say anything but thank you when I take my hand off your mouth. I don't want a returned 'I love you' out of obligation. If you love me, keep it to yourself 'til the moment you can't hold it in anymore, which is what just happened to me. And if you *don't* love me…just give me tonight and then let me down in the morning. Ok?"

He nodded.

"I'm going to remove my hand now."

"Thank you," he said, unable to contain his smile.

"Good boy." She patted his cheek.

There was no question, he loved this little chatterbox. From the first time that big smile beamed at him at that coffeeshop, he'd fallen. The realization that he was head over heels for Evie grew stronger over the months. To know she felt the same made thirty-one the most important birthday.

"So, do you want to wait 'til after dinner to have your dessert, or have it now?"

He looped his arms around her waist, tucking her against his chest and bending to kiss her neck. "Now, please."

"Colm." She squirmed out of his hold with a laugh. "Not *that* dessert."

"Ok."

"Oh, there will be *that* dessert. Trust me." Her voice went low and sexy as her fingers fiddled with the buttons of his shirt. "This dessert will just be the appetizer."

Evie opened the bakery box and removed a yellow cake with chocolate frosting. His favorite. *Happy Birthday Colm* was scrawled in orange icing gel across the cake's surface. After he blew out the candles, she plucked a carton of French Vanilla ice cream out of the bag. Another one of his favorites.

As he finished the last bite of their shared cake and ice cream, she clapped with the giddiness of a five-year-old. "Presents!"

"You're so excited." Laughter vibrated from him. "It's like you're getting the gift."

"I know people say this and they are usually full of you-know-what, but I really mean it. I love giving gifts. Like, I think I get more out of that than receiving them."

"You can say bullshit, I won't tell anyone."

"Open!" she commanded, handing over the sparkly bag.

Chuckling, he removed the shiny gold tissue paper and pulled out an oversized mug with *Colm* written over a beautiful image of a valley from Northern Ireland. His heart poked him with the words *tell her* as he studied the mug.

Next, he dug out a wooden pencil case like he'd had when he was a kid. Only *Colm Gallagher* was engraved on this case. When he opened it, there were five pens with *Colm* etched on them. His heart screamed *TELL HER NOW!*

"Evie."

"I know. It's a silly gift, but I thought it would be nice for you to have some of the souvenirs with your name on it. I know you could never find them as a kid or an adult."

"I love you."

Her face exploded in happiness. "Really?"

"So much." He grabbed her, taking her mouth with his.

Her arms encircled his nape. His hands drifted down to her ass. Grabbing it, he lifted her up and her legs folded around his waist as they kissed deeper, their tongues twisting. She whimpered as he trailed kisses down her neck. God, he was addicted to the noises she'd make when they kissed. He carried her to the couch and lowered himself atop her.

Forget dinner. The only thing he wanted to do tonight was make love to his Evie. He didn't care about a reservation. He didn't care about his to-do list. The only thing he cared about was lying below him, eyes wide and heart open, kissing him. Loving him.

"I love you, Evie Johnson," he murmured, breaking their kiss. His hands brushed her cheeks, reveling in her softness. He'd never said I love you to anyone beside his mother. That was so different than what consumed his heart with Evie.

"I love you Colm Gallagher."

Her blue eyes were so trusting. So adoring. He couldn't believe her gaze was only for him.

He devoured her mouth. His hands slipped below her dress to the lacy fabric of her panties. He hooked the waistband, and she raised her hips allowing them to slide off. Panties tossed, he parted her dampened folds and found his target. His fingers caressed her clit in slow strokes, reveling in how her hips moved in response.

She was so responsive to his touches. Even if she hadn't let him know with the writhing of her hips, flush of skin, tug of his hair, or moaning yesses, he somehow knew the path to take.

"Oh, Colm," she gasped with climax.

"That was just a warm-up." A wicked smile stretched across his face.

Evie placed her hands on his chest stopping him as his head bent between her legs. "Wait."

"What's wrong?"

Her manicured finger traced her lips curled in a seductive grin. "Let me warm *you* up, birthday boy."

She sat up, pushing him to a kneeling position on the couch. With a nipped kiss to his lips, her hands snaked down his torso to his belt buckle, slipping it open. Sultry playfulness filled her eyes and she licked her glossy pink lips. Pulling his jeans and boxer briefs down, she wrapped him in a slow-paced massage.

"Evie…" Her name uttered from deep in his throat.

Pressure bloomed through his length with the rhythmic movement of her hand. With a devilish grin on her face, she bent forward and licked up his arousal.

"Fuck," he groaned, lost in the sensation of her mouth enveloping him.

The caress of her tongue as she sucked inched him closer

and closer. He looked down to watch her and brushed back her hair, holding it as she worked. The little noises she made brought him to the edge.

"Fuck. Evie…stop," he rasped.

She released him, falling back on her heels. "I'm sorry. Did I do it wrong?"

"Oh baby," he panted, cupping her cheek. "No. You are very good at that. I just don't want to finish in your mouth. Not tonight. I want…I *need* to be inside you."

He jumped off the couch and pushed his pants and boxer briefs to the floor. Stepping out of them, he unbuttoned his shirt before pulling her up and unzipping her dress. It pooled at her feet and her bra was quick to follow.

He stepped back to let his eyes meander over her plump breasts and tiny pink nipples that hardened just at his gaze. Her shapely hips and tight little ass that begged to be gripped as he took her. Her heart-shaped mouth that not only moaned her own pleasure but wrecked him with the pleasure it gave. And her most delicious pussy. The combination of her sweetness and seductiveness was addicting.

"I think we're going to miss our reservation," she giggled.

"Yup," he said, determined and not the least bit sorry.

He pressed her back to the couch, crawling on top of her. His mouth captured hers and her legs wrapped around him as his lips moved down her throat, past her collarbone to her taut nipples. The sweetness of her skin melded with her needy whimpers spurring a fizziness within him. God, he could get drunk off of her.

He alternated between gentle licks, quick nips, and hard sucks of her nipples. Her fingers tugged his hair and she rubbed against his erection until his anticipation roared. He needed to be inside her. *Now!*

With a final suck of her left nipple, he pulled back to grab a condom.

She stopped him. "I'm on the pill. It's been over a year since my last sexual partner, and I was tested. I'm safe. We're exclusive."

Was she saying what he thought she was saying? He'd never had sex without a condom. Sex had risks. Even with birth control things could happen. Condoms gave an extra layer of protection.

He blinked. "Are you sure?"

"Yes."

"I love you," Colm said in heated desperation as he crawled over her. Slowly he pushed inside, allowing the feeling to wash over him like the first trickles of a refreshing hot shower. The velvety softness of her naked wet heat ignited an explosive sensation in every nerve.

Evie tipped her hips up, allowing him to push in deeper. Seated deep within her with no barriers between them an inferno raged, threatening to consume him in the heat of her core. At that moment, he'd let himself be burnt alive.

"Evie," he growled.

"I know baby, I feel it too," she panted, her nails biting into his back.

Her legs wrapped tighter around him and his finger slipped between them, stroking in that lazy circular fashion that always made her back arch and nails dig into him. Feeling the clenching of her pelvic muscles around him, he matched the slow caress of her clit with the pace of his hips.

"God!" Her whimpering cry was bathed in relief.

Her climax quaked around him spurring his own chase for release. As his hips grew frantic pushing towards that last delicious thrust into orgasm, his gaze shifted away.

"Colm." Her hands clamped his face, moving his gaze to hers. "Look at me…please."

Nodding, he complied. He saw so much in her eyes. Trust. Happiness. Belonging. Love.

"Evie," Colm grunted, crashing into release, his eyes fixed on hers. As his satisfaction shuddered, she bestowed a soft kiss on his lips, and he nestled into the crook of her neck. There, he grew still as her soothing fingers ran through his hair.

After going to the bathroom and cleaning them both up, he lay back down with her, pulling her in close. Yanking down a throw blanket from the top of the couch, he tucked it around them.

Evie snuggled in deeper into his chest. "So, I guess we're not going to dinner," she teased.

"If you're hungry I can get us more cake and ice cream."

"Two orgasms followed by cake and ice cream. If you do that on your birthday, I can't wait to find out what you do for my birthday in January," she said, kissing his chest.

"Why do I feel like you are a month-long birthday celebrater."

"Well, mom and I do call it Eviuary."

He kissed her temple. "Well, since your birthday is the thirtieth, then I'll have thirty days to celebrate you with orgasms and cake."

"Best boyfriend ever!" she cheered with clapping hands.

"Ha!" he rumbled. "So, do you want me to get the cake?"

"No. I want to be held by you more than I want cake."

"Evie Johnson, do you love me more than baked goods?"

"Yes, but not more than corgis. I mean, I don't have an apron with cartoon Colms on it."

"Yet." Wry confidence curved his lips upward.

"Aren't we full of ourselves."

"Of course, I have you in my arms."

Her face erupted with that big smile. "I can't tell if you're kidding or being serious."

"Serious."

"Ok." A deep crimson swallowed her smiling cheeks.

It was the truth. With Evie in his arms, he was the luckiest man in the world. What had he done to earn this? To earn, her? To earn her love? That blew his mind the most. Not only was she here with him but loved him. Evie was in love with him.

"Why did you make me look at you?" he asked, stroking his fingers lazily down her spine.

Her face tipped towards his. "You have wandering eyes. You don't always look at me. It's okay, it's not a complaint, but in that moment, I just wanted to watch your eyes as you…came." She whispered the word.

Colm smiled at how during sex she'd unleash this sex goddess only to button back up to his sweet little chatterbox after. It was a side only he got.

"Does it bug you that I don't always look at you?"

"No," she affirmed. "But when you do look at me, it's like Christmas. Like a gift only for me. It's special and it makes me feel…well, *special.*"

"You are special."

"I sometimes don't feel that way, but when you look at me, I do."

His smile tightened with realization. "Do you sometimes feel not special because of your dad?"

"Yes. I know it's ridiculous, but part of me feels if I was more…then he'd want me."

"He doesn't deserve you." The muscles of his jaw clenched. Violence wasn't the answer, but there was a tempting urge to sucker punch Evie's dad.

"Colm."

"Nope. I'm sorry Evie, but I can't. Seeing how he's hurt you. I can't." His tone was sharp but softened at her slight frown. "The idea of anyone making you feel this way infuriates me. I just want to protect you and prevent sadness from eclipsing that smile." His fingers traced her lips.

"Sad things will happen."

"I can try."

"I know you'll try, and I'll do the same for you." She caressed his face.

The rigid muscles of his body relaxed with her touch.

"I know it's strange that I'd still want someone that doesn't want me. I know my dad is cruddy," she sighed.

"It's not strange. I don't miss my dad because there isn't much to miss. I do miss the idea of a dad, though. So, I understand."

"I wonder if it's him, or the idea of him that I miss."

"It could be both for you. Your dad was a little more involved than mine." Colm felt a dull ache in his heart. It was strange to miss something you never had.

Evie placed her hand on his heart as if somehow, she knew it hurt. "He doesn't deserve you either."

"Agreed."

Their gazes intertwined. The love he felt for her hugged him tight. She was everything he'd wanted and didn't know he needed all wrapped up in a small but mighty package. Soft, but strong. Sweet, but spicy. Serious, but playful. Dynamic, but not showy. Talkative, but attentive.

"Even if I don't always look at you, you are always special in my eyes." He hoped she wouldn't just hear his words but feel them.

CHAPTER SIXTEEN

In The Goodbye- Evie
Present - Eighteen Days After The Wedding

T he sun hung low as Queen Elizabeth scampered across the cool sand of Rosie's Dog Beach. The gentle water of Alamitos Bay lapped at the shore, mixing with the happy barks of dogs running, wrestling, and chasing.

Colm and Evie usually took Queen Elizabeth to the dog beach or dog park at least once a week. They'd run around with her or toss toys for her to chase. If Queen Elizabeth made a fellow canine friend, then they'd stand there watching and laughing, his arms wrapped around her middle, his laugher vibrating through her. Sometimes they'd bring a blanket snuggling up on it while Queen Elizabeth trotted between doggy friends and them. But the last few months, she would come home to an empty townhouse and a note saying he'd taken the dog to the beach. Without her.

A sharp longing panged with the memory. Hand over her heart, she watched Queen Elizabeth dash away from a chasing bulldog. Missing Colm should be part of him being in Costa Rica. But she wasn't missing him. She was missing *them*.

"Come on girl," Evie whistled.

Leash hooked, they strolled towards the path between the beach and parking lot. Blue paint stripes divided the path into lanes for walking/running and biking. Not ready to go back to the emptiness of the townhouse, they joined the evening power-walkers, joggers, and couples with dogs. The last breath of sunlight lit the sky in burnt orange.

"Evie," A breathless voice called.

She turned to see Wyatt, his hands on his hips, gulping air. Even sweaty he was handsome, and she was annoyed with herself for noticing that as he sauntered closer to her.

"I thought that was you when I ran by."

"Yup. I'm me." She cringed at her words.

"Ha!" he hummed with laughter. "Is this the famous Queen Elizabeth?" Wyatt lowered to his haunches scratching Queen Elizabeth's ears, and her body melted into his touch.

"I didn't know you were a runner."

"Yup." He stood. "I ran track in high school and college. I was grateful that your *War & Peace*-sized guidebook had a list of the best running paths and hiking trails."

"It's not *that* big," she *tsked*.

"Ok, maybe it's more *Harry Potter and the Deathly Hollows*-sized." he chuckled. "It's big, but worth the read."

"Well, I'm glad you're finding it helpful."

"I do. Thank you."

"I should probably finish Queen Elizabeth's walk before it gets dark." Evie looked at the setting sky.

"Mind if I join? I was just about to walk for my cool down. I could keep you company. Plus, it's getting dark, as you said. Josephine would murder me with her bare hands if she knew I left you alone after sunset."

Evie bit her lip as she engaged in an internal tug-of-war. Wyatt had been kind to her since they'd met. She liked talking to him. But something felt wrong about this, like she was doing something naughty, even though she wasn't. She was just walking with a new friend. At happy hour, she'd watched Wyatt place his palm on Mandala's lower back as they'd walked to the bar later in the evening to get another round for everyone. It was just who he was. Wyatt was just a nice guy. That weird alarm bell sounding inside her was nonsense. Maybe it was the tropical depression of feelings about her relationship with Colm skewing reality.

"Sure," she said with a small smile.

They shuffled their feet along the cement path dusted with blown sand from the beach, discussing Evie's favorite hiking spots in the area. Wyatt asked many questions: How often did she hike? What time of day did she like to hike? What was her favorite hike? What was the longest hike she'd done? For the first time, Evie thought this is what it must be like talking to herself. As they reached the parking lot, Wyatt asked if she and Queen Elizabeth wanted to join him for a latte at one of the coffee shops in Belmont Shore, just a few blocks away. She ignored the voice in her head—which sounded strangely like Papa's—telling her to "Say goodnight and go home."

"Iced English Toffee latte for the lady," Wyatt said, placing Evie's drink in front of her.

"Thanks."

Wyatt nodded in reply taking the seat across from her at the orange metal bistro table outside Pietris.

"I took the liberty of buying us a baklava croissant to share and I bought a peanut butter cookie for Queen Elizabeth to have a treat, if you're okay with that." He dangled two paper pastry bags.

"That is my favorite!"

"I gathered from the bold and underline under the capitalized *must have* in the guidebook."

"You're never going to let me live down that guidebook, are you?"

"Nothing to live down. It's my new favorite book. I've sought its counsel at least once a day."

Trying to hide the slight embarrassment heating her cheeks, Evie sipped her latte. She wasn't embarrassed that she'd made a forty-page indexed PDF document of all the places she'd declared the "best" or "almost the best" in Long Beach. It was how often he referenced it that caused an uncomfortable tension in her belly.

"This is sinful," he groaned with a bite of the pastry. "You were right about this place."

"Colm and I come here a lot. Besides the yummy baked goods and lattes, they have a great brunch. Lots of vegetarian options for Colm. His favorite is the vegan scramble."

"That's a new record. You went a whole fifteen minutes without mentioning the boyfriend," he said, a soft snark in his voice.

"What?" Her forehead creased.

"Colm comes up a lot. When we were talking about hiking, you weaved him into almost every answer. Most of our conversations are salted with Colm tidbits. You're like a ninja in the skillfulness to connect every topic to him."

"Well, he *is* my boyfriend." Her voice was as defensive as a hockey goalie.

Wyatt held his hands up in a truce gesture. "I'm sorry. That came off ruder than I intended. You just mention him a lot. Josephine says it's not normal for you to have Colm on repeat in your conversation. I'd imagine the separation is tough on you and that mentioning him so much might make you feel closer when he's so far away."

"You've talked to Josephine about this?"

"Not like *that*. Not in a gossipy way. I was just asking her about some of the people I've met. I mentioned I've heard a lot about your boyfriend. I'm excited to meet him when he comes back. She said you were talking more about him than usual, but that was to be expected when missing somebody."

"I do miss him," Evie murmured.

"I know I'm a new friend, but you seem extra sad. How are you doing with him being gone? Really?" Wyatt's gaze bored into her, coaxing the looming tears.

"I miss him…but I miss us more," she croaked, fighting back tears. "It isn't just being apart. Something's changed and the person I'd talk to about it is dead."

Wyatt reached across the table to take her hand, his thumb skating across her skin, soothing and accepting her sadness. "Your mom? Josephine told me."

"She died last year." She swallowed thickly. "I miss her so much and the person I should turn to isn't here. I don't think he's been here for months. Costa Rica just punctuates it."

"Oh Evie." His tone was tender as he stood up and moved to her side of the table.

He knelt on the cement patio floor and wrapped his arms around her. She melted into his steady embrace, letting it all fall out of her, wishing it was Colm holding her. But a sad voice whispered inside her a looming truth…that Colm may never hold her again.

CHAPTER SEVENTEEN

In The Hello - Colm
Four Years and Nine Months Ago - The First Corgmas

"We need to talk about your definition of an ugly Christmas sweater." Jonathan shook his head with disappointment meeting Colm in the parking lot of Evie's apartment complex.

Colm gestured to his grandpa-style muddy brown wool sweater. "It's ugly."

"True, but there's nothing Christmas about that sweater," Jonathan scoffed. "Not like this piece of Christmas magic I'm rocking." He pointed to the red and white sweater embroidered with Reindeer holding *On Strike* and *Fair Wages* signs while Santa sat frowning in a motionless sleigh.

"I borrowed it from my grandfather. He wears it most Christmases."

"You're so literal sometimes, fuckhat. You're lucky Evie is already in love with you." Jonathan patted Colm's shoulder, laughing as they took the stairs leading to her apartment.

It was Evie's annual Corgmas party. A corgi-themed Christmas party she'd held the second Saturday of December ever since she moved to Long Beach. It was the first party he would attend with her. The added pressure of it not being just a party, but one she hosted, knotted his stomach all day.

The largest group activity they'd been to was a happy hour three weeks ago with some of her work friends. After forty-five minutes, Colm feigned a headache and ducked out early. Small groups were difficult, but parties were a mountain almost too large for him to climb.

He'd spent most of the day in his apartment, alone, in preparation for tonight. He'd even declined Evie's offer to come over early to help set up. It was the first lie he'd ever told her, saying he had something important to finish for his students.

Now, with a surprise gingerbread latte clenched in his hand, his heart pounded like a war drum. He knocked.

"Colm!" Evie bounced in greeting wearing a fitted sweater with Santa being pulled by a team of corgis. A sparkling red Santa hat sat atop her head. Her hair was pulled into two long pigtails tied with red ribbon. She was like an explosion of Christmas.

I am a fuckhat. Colm grimaced at his boring sweater.

"Thanks for the invite. I brought booze." Jonathan hugged Evie, handing her a bottle of red wine.

"So sweet." She ushered them in and rose on tiptoes to kiss Colm. "I'm so happy you're here."

"I brought you a gingerbread latte." He handed her the drink.

"Best boyfriend ever!" she squealed with delight.

"Even if his fashion sense is more *Grumpy Old Men* than *National Lampoon's Christmas Vacation*?" Jonathan snarked, pointing to Colm's sweater.

"Jonathan, be nice, or I won't point out any of my single

lady friends tonight." Evie wagged her finger. "Plus, it's totally ugly, even if the man wearing it is the cutest." She brushed her fingers across Colm's cheek sending accepting and loving heat through every inch of him.

"I'm going to need an insulin shot being around you two."

"Well, if you're a good boy Santa will bring you one," Evie quipped. "Now, let me give you the lay of the Corgmas land."

Christmas had quite literally thrown up in Evie's apartment. Red pillows with Santa-hat-wearing corgis dotted the evergreen couch and oversized chair in the living room. Twinkling white lights outlined the ceiling perimeter and doorways. Red, white, and gold poinsettias in glittery candy cane pots lived at the center of various surfaces around the apartment. A mixture of classic Christmas music and covers by pop singers played in the background. A six-foot tree sparkled with colorful lights and shiny ornaments in the corner.

Stations were set up for everything. A buffet spread of homemade appetizers lined the kitchen counter. A hot chocolate bar was created on the small side counter next to the stove with sprinkles, chocolate shavings, marshmallows, crushed graham crackers, whipped cream, and different syrups. The actual bar was set up on her balcony, with ice-filled coolers of wine, beer, water, and soda. Platters of corgi-shaped sugar cookies rested on a table draped with a shiny red tablecloth in the small dining area.

Evie fluttered around the room introducing Colm to different people, checking on guests, and freshening up the snacks. When she slipped away, always with a kiss or squeeze of his hand, he sunk into the corner of whatever room he found himself.

Alone in a cluster of her friends, his eyes drifted to her

bedroom door. The group's crossfire conversation whizzed by him. Each muscle tightened as a rigid smile rested on his face and his eyes fixed on the salvation of her bedroom.

At first the group was talking about favorite holiday movies, then Leo and Josephine started talking about skiing in Big Bear as Martin tittered about some new parking regulation downtown to Mandala. Then Josephine asked him if he wanted to be a professor someday like Jonathan. He froze, caught off-guard by the question.

Before he could answer, Martin interrupted, shouting across the room to Jonathan, who walked past with some blonde in a sexy Mrs. Claus outfit. Someone else joined with boisterous laughter about something Leo said the other day at the hospital. Then another blonde with a pointed bob haircut that everyone called Jane said something about birds, making Josephine laugh.

He finally answered Josephine's original question with a "Nope." She just blinked. With a tight grin, then she turned to Leo asking about holiday plans—or was it hams? Colm wasn't sure, because two people were loudly singing "Santa Baby" off-key.

Words shot by him like verbal missiles. It was all scrambling together. Periodic glances of expectant eyes fell on him. He just nodded, not knowing what to say because he had no idea what they'd said to him.

The cacophony of laughter, shouts, squeals, singing, and conversation competed in a fierce tug-of-war for attention. The focus needed to maintain his composure zapped him.

He clutched his Coke Zero. Each squeeze of the cold soda can anchored him in the battle against his urge to hide in Evie's room.

Like a life preserver, Evie suddenly appeared, trash bag in hand.

"Hey," he said, walking to her.

"Having fun?" she asked with a sweet smile.

"Yep." It was the second lie he'd told her today.

"I'm just going to run this out to the dumpster. I'll be right back."

"Let me take it." He reached with a desperate hand for the bag.

"That would be a huge help. Thank you. I need to replenish the hummus."

"I got it." He nodded, praying his smile would hold just a little longer. Freedom was mere seconds away.

Evie planted a swift peck on his lips. "You're the best."

I'm the worst. Forced smile in place, he moved through the party to the door.

The muffled sounds of Christmas music and laughter grew faint as he ran down the stairs. The December air was cool compared to the oppressive mugginess inside. The inky night twisted around him. In the distance the gentle zoom of cars. Soft white light in the parking area illuminated his path to the dumpster.

He tossed the bag and turned to look at Evie's building. The light from her windows waved for him to return like a villain from a movie promising he'd be okay before feeding him a poison apple. The place that he'd been so comfortable in was now a minefield. One wrong step and he'd combust.

Colm wanted to be inside. To easily weave through the room charming Evie's friends as he jumped from conversation to conversation like a frog hopping between lilies pads. To be the man she deserved.

"I wish I could be that for you." He exhaled and with a mournful twinge in his chest, he turned and walked away. He just needed a little break. Just fifteen minutes. Nobody would notice. Just a few minutes to soak in the silence and reinvigorate his drained brain.

Colm walked. And walked. And walked. Through Evie's

complex. Then the neighborhood, lined with front porches wrapped in twinkling lights and front doors decorated with green wreaths and large red ribbons. Then another neighborhood.

With each step the tension dissolved. Muscles both relaxed and woke. The quiet settled inside him with each intake of breath.

Eventually, he made his way back to Evie's apartment. The street alongside her complex and the guest parking spots were now empty. The light still shined from her apartment, but no muffled music or voices filtered. As he reached the sidewalk leading to her stairs, Jonathan appeared on the steps holding two trash bags.

"What the fuck, buddy? Where've you been?"

"I went for a walk," Colm said.

"For an hour and a half?"

"What?" He pulled out his phone and saw that it was one a.m. There were texts from Evie asking where he was. His chest tightened and stomach churned.

"You haven't told her, have you?"

He avoided Jonathan's gaze and stared up the stairs to Evie's front door.

"Fuckhat! You love her and you haven't told her? She deserves to know. I think you hurt her tonight."

"I hurt her?" Panic seized him.

"She didn't say anything, but I heard her crying in the bathroom after everyone else left. She came out with that 'nothing's wrong' smile plastered on her face. But I heard her cry, and I knew you hadn't told her. If anyone would understand—if anyone would partner with you to handle these situations—it would be Evie. You need to go upstairs, tell her, and fix this. She thinks you just left." His tone was firm but supportive as he rested his hand on Colm's shoulder.

"I…"

"Save your words for her. She's alone up there. I was the last to leave. I hung around to help her, and in case you showed up. Go up there and talk to her. Listen, you can fix this. It's not broken. That woman loves you. God only knows why, fuckhat." There was a playful tug of his lips.

"I *am* a fuckhat. She deserves better than me," he sighed.

"No. You two are perfect for each other. She just deserves the full you, and you deserve to *be* the full you with the woman you love. I've lived through both your previous girl-friends. Nice girls, but not anyone I could see you with. Not anyone that could fully embrace you in all your fuckhat glory." Jonathan nudged Colm's ribs. "Evie, though. I'll say this…I've already started drafting my best man speech."

There was no doubt that Evie was his forever. He just worried that he wasn't hers. Evie deserved the boyfriend he'd imagined himself to be, not who he was. A boyfriend who would be by her side, not slinking away in the dark, wandering the streets instead of mingling at parties.

Jonathan punched his arm. "Get out of your head. Get up there. Let me know how it goes."

The Christmas lights glowed, but the remaining lights in the apartment were off. Evie sat on the couch in sleep shorts and her University of Missouri hoodie. With the click of the opening door, her face lifted from her knees. She gave him a weak smile.

"I'm sorry," Colm's voice cracked.

"What happened? You took the trash out and never came back," she sniffled. There was no accusation, just questioning.

"I needed a break."

"From me?" There was a worried bite of her lower lip.

"No." He shut the door and moved to kneel in front of her, his eyes pleading for understanding. None of this was about her. The only thing that kept him there tonight was her.

"What happened?"

"I should've told you before this," he started, exhaling a stuttering breath. "I'm on the autism spectrum. They call it Autism Spectrum Disorder Low Needs. It's what used to be called Asperger's. I was diagnosed when I was seventeen. I have difficulty in social situations. It drains me and I often need breaks."

"Drains you?"

Colm sighed, "I work twice as hard as other people in social situations. I have trouble keeping up with the conversation. It gets overwhelming. After a few hours, I feel like I've run a marathon with a backpack of cement blocks strapped to my back. My brain can't process simple things. My muscles get tense and fatigued. I can't concentrate. I just want to crash."

Her face scrunched in realization. "When you snap your fingers when you talk, you're stimming."

"I don't always notice I'm doing it, but stimming sometimes soothes the anxiety spidering through me."

"Colm, why didn't you tell me?" she asked, hurt etched on her face.

"I didn't want to disappoint you. To have you look at me differently. To stop looking at me the way you do. I wanted to be the man you deserve. The man you…"

"Colm Gallagher," she huffed, cradling his face in her small hands to pull his gaze to hers. "Look at me. You are still the man that showed up here with a gingerbread latte for his girlfriend. The man that always stops to pet dogs. The man that has dinner with his mom weekly and fixes things at the apartment for her. The man that watched *A Mickey's Christmas Carol* with his girlfriend, even though I think a little bit of your soul died that night. The man with a heart too big for this world. And above all, you are still the man I love. I'm a little mad that you didn't tell me, that you didn't trust me to do what I said I would do—love you. The only thing that could change you in my eyes is if you said you murdered a puppy or gave up carbs. I don't think I could be with a man that didn't go to bakeries."

There was anger and hurt in her eyes. But mostly there was love. No pity. No disappointment. No regret. So often when Colm shared with others about his autism, they'd look at him with something other than acceptance. He became less a person and more a something. Something for them to fix. Something to make better.

"I'm sorry. I should have told you sooner."

"Part of me wants to scream 'Yes, you should have.'" There was a quiet fierceness in her. "But I understand if you weren't ready to share. If you needed to skip the party, I would have understood."

"No," he protested. "I wanted to be here. I don't want to miss things that are important to you. You asked me to be here. I wanted to be here. For you."

Evie kissed him, soothing away the tension in his muscles. "I know. I love you for that, but we need to think about us. Not just me. We can come up with a plan. I just need you to promise me that moving forward you'll talk to me. I can't be a good partner if I don't know."

"Jonathan said you were crying," he lamented, raising his hand to her face, tracing where teardrops had been.

"It's okay. It's fine. I know now, and we can make a plan."

"Please, don't act like everything is fine when it's not."

"Colm, I can be understanding and hurt at the same time. Both things can be true."

He nodded.

"Now, please get on this couch and hold me," she demanded.

Colm complied, slipping beside her on the couch and

tucking her small frame in his arms. The rigid muscles in both their bodies dissolved with their closeness.

"I am so sorry I made you cry." A quiet quake laced his voice, but no tears came.

Crying wasn't something Colm did. He'd cried twice in his life. The first time after falling off his bike and breaking his arm when he was seven. The second after his dad left. Not because his dad left. It was due to the new role Colm was assigned. The man of the house. At night, alone, beneath his Teenage Mutant Ninja Turtles sheets, he'd hid his not-yet-a-man sobs in the pillow.

Now, at thirty-one, he wanted to be the man he'd failed to be at ten. To be the man that Evie deserved. A man that wouldn't make her cry.

You've already failed. The truth stung.

"I know you're sorry, baby," she said, kissing him. "First. Yes, I'm hurt. Not that you left the party, but because you didn't say anything. Even if you weren't ready to tell me about being on the spectrum, you could've told me you needed to duck out. Instead, you took the trash out and disappeared for ninety minutes. We both have dads that abandoned us, so things like this can be triggering. I need you to promise you'll tell me when you're leaving."

"Ok." Colm squeezed her tighter.

"Second. We're a team. Let's work out a plan for how we'll deal with social events. We can limit the time or pick only certain events for you to join me at. We can even have a safe word," she suggested.

"Ok." Colm felt incapable of saying anything else. The word such a poor response for all she was offering. Love. Understanding. Belonging. They were a team.

"Third. I love you."

"Ok."

Evie knit her brows in mock annoyance. "Fourth. Learn a new word."

"Ok." There was a playful curl of his lips.

"Colm." She pinched him.

It didn't hurt at all, but he mocked winced. Then captured her mouth for a slow kiss. "Fifth. I love you."

Their lips found each other in languid kisses that intensified like a growing storm. God, he wanted her…every inch of her. Even more he wanted to give every inch of himself knowing that she would accept him. All his parts. Even the ones that didn't fit, but somehow fit with her.

She crawled onto his lap, straddling his waist. His hands roamed beneath her sweatshirt, bathing in the softness of her silken skin. As their kisses deepened, her hot, slick tongue tangled with his. His body craved for no barriers between them. To feel skin on skin. To savor the soothing sensation of her touch.

"Colm, I need you," she whimpered, grinding against him.

"I need you too," he groaned like a man starved. The only thing to quench his hunger was her…all of her.

He tugged her sweatshirt over her head, tossing it to the floor. Hot kisses trailed down her neck as her head fell back allowing him greater access to the delicious taste of her throat. Her hands moved to the hem of his sweater, yanking it up. As hands explored and mouths tasted the rest of their clothing found its way to the floor.

Naked, she settled back on his lap. Ravenous kisses and pleading moans filled the room. The wet heat of her core pressed against him. The contact of their naked bodies wasn't enough. All he wanted was to be deep within her. For her sex to clench around him, claiming him, solidifying her promise that they were a team.

To belong to her, only her.

"I'm yours," he rasped, the desire pulsing through him.

"I know baby." She slid herself onto his arousal.

"Fuck." His groan was both wanton and relieved.

She moved in a slow rocking fashion on top of him. Each pump of her hips thrummed desirous satisfaction within him. How could he both want more and be contented at the same time? His hands clung to her waist quickening her movement.

Cradling his face with her hands, those satin lips of hers pressed against his in a consuming kiss. Their lovemaking both slow and frantic, his eyes never left hers as they moved in tandem inching closer to their release.

"Colm," she gasped, her hips moving faster.

"Evie."

Her back arched. The orgasm shuddered through her. He wrapped her tight, pressing her trembling body into his chest. With one last pump his own release came. Still holding her close the aftershocks of his climax ripped through them both. Evie's head rested on his shoulder, melting into his embrace. Colm was unable to tell where he started and she ended. They were one.

For several minutes they just remained like that. A sated and spent Evie slumped against him, her heartbeat matching his. Colm placed a tender kiss against her hairline, brushing away wayward pieces of damp hair.

Her face tipped up to him. "I love you so much." Tears spilled at the corners of her eyes.

The rough pads of his fingers dashed them away. "I love you too." God, he wanted to cry, but no tears came. He worried his heart would burst at the idea of his Evie crying, even with overflowing love for him.

Evie slid off his lap. Every inch of his body mourned the loss of their connection.

They situated themselves on the couch. Colm on his back with Evie sprawled over him like his new favorite blanket.

"Was that our first fight?" she queried, looking at him with a satisfied smile playing on her lips.

"If it was, I don't know if we did it right," Colm grinned.

"I kind of like how it ended," she teased, pressing her smirking mouth against his chest.

"I don't think women that 'kind of like' something make the noises you did."

Evie buried her face into his chest. The dichotomy of Evie during and after sex was a sweet contradiction.

She looked up, her face serious. "I want to tell you something."

"Ok." He held his breath.

"I'm scared of the dark."

He wanted to smile with his released breath but the look on Evie's face told him there was more. That this wasn't just a childhood fear like him and snakes.

"I'm scared mainly when it's dark and quiet. Growing up in Missouri we'd get really bad storms with tornadoes. When I was thirteen there was a really…*really* bad tornado. It was in the evening," Her voice shook, but she continued. "The alarm sounded. We could barely hear it over the rain and wind outside. It was just me and Papa. Mom was at work. We ran into the basement. It was so loud. Like being in the throat of a roaring tiger not knowing if you'd be spat out or swallowed. Papa just held me tight, telling me we'd be ok as we hid under his workbench. Then it got quiet. No howling winds. No pounding rain. No distant siren. Papa's hands fell, but he remained behind me against the base of the bench. I thought that meant it was ok." Her gaze shifted away from him. "It wasn't ok."

Hand on her chin, he guided her gaze back to him. "Evie, what happened?"

Fat tears rolled down her face. "When I turned, he was slumped against the bench. The storm was gone, and we were safe... but he still died. It was a heart attack. They call it a widow maker."

"Oh baby. I am sorry." He brushed away her tears trying to soothe the sadness away.

"I tried to wake him, but it was too late. I tried to go upstairs to call for help, but the door wouldn't open. The storm had destroyed parts of the house and the fridge had been blown against the door. I was trapped."

"For how long?" He didn't think he could hold her tighter, but he did.

"Until morning," she wept.

He clung to her, the grip of his hold not just for her sake, but also for his. He felt every ounce of her pain.

"I'm so sorry. I'm so sorry. I'm so sorry." His clumsy, sorrowful words spilled out like water from a tipped over glass.

She lifted her face, the tears replaced by concern. "No, Colm. I didn't tell you to make you upset. I just...I wanted you to know. Because I want you to know all of me. You shared something important about you. Something that I know you don't tell a lot of people. Something that has had an impact on your life. What happened in that basement has had a large impact on me. We both have things that can sway a single moment of our day, but together we can face them. I can't just say we're a team and not share my stuff."

"Evie...I..." The words failed him, as they so often did.

"Just say, 'Thank you for sharing.' It's what I do when someone shares something too much to process. I kind of dumped a bucket of childhood trauma on you." Her face pinched. "We really are bad at fighting."

A silent chuckle escaped, "Oh, Evie. I love you."

"I love you, Colmy Bear."

"Colmy Bear?"

"I'm trying it out. No good?"

"Terrible." A smile stretched across his face.

Evie's fingers threaded with his. "We're a team. A strong team needs to know each other's strengths and challenges."

"We're a team." Colm pressed his lips against her temple. "Always."

CHAPTER EIGHTEEN

In The Goodbye - Evie
Present - Twenty-One Days After The Wedding

Today Evie felt as if she wandered through a haunted house, each memory primed to jump out and grasp her in its clutches until she broke. It was the deathiversary. It started at eight a.m. when her phone pinged with a message notification. For a moment she thought it was Mom. But the sobering reality drenched her in its icy waters. Mom was dead. It was a message from Leo with a simple *Love ya babes* and prayer hands emoji.

On Queen Elizabeth's morning walk, they stopped at a small park. Sitting on the iron bench, Evie breathed in the not-yet-steamy morning air and watched a group of children on the playground. A sharp ache clogged her chest with every squealed, "Mommy!" from running children.

A flower delivery from Josephine with a card saying *Thinking of you* was waiting on the front stoop when she returned from the walk. The white roses sat on the kitchen island while Evie smeared creamy peanut butter across each nook and cranny of a toasted English muffin. Instead of eating at the table she opted to lean into a vegetative state in front of the TV.

Three channels in a row had Vin Diesel movies. Cringing, she flipped to Bravo hoping to lose herself in the nonsensical drama of any of the Real Housewife cities. It worked for a few hours, until the episode where Vicki from the *Real Housewives of Orange County* lost her mom. She had never cried watching the *Real Housewives* before, unless it was from laughter.

Wiping her eyes, she turned the TV off and checked her phone. The only new text was from Terrance, checking in. They'd stayed in touch since mom's death.

It was also Saturday. Date night with Colm. The last three hadn't gone well. There had been a *Good Morning* and *Goodnight* text each day this week with the obligatory *Hope you had a good day*, but nothing more. Evie thought he'd text more today, but outside of a *Good Morning* that came in before she woke, there was nothing.

There had been social media posts with Sarah, though. A slew of cityscape and rural landscape photos tagging him, and a selfie of them at lunch filled his Instagram feed. They were touring a coffee plantation an hour or two away from San Ramón.

"Ugh," she grumbled, tossing the phone away from her. "No more social media."

Colm *should* be out enjoying Costa Rica. He deserved it. Nothing was going on with Sarah. But why did she have to be so pretty? Dark eyes that you could lose yourself in. Flirty curls that looked as soft as silk. The two of them looked like the leads in a rom-com. Why did he have to be out with her? Why, of all the days, did it have to be *today*?

Evie clamped her eyes tight wishing that it was already tomorrow, and this was all over. Hoping that tomorrow she'd wake and that aching hollow feeling in her heart would be filled.

Costa Rica was only an hour ahead of California, so it was five-thirty p.m. there. She picked up her phone and dialed. Their video chat wasn't scheduled until eight p.m. California time, but she hoped that Colm had returned to Sylvia and Antonio's house from sightseeing. Maybe they'd talk early. All she wanted was to hear his voice. To see his face. To have him say, "It's okay to be sad," while soothing her.

All she wanted was her person. No matter what had been happening, no matter what had shifted, he was still her person. If she clung to that, maybe she'd have enough strength to get them back to the time when their phones were filled with more than *Good Morning* and *Goodnight*. To when he looked at her like she was special, and not like she was broken.

There was no answer. Frowning both at the unanswered call and at herself, she tossed her phone to her side forcing herself to be patient and wait for their scheduled video chat. He'd be there. Colm never broke plans.

At eight p.m., she dialed again. No answer. Twenty-minutes later, no answer and no call. This repeated for two and a half hours. Evie sat glued to her phone, debating between calling again or waiting until the clock hit eleven p.m.—midnight in Costa Rica.

This wasn't like Colm. Panic snaked through her. She didn't know who to get a hold of. He hadn't provided her with contact info for Sylvia and Antonio. Checking his social media, Evie saw him tagged in a selfie with Sarah in the back of a taxi with the caption *What a day!* It was posted ten minutes ago. He was safe.

With Sarah.

Tears fell as she turned off her phone and went to bed. Despite having Queen Elizabeth nuzzled at her hip, she felt alone. So alone.

CHAPTER NINETEEN

In The Goodbye - Colm
Present - Earlier The Same Day

Colm sighed and closed his eyes, leaning his head against the worn leather headrest of the bus seat. The cacophony of loud chatter, snoring passengers, music from cellphones, and coughing roar of the bus's engine assaulted his senses. It was another twenty minutes until they arrived at their stop, and then a fifteen-minute taxi ride before they would end up at the front gates of El Rojo Frijol Plantation.

It was the first of two coffee plantations he'd visit with Sarah today. They'd tour, taste-test, and purchase some coffee. In between plantations, they'd do lunch at a small café that was only a ten-minute walk from the first plantation. Then they'd have dinner in town before boarding the bus back to San Ramón and arrive home just in time for his date with Evie.

The plan for the day was committed to his brain. Not just the sightseeing with Sarah, but his plan for date night. The call with Evie last week was tense and short. Most of it akin to swimming through muddy water trying to find her. She didn't seem to be present. There was a jagged edge to her mouth. A tired sadness in her eyes.

After the call, he'd replayed every word, turn of eye, and inflection as if he were a coach analyzing post-game footage to find every misstep, in hopes of securing better performance next time. It just all went sideways so fast. She said she was tired. She looked tired. But he worried the exhaustion wasn't just from the day or lack of sleep, but from him. From them.

"You're miles away." Sarah nudged him with her elbow. "What are you thinking about?"

"Evie."

"Shocker," she mocked, rolling her eyes.

"Ha," he grumbled, his forehead creased in dismissive annoyance.

"So, besides the music and candles what's the plan for date night? Will there be dirty stuff?" she teased and waggled eyebrows.

"Phone sex? No," he scoffed.

"Don't give me Puritan eyes."

"I'm not. Evie and I aren't phone sex people."

"I'll resist asking for your take on *phone sex people*. Have you two *tried* phone sex?"

"No."

"Then you don't know if you're *phone sex people*." Sarah made a sultry inflection on "phone sex people," shimmying her body in her seat.

"Why do I tell you things?" he groaned.

A cheeky smile lit her features. "Because I'm brilliant and you'd be lost without me."

He had shared with Sarah his concerns about the disconnect with Evie. Not all the details, but some. She'd been attentive, offering suggestions and calling him a moron if he messed this up. She was like the female version of Jonathan, only she didn't call him a fuckhat, which was a nice change.

"I've drafted a list of possible discussion topics and questions to ask her," Colm said as the bus rolled to a stop.

"How very job interview of you," she snarked, but her expression shifted into curiosity. "Can I see?"

He reached into his pocket and dug for his phone. Where was his phone? It should be in his pocket. It was there when he'd walked down the stairs this morning. He'd had it in his hands until…

"Fuck," he muttered.

"What?"

"My phone is on the dresser. Ricardo wasn't paying attention and knocked into me with a pitcher of juice this morning. It went all over me. It threw me off. I must have left my phone on the dresser when I went to clean up and change."

"It's all good." Sarah dismissed his concern with a wave of her hands as they streamed off the bus with other passengers. "I've got my phone. We can use it to navigate, hail those illegal rideshares, and for lots of social media posting."

"I don't like not having my phone. What if…"

Sarah placed a warm hand on his forearm. "Relax. It's all good. I've got mine. We're okay. If you're worried about your list, we can draft a new one at lunch. If you're worried about Evie knowing where you're at, I'll post lots of pictures and tag you in them. I can even DM her to let her know."

The rigid muscles of Colm's shoulders relaxed. "Yeah. Could you message her now?"

"Sure." Sarah's brows locked in frustration. "As soon as I get Wi-Fi. Let's go into the town before we head to the plantation. I'll tap into someone's Wi-Fi and send the message so you can relax."

"Ok. Thanks. I appreciate you."

"Hey, you're my wingman and I'm your…whatever the

lady equivalent is for a dude in a relationship in need of some spotting. Ha!" she barked. "Spotter. I'm your spotter."

If only that had been the end of the plan being ripped to shreds. The taxi to the first plantation dropped them two miles away from the gate. They arrived sweaty and thirsty. Sarah just kept saying, "It's an adventure," while his fingers snapped and his pulse quickened.

Breathe for two, out for four. Colm's fingers clutched the small porcelain cup as they sat under the lattice pagoda that served as the plantation's tasting room.

"This is so good," Sarah awed, breathing in deep the dark roast's aroma.

"Yup." His eyes flicked to the attendant bringing their next samples. "Do you have Wi-Fi?"

"No, Señor," the attendant replied, replacing their cups with fresh ones.

Sarah placed her hand on his. "It's alright. The café will have Wi-Fi and we'll check if she got my message."

The little café where they'd planned to eat lunch after visiting the first plantation was closed. A note tacked to the front door said that the family that owned it had closed for the day to attend a wedding in San José. Colm groaned. Sarah shrugged and hailed a rideshare to take them back to town for lunch. With each of the twenty-five minutes they had to wait, he grew more anxious. Rideshares in Costa Rica functioned like a black-market transport option and often came with long waits or last-minute cancellations.

Arriving at a small restaurant in town, Colm and Sarah guzzled water and devoured their lunches beneath the shade of a giant blue umbrella. Wi-Fi was slow, but available. There was no reply from or indication that Evie had read the message from Sarah. He borrowed Sarah's phone and scrolled Evie's feed. Nothing had been posted for the day.

"She's probably out enjoying her Saturday, as you should be." Sarah frowned, taking the phone back.

"I hope so," he said, though he knew there'd be no enjoying herself today. *Not today.* He wasn't enjoying himself either, despite the attempted distraction of the trip to the coffee plantations.

What have I done? He squeezed his eyes shut tight as he bounced his leg under the table. He'd been distracted all day, remembering the events of a year ago. Holding Evie's trembling body. The loss. He should've never agreed to this outing. Today should have been spent with Evie. For the first time since arriving in Costa Rica, he wondered why he'd come here at all. Why had he signed up for a trip that took him away from home—from Evie—for *this* day?

"Ok, I got our ride for plantation number two. Let's get going," Sarah said, rising from the table.

"Maybe we should go…"

"Colm, you promised you'd go with me. This is the only Saturday I have free for the rest of my time." She crossed her arms in a slight pout.

"I just need to get a hold of Evie."

Her stance softened as she looked at him. "I know you two are having trouble, but you're extra heightened about this. What makes today so special? Is it your anniversary?"

"It's an anniversary of sorts." A somberness laced in his words.

"Dude!" Sarah punched his arm. "What the hell, Colm?"

"I know." He sighed. "I shouldn't have come with you, but I wanted a distraction."

"From what?" she pushed, sitting back down at the table.

He sat staring at his fingers rolling and unrolling the yellow cloth napkin. The words couldn't be said out loud. He'd barely let himself think the words.

Sarah studied him for a while. Her slight scowl relaxed as

she reached across the table to still his hand, squeezing it. "Hey, why don't we go. I can check the bus schedule and we can take an earlier one back."

"What about the second coffee plantation?"

"Once you've seen one coffee plantation, you've seen them all." She tossed her hands in the air. "Let's head over to the bus station. We'll get back early so you can call Evie—don't faint at this—*before* the pre-scheduled time." She clutched her chest in faux dismay making him smile.

But hours later, Colm sat in a different restaurant in a town twenty miles from San Ramón. The four p.m. bus they'd boarded broke down five miles from Naranjo. Forty-five minutes of waiting on a sticky bus led Sarah and Colm to hike towards the town in hopes of finding any transport back to San Ramón. Hell, at this point he'd fucking walk there.

Lanterns dangled from a red striped awning, illuminating the small metal table where he sat. His legs quaked violently beneath the table. The motion a failed attempt to sooth the anxiety rioting within him. It was eight thirty p.m. in Costa Rica. The date with Evie would start in thirty minutes and the spotty Wi-Fi wouldn't allow him to video chat from Sarah's phone. He couldn't miss it. Being unreachable all day was one thing, but he couldn't miss their scheduled date. It couldn't happen.

Why the fuck had he left his phone!? Although, what good would it have done having it? Sarah hadn't been able to get a signal or dependable Wi-Fi since they'd left the café after lunch.

"I'm a goddess," Sarah proclaimed, plopping down across from him. "I got us a taxi."

"Great. Let's go." He stood, but Sarah motioned for him to sit.

"The driver will pick us up in thirty minutes to take us to

San Ramón. I guess he's got two local runs to make first, but then he'll take us."

Colm sighed, "There isn't any other way?"

"I can't use a rideshare app with no signal. Relax my dude. This is our best option. Let's eat some dinner to kill time. Then we'll meet the taxi and get you back for Evie time. I know you'll be late. It will be all right. She'll understand."

Colm wanted to trust Sarah, but nothing today had gone to plan. Nothing! Today was a shit day. Fitting, considering this day last year was the fucking worst day of his life.

His last ounces of energy depleted rapidly as he worked to keep his emotions contained. To not cry. To not scream. To not kick over this table just to hear the dishes crash to the sidewalk. To not punch the window and feel the bite of shattered glass rip into his knuckles.

He fucking hated today. Fucking hated broke down buses. Fucking hated taxi drivers. Fucking hated Instagram messages. Fucking hated a lack of signal and Wi-Fi. Above all, he fucking hated himself.

The taxi threaded through the streets of San Ramón. The driver had been forty minutes late and every traffic mishap that could happen, did. It was after midnight. Colm was three hours late for his date with Evie.

Sarah rubbed his back. "It will be alright. Evie will understand."

He shrugged her off. He didn't want comfort. He didn't deserve it. This was punishment for his selfish action. For focusing on how to distract himself today rather than how to take care of Evie and be the man he wanted to be. Instead, he was like his father. Too focused on himself to be there for the people that depended on him. The people that loved him.

I hope she still loves me. A sharp pain pricked at his eyes and sliced in his chest.

At twelve-thirty p.m. Colm ran up the stairs of the sleeping house. The only noise a soft hum of music from Ricardo's room at the front of the hall. With swift steps he moved down the hall and ducked into his room.

The fucking phone sat on the dresser beside a white vase full of fresh yellow flowers. Antonio got fresh flowers each Saturday morning, filling different vases around the house. He'd done that since he and Sylvia were first married. The symbol of a simple act of affection from a man deeply in love with his wife. A man unlike Colm, one who wouldn't disappear for an entire day when he should be there.

His phone was filled with missed calls and messages from Evie. Sinking to the floor, he dialed. No answer. He dialed again. Each call went direct to voicemail.

"Why is your phone off?" he growled and redialed, hoping it would magically turn on.

His heartbeat raced like a starved lion chasing the first gazelle seen in weeks, its hunger quelled only by her voice. Its fatigue soothed only by her touch.

"Please, baby…pick up," he begged, but there was no answer. He just kept dialing.

CHAPTER TWENTY

In The Hello - Evie
The First Christmas - Four Years, Three Months and Three Weeks Ago

"The cutest babies! Scarlet, you're so right," Mom chirped, her soft voice drifting in from the balcony where she sat drinking coffee with Colm's mom and Terrance.

Evie had invited Colm and his mom, Scarlet, to join them for Christmas dinner at her place. There'd be a double feature of *Die Hard* and *It's a Wonderful Life* after dessert, acknowledging the two families' traditions and appeasing both mothers.

The five of them had blended as if they'd always meant to go together. The moms connected over a shared love of Bravo, mystery novels, and equal affection for each other's child.

It was a perfect first holiday. They played Catch Phrase over appetizers and mulled wine while dinner cooked. Mom had insisted on cooking, allowing Evie to take control of dessert. The weather was warm, so they'd eaten on the balcony at the patio table. The conversation flowed as they devoured homemade pumpkin soup, biscuits with apple butter, butternut squash stuffed ravioli in pine nut cream sauce, grilled focaccia bread, and warmed spinach salad.

"Agreed Diane! How cute would those McBabies be," Scarlet gushed from the balcony.

"Are they talking about us having babies? Also, did your mom call them *Mc*Babies?"

"Yup," Colm said, smiling as he pulled down the small dessert plates from the cabinet.

"My mom spent my teens scaring me into abstinence with talk of how my life would be ruined if I got pregnant. Now, she and your mom are giddily hoping I get preggers."

"We would make cute babies," Colm whispered in her ear, his hot breath setting a delicious shiver down her body as his arms wrapped her into his chest.

Evie turned. "Colm Gallagher do you want to impregnate me?"

"Not right now. Our mothers and Terrance are ten feet away."

"But you do want to…someday." A flutter jerked in her belly like an uncoordinated dancer after drinking a gallon of Red Bull.

"Someday. Yes." His tone decisive, but emerald eyes questioning. "Do you want kids?"

"Yes, but not now. I still have a lot of things to do before motherhood. Are kids something you want soon?"

"No. Not now. I hadn't ever considered fatherhood 'til…" He stopped speaking, his green eyes fixed on her.

"Until me?" The loud thump of her heart muted the laughter filtering in from the balcony.

"Until us." He brushed her cheek. "We still have time, though. Lots of time to just be a couple. To see what our future looks like. I just want you to know that it's something I've been thinking about more. Not just babies, but a future with you."

"A future with us." She beamed.

He dipped his face inches from hers, murmuring, "If that future involves that big smile of yours on tiny little Evies and Colms, then I'll be a lucky man."

She melted into his kiss, his arms pulling her in tight. Warmth spread along her veins. Was she really talking to her boyfriend of almost four months about hypothetical future babies in her kitchen? Was she really completely okay with this?

Absolutely!

"Oh, Colmy Bear," she purred nuzzling into his neck.

"That nickname is terrible." His chest vibrated with laughter.

"It's sweeter than My Little Chatterbox." She nipped his lower lip.

"You *love* being my little chatterbox." His hands settled on her lower back as he drank up her kisses.

How she loved being his anything when he kissed her like that.

A throat cleared. "You two may want to extricate yourselves from one another to join us with the dessert. Your moms have started planning your wedding and have gone down the Pinterest rabbit hole. They're currently debating a fairy tale or traditional Celtic theme." Terrance's face pinched with bemused apology.

"Are they aware we're not engaged?" Colm asked with a slight grumble.

"Oh, you naïve man. You two introduced your mothers

and you didn't think this would happen? I'd imagine you're in store for your mom sending you sales notifications from Zales and Jared's for at least the next....well, 'til you two actually get engaged. Then, after that it will be BabiesRUs advertisements."

Colm stood; mouth open. He'd said he'd been thinking of their future, but Evie knew the prospect of someone else planning it horrified him. As plan oriented as he was, he also needed to be the one drafting and executing that plan. She'd learned that more over the last few weeks as they'd navigated the busy holiday season as a team, united in their plan to weave through the social situations that challenged and drained him.

"Don't worry, baby. I'll distract them," she assured with a pat of his cheek. "Ladies, I've got dessert! Also, can we talk about the latest episode of *Vanderpump Rules*?" Evie walked out onto the balcony carrying the gingerbread cheesecake she'd made.

"Brittany should break up with Jax," Mom said, sipping her coffee.

"I can't believe she'd stay with *that* cheaty-cheaty bang man!" Scarlet added in agreement.

The two women ping-ponged discussing their theories of the childhood traumas and personality quirks fueling the antics of each cast member of the reality TV show. Evie weighed in with probing questions to keep them going, while Terrance shook his head laughing and Colm smirked between bites of cheesecake.

Colm leaned in, whispering, "If we do have babies some-day, I hope they inherit your evil genius skills to sway conver-sations."

Someday. A mountain-size smile stretched across her face.

Joint Christmas, someday. Waking up with Colm every

day, someday. Children, someday. Married, someday. A home, someday. A rescue corgi, someday. A forever, someday. The loveliness of the word *someday* washed over her. One day, all the somedays that danced in her heart would become today.

CHAPTER TWENTY-ONE

In The Goodbye - Evie
Present - The Morning After Colm Missed Their Date

Evie woke up groggy, her head pounding and heart aching. It was that special hangover that festers after a night of too much crying. Rolling over in bed, she grabbed the phone, the black screen reminding her she'd turned it off last night. She never turned off her phone. It felt cruel to do that, to eliminate any way to get a hold of her, but last night was too much. Too much waiting for him. Too much reaching out to someone not answering.

"What should I do, girl?" There was a deep exhale. Queen Elizabeth padded up the bed, placing her wet nose in Evie's face.

Massaging the corgi's velvety ears, Evie thought about mornings spent in this bed with Colm. Queen Elizabeth nudging them both awake and each of them trying to coax the other out of bed to walk her. Most mornings, Colm would lose. With a kiss, he'd murmur, "I got this." Then he'd roll out of bed to pull on shorts and a shirt and carry Queen Elizabeth, like the pintsized monarch she was, downstairs.

The memory thawed Evie's resolve. She picked up the phone, turning it on. There'd be a message, no doubt. An explanation. An apology. Some reason he'd forgotten her. Some reason why he'd spent yesterday, of all days, with someone else.

The memory flashed of that selfie of Sarah and Colm taken around eleven-thirty p.m. Costa Rican time. A winking smile painted on Sarah's pretty features and an annoyed grin on Colm's. Sarah's wink almost mocked, "Haha girl, he's with me." But it wasn't really Sarah. It was that he wasn't here for her. Not the way he should be. Not the way they had once been.

The phone rang awake with an incoming video chat request. She paused for a moment before accepting.

"Hi."

"Evie," Colm said, an exhausted desperation in his voice. "I'm so sorry, baby. I'm so sorry."

"What happened?" She tried to keep her voice calm. Tried to be open to understanding. Tried to not let the nibbling jealousy and devouring hurt eat away her ability to listen.

"It was the day from hell," he sighed.

Stay calm, Evie. Just smile.

"Oh no. What happened?" she asked, her tone clipped.

Colm paused, staring at her. Dark circles rested beneath his green eyes. For a moment Evie's heart twinged. He looked as if he'd not slept in days.

"Everything that could have gone wrong did. I forgot my phone at the house. Then we had transportation issues. The bus broke down. By the time I got back to San Ramón it was after midnight here. Sarah sent you DMs earlier in the day and when we got into San Ramón, she'd texted to let you know. We didn't have a signal or Wi-Fi most of the day. Did you see them?"

"I did not," she said, tone flat.

Her hackles bristled with all the "we" language. Tight smile in place, she pulled up her messages and Instagram, finding the messages from Sarah. She hadn't checked notifications, only Colm's feed yesterday. The text from Sarah came in after she'd turned her phone off. This all should have calmed the monster inside of her bashing walls for retribution, but it did not.

"She sent them," he insisted.

"She did. I just didn't see them 'til now."

Colm let out an exasperated breath. "Why didn't you check your messages? Why did you turn off your phone?"

"Why did you forget your phone?" she snapped.

Was he really annoyed with her? Seriously? She'd been the one waiting. *She'd* been the one calling and messaging. *She* was the one here. *Alone.*

He flinched. "It was an accident. I forgot it."

"You don't forget things. You have checklists for *everything*," she hissed.

"I know. I was…" He closed his eyes. "…I'm sorry."

"It's fine," she sighed, tossing up her hands in defeat. It was always fine. But the monster inside her was unsatisfied with this answer. It wanted heads to roll. It wanted to not hurt anymore.

There was a long pause. Both waiting for the other to speak. In a game of who would break the silence first, Evie always lost. She sucked in a steadying breath and forced her features into a smile.

"So, how was the coffee plantation?"

"Evie. Don't." A severe firm line anchored his features.

"Don't what?"

"Play fucking *Happy Evie* with me. Don't pretend it's all okay when it's not."

"I'm not…"

"Yes, you are. You can fool everyone else with your pretend smile. Not me. I've seen your fake smile too many times this last year. I can't do it anymore," he cut her off. Anger glinted in his eyes.

"If you can't stand looking at me, maybe *you* should hang up and go hang with *your* new best friend Sarah." The venom in the words tasted sour in Evie's mouth.

"Don't be ridiculous, Evie."

"Ridiculous?" she shouted. "*Ridiculous?* Since you've been gone your social media is full of nothing but Sarah. You're off doing whatever with her, while I get minimal text messages and a weekly call where we barely speak—or that you completely miss—like last night."

"I told you what happened!"

"I wonder if there was part of you that wanted to forget your phone. Wanted to forget me. I feel like an afterthought." A quiet quake engulfed her words.

"Evie, you're being…"

"Colm, I swear to fucking god if you say I'm being ridiculous one more time I'll hang up," she spat.

He winced, as if she had slapped him. "My only thought yesterday was of you. I was up all night trying to call you. You didn't answer. You turned your phone off. *You* shut me out. Again."

"Your only thought was of *me*? You left me," she snarled. "You fucking left me. I needed you and you left."

It wasn't about yesterday. It was about the quiet moments over the last year that had built to a sense of being left behind. Of a slow abandonment. The sensation that swirled in her belly like a viper hissing its poison was finally given a name. Abandoned.

"I went to a coffee plantation!" He threw his hands up.

"I can't," she croaked.

"Can't what?"

"I can't do this anymore." A storm of tears raged.

"Evie, do *what*?" Worry rippled through each syllable.

"I can't be us anymore."

They hadn't been "us" for several months. More and more, loneliness enveloped her over those months. Too many nights going to bed alone. Too many parties attended alone. Too many dinners spent sitting across from one another with nothing more to say than "This is good." Too many "I'm fines" and "It's okays." Too many times they'd walked side-by-side, her hand dangling beside his, yearning to be held.

"Evie."

"I can't. I can't. I can't," she wept.

He shook his head over and over again. "Evie. No. No. No. Baby look at me. Please. We can fix this. We can…"

"We haven't been a *we* in a long time."

"Please. Evie, I love you."

"I love you, too. That's why this hurts so bad. If I didn't love you, I wouldn't miss you. I don't want to keep missing you even when you're here. I don't want to feel alone anymore." She sucked in a breath, forcing a certainty into her voice that wasn't there. "I can't do this anymore. I'm sorry. Goodbye, Colm."

"Ev…"

She ended the call and turned off the phone. If she didn't, she'd pick up when he called back.

Lying in the center of the bed, she cried. In films and books, the newly single person always talked about starfishing in the center of the bed. Until last year, she'd always slept in the middle of the bed with Colm, cushioned against his strong chest. All night, they'd sleep snuggled together. Even after Queen Elizabeth came along.

Evie rolled over to the right side of the bed. Being in the middle without Colm hurt too much.

A life without him would be hard, but a life with him there but not there would be a slow death of her heart. It was the middle together or the right side and truly alone. There'd be no compromise with the ghost of "them" sleeping in the middle as they lay on opposite sides.

CHAPTER TWENTY-TWO

In The Goodbye - Colm
Present - One Minute Earlier

Colm shook his head. "No. No. No."

He dialed again. No answer. Again. No answer. Again. No answer. Again. No answer. "FUCK!" he screamed, chucking the phone across the room. "Fuck. Fuck. Fuck," he growled, hitting his head on the headboard behind him.

He rose to his feet and paced the small room. The race-horse speed of his heart choked him. Bitter bile pushed up his throat at the realization of what just happened. He'd lost Evie.

No. No. No. His fingers raked into his short blond strands. This couldn't be happening. This couldn't be how they ended.

He turned and ran out of the room, down the hall to the bathroom where he fell to his knees in front of the toilet. It all came up. The pain. The worry. The grief. The fear. The failure. It all came out. It stung and burned his throat as he heaved twelve months of the unspoken.

"Let it out," Antonio said softly, his palm on Colm's back.

After several minutes, nothing was left.

"Here," Antonio said with a sad smile, handing him a wet washcloth.

He wiped his mouth and turned to face Antonio, The happy crinkles around his dark eyes replaced with remorse.

"I'm sorry."

He wasn't sure if he was still apologizing to Evie or to Antonio. No doubt Antonio had heard him fling the phone, swear, and rush down the hall.

Antonio sat on the yellow linoleum floor and reached a hand to Colm's shoulder. "No need to apologize. I'm not going to ask if you are okay, because it is clear you are not. What happened?"

"I think…" The words caught in his throat, but he'd push them out. "…Evie and I broke up." An unfamiliar hot liquid ran down his cheeks, and he raised his fingers to his face. *Tears.* This would be the fourth time he'd cried in his life. Twice as a little boy, once a year ago, and now today.

"Think is good."

Colm's head jerked towards Antonio. "What?"

"Think means doubt. You didn't say you *know* you broke up. You think, which means it's not certain. What's not certain can be changed. Can be fixed."

"I don't know if it can be fixed," he sniffled.

"Do you want it to be fixed?"

"Of course," he said, a quick desperate pace to his words.

"Then we'll find a way."

"I don't know what to do."

Colm raised his hand to the sharp pain in his chest. Darkness loomed with a life without Evie. She wasn't just the sunshine, the sky, and the warm breeze, she was his whole fucking world.

"To fix something, we need to know when it first went haywire. When did things first start going wrong?"

"I don't know."

That was a lie. He knew what happened. It was a year and one day ago. The turning point on the map of their relationship. The start of their long goodbye.

"I think you do. You may not want to face it just yet, but if you're going to fix it, you must face it."

"I failed her," Colm whispered his confession.

CHAPTER TWENTY-THREE

The Start of Goodbye - Colm
A Year And One Day Ago

Colm turned at the sound of Evie's heels clicking down the oak stairs, letting the tingle of anticipation dance through him. After four years dating, a year of which was living together, he shouldn't still have those unmanly butterflies in his stomach, but he did. The breath would still swoosh out of him when she'd smile up at him from a book, walk through the front door after work, or lift her head up in the morning batting those blue eyes to convince him to walk Queen Elizabeth.

Each day he fell just a little more in love with her. He kept waiting to reach the bottom of the well, but he never did.

"Date night," Evie said in her sing-song voice, reaching the bottom step in a mint green dress. Her hair was swept up in a high pony that allowed fallen tendrils to frame her face. Emerald earrings that he'd bought her during their trip to Vancouver last week dangled from her ears.

Colm closed the distance between them, taking her lips in a slow kiss. "You're so beautiful," he said twining a tendril of her hair around his finger, watching a blush caress her cheeks.

Part of him wanted to lift her up and take her back upstairs. Making love to Evie was the perfect date night. They'd had many that started off with good intentions of a night out but ended up in bed. Those were the best. Tonight, though, he had plans. They were going out.

"You look pretty dapper yourself," she cooed, running her fingers up his pale blue button up, the heat of her touch scorching his skin beneath the fabric.

"We should go before I take you back upstairs," he warned with a wicked rise of his lips.

"Oh, my naughty Colmy Bear."

"That name is still terrible," he chuckled.

"You didn't seem to mind it this morning when I whispered it in your ear before going down on you." Evie winked.

The memory coursed hot lava along his veins. Yep, they needed to go, or they'd never leave the townhouse. Hell, they'd never leave the bed.

"We have a seven o'clock reservation. Let's get going, my little chatterbox." He kissed her forehead.

"You're no fun," she teased with a pout, releasing him before walking to the kitchen counter to grab her phone. "Oh, I have two missed calls from Mom. She must have called while I was getting ready."

"Date night. Remember? No calling your mom 'til after." Colm grinned, plucking his keys out of the little rainbow striped pottery bowl they'd painted at A Purple Glaze, a pottery painting place in Belmont Shore.

The townhouse they'd moved into a year ago was decorated with trinkets from their life together. It was a little bit her and a little bit him, but uniquely them. Framed pictures from trips, events, or dates dotted the cream-colored walls. Evie's Queen Elizabeth and corgi salt and pepper shaker sat on their table flanking the napkin holder his mom gave him as a gift when he'd moved into his first apartment. His travel books sat snug beside Evie's romance novels on the bookcase they'd bought at IKEA and assembled together. On each shelf and surface lived the memories of their life together and their many adventures.

Tonight's adventure was Mama Gurga's. After their first date, it had become their place. They'd get dressed up like it was their first date, sit at the same table, and enjoy the evening together. The only difference is that now when he walked her back to the car, he made sure she was thoroughly kissed before getting in. Never again would he miss a chance to kiss her like he'd done on their first date.

"Evie, when are you going to leave this guy and run off with me?" Toni, owner and head chef of Mama Gurga's, greeted them with a charming smile from the hostess stand as they walked through the door, his bulky frame open for a welcoming hug.

"I think Mrs. Gurga would have something to say about that," Evie giggled.

"Please, take him," Mrs. Gurga clucked, her ample hips checking her husband as she took two leatherbound menus from the dark walnut stand. "We've got your usual table."

"Thanks," Colm smiled.

Over the years of coming here, and thanks to Evie, they'd developed a casual acquaintance with the café's owners. Every place they went on the regular Evie collected a menagerie of people. They were never a faceless couple. Evie's warm chatterbox ways made friends wherever she went. It might be bias, but he imagined everyone fell just a little in love with her.

Yep, he was totally whipped. Jonathan gave him shit

about it mercilessly. "You're totally gone, fuckhat." He knew it, and he gave zero fucks. The only thing he cared about was the woman whose silk-soft hands clasped his as they moved through the restaurant to their usual table.

"Mama, they don't need the menu. I have a special dish for them," Toni tutted, following behind them.

"Toni, they may want to look at the wine list," she insisted, her apple cheeks blushing in a smile.

"Look at the wine list," Toni scoffed with a full belly laugh. "Mama, he'll have the IPA and she'll have the pink champagne cocktail. It's always the same drink order."

Evie's forehead puckered in embarrassment. "Maybe we should change it up once in a while."

"If you want, but why mess with a good thing," Colm said, holding her chair.

"Agreed. Why mess with perfect?"

"A man that knows when he has a good thing," Toni praised with a loud smacking kiss against his fingers. "Tonight, I have a grilled peach and buffalo mozzarella salad in a champagne vinaigrette for your starter, a pumpkin-stuffed ravioli in a white wine cream sauce for entrée, and my famous pumpkin cheesecake with cappuccino for dessert."

Evie's eyes lit up. "That sounds so yummy. It's not pumpkin season yet, how did we luck out?"

"A special treat for *our* favorite customers. Bastian will be by shortly with your drinks and starter. Come on Mama, let's leave the lovebirds alone to get lost in each other's eyes. Maybe I can get lost in yours," Toni smiled, holding out his arms to his wife.

"Maybe you just get lost," she teased with a cheeky smile, taking his arm and strolling away.

Evie arched her right brow in playful accusation. "A special meal? Colm, what did you do?"

"What?"

"Did you conspire with Toni to make a special meal to celebrate my promotion?"

"Maybe." His lips curled in a sheepish smile.

"You're too sweet to me," she said, sneaking out of her seat to come over and wrap her arms around his neck, pressing smiling kisses. "I love you so much."

That love washed over him like a gentle summer rainstorm. Over the last four years, he had blossomed in the sunshine of her love. That night on her couch after the first Corgmas, she'd said they were a team. And a team they'd become, facing each day together—the good, the bad, and the in-between.

Tonight, they'd celebrate the good. After seven years of working at Grace Memorial, Evie had been named the Director of Social Work Services. Each day she gave so much to the staff and patients at the hospital, yet still managed to come home and give more to him. To them. All he wanted was to give everything he could in return.

Colm splashed cold water on his face in the restroom at Mama Gurga's. Steadying himself, he patted his face dry with a paper towel. He pulled the black velvet ring box out of his pocket and mouthed the words *Will you marry me* in the mirror. The ring had been custom made special for Evie.

The original plan had been to propose while in Vancouver atop the treehouses at the Capilano Suspension Bridge, the Pacific Northwest rainforest canopy over their heads as classical music sang from hidden speakers in the trees. He'd researched for months. The location was like something out of a fairy tale, and Evie deserved a fairy tale. It was a perfect plan, but the ring wasn't ready in time.

A new plan was hatched. The only people that knew Colm was planning to propose were Jonathan, Evie's mom, and Leo, who was far more helpful than Jonathan with the ring design.

It wasn't needed but he'd asked Evie's mom for her blessing two weeks ago. "Oh, my word, yes," she'd squealed her approval. For the last two weeks Colm held his breath each time Evie spoke to her mom, scared Diane would spill the beans. If he didn't ask soon, she would no doubt ruin the surprise. There were already two missed calls from her. It would only be a matter of time before she'd call again.

"You got this." Grinning, he slipped the ring box into his pocket and headed back to the table.

As Colm approached, he saw that the rosy flush that had caressed Evie's cheeks was replaced with stark white. There was no warmth in her eyes, no sunshine in her expression, no smile. The only life, a slow tremor in the hand clamped around her phone.

"Evie? What is it?"

Evie just shook her head. A muffled voice was calling her name from the phone.

Unwrapping her fingers, he pried it from her hands and put it to his ear. "Hello?"

"Colm?"

"Terrance? What's wrong?"

Colm's eyes fixed on Evie, whose head just kept shaking no.

"Diane's been in an accident. Her car was in a ditch for hours. She died…She's dead. I can't believe she's dead." The words were rapid and laced with pain.

The questions stampeded in cadence with the beat of his racing heart. *The two missed calls. Were they from Terrance trying to get a hold of Evie using Diane's phone? Or were they Diane, using her waning strength to call Evie before taking her last breath? What if I hadn't told Evie to wait to call back? Would they have had a chance to say goodbye? Could Evie have sent help? Would Diane be alive?*

"I'm sorry," Colm cleared his throat, pushing away the guilt. Evie needed him. He needed to be the man Grandfather Bill told him to be after his dad left. *Take care of her.*

"You're there with Evie? You'll take care of her?"

"Of course, Terrance." He felt as if he'd failed her already.

"I have more calls to make. I'll call in the morning with funeral details. Diane had everything already planned so nobody had to make any decisions. Isn't it just like her to take care of us even after she's gone."

Colm nodded as if Terrance was in the room.

"Hold on to her, Colm. You never know when it's your last chance to do so," Terrance said, ending the call.

Colm placed the phone on the table. Lowering to his haunches, he placed his hand on Evie's chin, guiding her gaze to his. "I am so sorry, baby."

It seemed like that was all she needed to hear to let herself crumble in his arms sobbing.

Cleared throats, hushed voices, and clanking dishes around them reminded Colm that they were in public, but he didn't care. All he wanted was to hold her. To never let go. He knew Diane's death wasn't his fault, but responsibility wagged its finger at him.

"Colm, is everything okay?" Mrs. Gurga murmured, gingerly placing a hand on his shoulder.

Colm raised his head. "Evie's mom died. We just found out."

"Oh sweetie…" Mrs. Gurga turned to Evie and encircled her in her arms. "I am so sorry. Don't worry about dinner. You two head home."

"No, it's alright," he said reaching for his wallet.

"Put that away. And please, call us if you need anything," she insisted.

Colm rose to his full height, taking Evie's hand to help her up.

"I'm sorry for causing a scene," Evie apologized, her voice tiny. There was a slight sway of her legs as she stood.

"Sweetheart, don't—" There was a gasping pause. "Evie, are you okay?" Mrs. Gurga's voice flooded with panic as her eyes shot from the chair where Evie had been sitting to Evie.

Colm looked down to the small pool of dark red liquid on the light brown chair. *Blood?*

Evie's eyes wobbled following Colm and Mrs. Gurga's stares. "I'm sorry. I will clean—"

Colm reached out to catch her as she fainted. "Evie!" he shouted, scooping her up in his arms. Blood trickled down her legs.

Mrs. Gurga placed a steady hand on Colm speaking in a slow measured pace, "It will be alright. Toni was a medic in the army. We'll call an ambulance. Bastian, get Toni. Now."

Hours later in the emergency department, he sat with his face in his hands in a blue plastic chair beside Evie's bed. She slept in the fetal position, her back towards him, the hospital blanket tucked tight around her.

Leo was getting her a second blanket. Grace Memorial was the closest hospital, but Colm would have insisted they go there regardless. Leo was working the ED tonight and he'd make sure she was taken care of.

"Hey," a somber-eyed Leo said, opening and closing the

privacy curtain as he entered with an extra blanket and draped it over her. "To keep our little Evie warm."

"Thank you," a groggy Evie whispered.

"Terrible patient. You're supposed to be sleeping," he chided with a warm smile.

Evie turned and sat up in the bed. "It's hard to sleep in the ED."

"You can always show Thor here where the best napping spots in the hospital are. I'm sure he'd carry you." Leo smiled at Colm.

Most of Evie's friends were nice, but Leo was Colm's favorite. Other people just tolerated him because he was Evie's boyfriend, but Leo and his boyfriend Martin liked Colm on his own. They'd talk directly to him, not through Evie like Josephine. Leo and Martin weren't just Evie's friends, but *their* friends.

The privacy curtain swung open again and a tall man with rumpled brown hair and one collar of his shirt sticking up entered the room holding a tablet. Clearing his throat he addressed them, "Ms. Johnson?"

"Farrukh." Leo turned with an arched eyebrow. "You can call her Evie. I know she's a patient right now, but you've known her since you were a resident in doctor diapers."

Farrukh looked around the room at Colm, Leo, and back to Evie with a worried furrow. "Ms. Johnson…Evie…would you prefer to speak alone?"

"You know she's going to tell me everything five minutes after you leave and good luck getting the behemoth of a man back there away from her. Just spit it out." Leo placed his hands on his hips.

Evie always said the nurses ran the hospital and seeing how the doctor cowered at Leo's glare, Colm knew that was true.

Farrukh cleared his throat at Evie's consenting nod. "I've

looked over everything. The fainting was likely a psychosomatic reaction to the shock of your mother's sudden death. We found no other medical reason for that. You had also reported having pelvic cramping earlier in the day, so we ran some tests," he paused, taking a deep breath. His dark eyes filled with remorse. "I'm so sorry. It appears you're having a miscarriage."

"Pregnant?" Colm looked between Evie and the doctor. "But Evie is on the pill."

"It happens sometimes. Missed pills or antibiotics can affect the pill's effectiveness," he explained.

Colm leaned back remembering Evie being sick a few months ago. The doctor prescribed her antibiotics. He knew her periods were a challenge for her, even with the birth control. Of course, she'd never say it, but over the last four years, he'd noticed her wince and clutch her lower stomach at times. He'd even seen her do it earlier today but hadn't said anything.

Why hadn't I said something?

"A baby?" Evie's voice shook.

"Not anymore," Farrukh said, cringing after the words fell out.

Leo yanked the tablet from the doctor's hands. "Farrukh why don't you take a coffee break. I can go over things with Evie and Colm."

The doctor's features relaxed. Turning to leave, he then swung back. "I'm so sorry Evie. About your mom and…this."

Leo shut the privacy curtain once the doctor left. A mixture of attempted stoicism and grief etched on his face. Evie and Colm remained in their fixed positions. Her sitting in the bed, eyes cast down to her hands, shaking her head. Colm's hands on his knees looking between Evie and Leo.

Evie pregnant? No. Not anymore. There'd been a baby.

Their baby. But it was gone. In a few minutes Evie went from beloved daughter and unknowing expectant mother to orphan and grieving parent. In a moment Colm went from a man about to propose to the woman who was his world, who carried their future in her womb, to a man that lost so much and almost lost everything.

She's still here. She's your everything and she's still here.

"I was pregnant?" Evie broke the silence. Her hands rested on her lower abdomen.

"Babes, I'm sorry," Leo said, his tender gaze looking at Evie before pivoting to Colm. "I'm so sorry, Colm."

Words could not come. Too many emotions rushed within him. The loudest of which was Terrance's words to hold on to Evie. He turned and reached to touch her, but she flinched at the contact. Quickly he took his hand away, resting it back on his knee.

His legs bounced trying to soothe the riot of feelings. *She flinched at my touch.*

After Leo went over instructions and gave Evie a mild sedative, she'd fallen asleep. They'd be discharged later, but Leo wasn't pushing them out right away. The ED was quiet, so the bed wasn't needed. Jane, one of Evie's nurse friends, offered to sit with Evie as she slept so Colm could stretch his legs.

It was two a.m. The hospital was hauntingly quiet, save a lone housekeeper mopping the long corridor outside the ED. Colm wandered the halls until he came upon a small alcove with two vending machines.

Peanut M&Ms were Evie's candy of choice. If there wasn't a bakery open to pick up a chocolate chip cookie, he'd get her favorite candy. Digging loose change from his pocket, he punched in the selection. The yellow bag middle-fingered him, dangling from the rack, refusing to fall.

"Of course." Colm slammed his fist against the machine.

With each slap and slam of his shoulder and hands against the machine emotions dislodged, but the bag of candy remained, mocking him. The frustration in tonight not going as planned came out. The fury for taking away Evie's last chance to speak to her mom came out. The ache of feeling Evie's pain coursing through him came out. The grief came out. The fucking grief.

He'd failed in doing his one job. Of taking care of her. If he'd told her to call her mom, maybe none of this would have happened. If he'd not been so worried about keeping the plan, none of this would have happened.

Colm kicked the machine. The raging storm roared out of him.

"Colm." Leo's hand settled on his shoulder.

"The Peanut M&Ms are stuck," Colm said, pointing to the uncooperative yellow bag.

"I got you." Leo stepped to the side and smacked his hips against the machine, dislodging the bag of candy and pulling it out. "There's a trick to this machine. Evie figured it out five years ago."

Colm took the M&Ms. "Thanks." Colm looked down at them. Was he really bringing Evie Peanut M&Ms after losing her mom and their baby all in the same night? What was he thinking?

"She may not feel like eating for a few days, but when she does, she'll appreciate this," Leo reassured. "I'm not going to pretend I have any idea of how either of you feel right now. What I do know is loss. I've seen enough of it working here over the years. The looks on both of your faces when you found out about the miscarriage. Neither of you knew she was pregnant. You went from the elation of finding out you would be parents to the devastating realization you'd already lost. I know Evie lost Diane and the pregnancy tonight, but I also know she isn't alone in this. That you're hurting too."

Colm exhaled, trying to tuck it all back in. To keep it locked away, so he could be who he needed to be. The man that could steady Evie in this storm.

I can't fail her again.

"I know you're going to go into 'take care of her' mode. You're already there, but take a moment. You need to feel this. You need to let it out."

"I can't." Colm swallowed hard.

Leo pulled him into a hug. "You need to. Trust me. If you don't now, you'll break when she needs you."

Colm tried to resist, but Leo squeezed tighter locking him into that moment. Into letting some of it out. "I thought I was going to lose her." The words inaudible as Colm cried.

"But you didn't. She's still here," Leo soothed.

But I still might. The fear echoed within him.

Around four a.m. they arrived home. Leo had loaned her some hospital scrubs and offered to have her dress dry cleaned. She may not want the reminder of those clothes, but he'd keep them in case she changed her mind. Colm knew she wouldn't. He carried her purse, shoes, and jewelry in a plastic bag.

Queen Elizabeth shuffled over to the door as they came inside. The usual exuberant greeting dulled with sadness as if sensing the sorrow. Martin had stopped by the hospital earlier to get a key to walk Queen Elizabeth, giving them one less thing to be concerned about.

"I'll carry you upstairs. Leo says you should take it easy for a few days," Colm said, hanging Evie's purse on the hook.

"No." Evie shook her head, slipping off Leo's crocs. "I'll sleep on the couch tonight."

"Are you sure?" He watched as she shuffled over to the couch and began adjusting the pillows. He reached to help but stopped when he saw her determined glance to do it herself.

Instead, he grabbed her fuzzy yellow blanket dotted with cartoon corgis and tucked it around her after she lay down. It had been a gift from Diane.

Colm sat on the edge of the couch looking at her. She seemed so tiny and sad lying there. He fought the urge to pull her in to his chest. To ignore her protest and carry her upstairs to be with him. He wanted to hold her. Not just for her comfort, but his own.

But she didn't want that. *Evie wants to sleep here…alone.*

Guilt riddled through him. The flinch at the hospital when he'd touched her. She knew his failure. He didn't need to say anything. Evie always knew. She always understood him.

"I'm sorry Evie. I'm sorry I didn't let you call your mom earlier. I should have…" he swallowed back the threatening tears. "…let you call."

"It's okay," she whispered. "I'm really tired. I'd like to go to sleep now. We can talk in the morning."

"Okay." It wasn't okay, but maybe if they both said it was, it would be. He picked up Queen Elizabeth and set her at the end of the couch atop Evie's feet. "Keep mommy safe."

The word "mommy" sliced into him. It was so normal for them to refer to themselves as "mommy" or "daddy" when it came to Queen Elizabeth. Now, she had almost been a real mommy—until tonight.

He picked up Evie's phone, turned on the white noise app and set it on the coffee table before clicking off the light. He stood at the bottom stair, listening to her quiet whimpers and the shifting of Queen Elizabeth on the couch. Colm didn't need to look to know that the corgi lay in Evie's arms, snuggled into her chest.

He wanted to turn around. To take her in his arms. To beg forgiveness. To kiss her until this all went away.

She wants to be alone.

Colm walked upstairs to the darkness of the bedroom and pulled the ring box out of his pocket, staring at it as he sat on the edge of their bed. Only a few hours ago he'd stood in Mama Gurga's bathroom, his only care being whether or not she would say yes.

CHAPTER TWENTY-FOUR

In The Goodbye - Evie
Present - The Day After The Breakup

The late afternoon sun tiptoed into Evie's office through the half open blinds. Red rimmed eyes squinted at the computer screen. Had it really only been yesterday since she'd told Colm she was done? Part of her ached as if she'd been living with the pain of a Colm-free existence for months, even though it felt like a blink of an over-cried eye that he was gone.

Her phone remained off until this morning. She knew a collection of missed calls, unread messages, and emails from Colm waited inside. Receiving those messages would require a response. What would she say?

It was easy to pretend to be Happy Evie with others, but not with Colm. Not anymore. He wouldn't let her. At this moment, she wouldn't let herself.

Even when her dad messaged, Evie always responded. The messages were often an *Okay*, or *Thanks*. While she missed her dad and a piece of her would always want him to be part of her life, there'd never been a painful longing that ached in her chest like there was now. With dad, she'd accepted the relationship as it was, even if it wasn't what she wanted. But with Colm, it was unacceptable.

Twenty-four hours ago, Colm was a sliver in her life. She didn't want slivers. She wanted the full Colm. Every inch of him. Taking up all the space in her heart. Everything they'd been. Everything they could be. The closeness. Doing life together, not just existing together.

"Look at you, burning away the six o'clock oil," Wyatt teased.

She looked up to see him leaning against her office door frame, a to-go cup in each hand and a wide smile on his face.

"Hey," Evie said, leaning back in the plush leather chair and away from her thoughts of Colm.

"I brought you a late afternoon pick-me-up." He grinned and placed one of the cups on her desk beside the picture of she and Colm atop Sandia Peak in New Mexico.

Evie picked it up and inhaled. "English Toffee Latte?"

"With almond milk." He smirked, sitting in the brown leather chair in front of the desk. "I remembered from Pietris. Plus, I told the barista at the coffee cart it was for you, and they knew how to make it."

"I do frequent it." Evie sighed and took a sip, letting the warmth fill her. "Thank you for this. It's very kind of you."

"You looked like you needed a treat. You've seemed extra tired today and weren't your normal bubbly self during morning report."

"Oh no, was I grumpy?" she cringed.

With a wave of his hand, he dismissed the concern. "Nah. You just only clapped twice. You're usually good for at least three clapping outbursts each morning," he chuckled.

"Am I *that* bad?"

"No. You're just *very* encouraging. Like our own personal

cheerleader or soccer mom wearing a T-shirt with our names on it."

Evie frowned a bit, fiddling with her butterfly necklace. Encouragement was the most fluent of the love languages she spoke, but the way Wyatt phrased it made her behavior seem a bit ridiculous. Like she was someone people didn't take seriously.

As a department head, respect should come with the territory. Yes, she wore a lot of bright colors. Yes, she liked twirly skirts. Yes, she cheered people on. Yes, she baked cupcakes with edible glitter frosting for the staff.

Of course they don't take you seriously.

"Well, thanks for the latte." Her tone was clipped. She logged out of her computer and stood up to leave. "I should get going. I need to get home to walk Queen Elizabeth."

Wyatt reached for her arm, halting her steps. "Are you okay? You seem upset."

"I'm fine." She bit her lip.

"Evie, talk to me. We're friends. Did I say something?"

They were friends. New friends, but friends. At Pietris he'd listened to her about mom's passing and the weirdness with Colm. His strong arms had folded around her, taking in her sadness. It was nicer than Evie would admit to herself to be held.

"I'm sorry. I just don't want to be seen as a joke."

"Nobody sees you as a joke. You're more like a breath of fresh air. A lot of the department heads and deputies are a little prickly. Some are nice, but a lot are just so focused on their own department's needs that they don't take a moment to celebrate or encourage others. You do. It's nice. Frankly, it's needed." His thumb brushed soothing strokes down her upper arm.

Evie's eyes darted to Wyatt's hand.

"Sorry." He let go, clearing his throat. "I am sorry to have made you think you were a joke. You're not."

"It's okay." She smiled, rubbing her arm where his fingers had been as if the spot burned. "I should get going." She turned and unlocked the top cabinet to grab her purse.

"Yeah." He slipped his hands into the pockets of his lab coat, studying her. "It's more than my thoughtless comment, isn't it? You've been off all day. Is it Colm? I take it this weekend's date night didn't go well."

Evie sucked in a sharp breath trying to not crack. Everything wobbled. Heart. Eyes. Throat. Legs.

"I think we broke up."

Wyatt wasn't the first person she'd shared this with. Poor Queen Elizabeth played patient consoler, and she had spewed out everything to Martin and Leo's attentive ears. The loneliness. The tension. The rift.

"Wow. I'm sorry. It's stupid to ask, but how are you doing?" Wyatt blew out a breath.

"I'll be fine," she said, not sure if she was reassuring him or herself.

"Do you want to go somewhere and talk? I'm a good listener." He rubbed the back of his dark hair.

"Sorry McDreamy, she's got plans with me tonight," Leo snarked from Evie's office door, causing Wyatt to pivot.

"Leo…hey." Wyatt's forehead creased in annoyance.

"Wyatt," Leo said, crossing his arms.

The two stared off like male dogs ready to mark a tree. The last time she checked, she was not a tree, nor did she want to be urinated on.

"I should get going." Wyatt twisted to Evie flashing a small smile. "My offer stands. Anytime." With a nod, he slipped out of the office.

Leo crossed the threshold frowning. "I see McLecherous smells a wounded gazelle."

"Excuse me?" She gaped.

"He's been sniffing around you since the wedding and he's playing all the angles," he grumbled, picking up Evie's latte. "Are you drinking this?"

"I was."

"I'll buy you a fresh one. I need caffeine and sugar stat." He gulped the drink.

"I think you're wrong about Wyatt."

"I think you're *too* sweet for this world."

She crossed her arms. "Why does nobody take me seriously?"

"I take you seriously. I just think you give people too much benefit of the doubt sometimes." Leo leaned against the desk, gesturing with the coffee cup.

"Sure, telling me I give people too much benefit of the doubt screams that you take me seriously."

"Why, was that a little bit of feisty snark from my little Evie?" he mocked with a proud glint in his brown eyes. "But seriously, I don't trust the guy around you."

"Why?"

"Because I'm Team Colm and I'm not going to like anyone else sniffing around you."

"We broke up." A choking lump clogged her throat.

"Yeah. Martin and I talked last night. We don't think that's going to hold." Leo's face sobered from playful to serious. "Last night when you came over you needed me to just listen, so I held back 'til now. You can work this out. The two of you need to talk. *Really* talk."

"Leo, I—"

He raised a hand. "Nope. I've been in the front row watching the *Evie and Colm Love Story* for the last five years. The first four a sickly sweet Hallmark movie, though I know from that weekend the four of us went on that couples' trip to Palm Springs with the thin walls between our rooms that there is some Skin-a-Max antics happening between you."

Her cheeks heated.

"This last year, though, I've watched you two grow apart." Leo draped his arm around her shoulders pulling her in. "I was there that night. I saw both your hearts break. I was there when Colm beat the hell out of the vending machine to get you Peanut M&M's because he felt powerless and getting your favorite candy was the only thing that he could do to take care of you. I was there when he broke down. I never seen a man cry so hard."

Each word squeezed Evie's heart like a vise. This had never been shared with her. They'd never talked about it.

"That whole night was fucked up. You lost so much, but you weren't the only one that lost something. I don't think the two of you have ever talked about it and I think you need to. If I had to pinpoint the moment your love boat got turned around, it was that night," he said.

Despite being all cried out, fat tears fell. *Guess there are reserves.*

Leo rubbed comforting circles along Evie's back. "Let it out, babes. You need to talk about it. After that night, you never talked about it. Not to me, and I suspect not to Colm, which means he's probably not talked about it with anyone either."

"It hurts too much," she whimpered.

Leo held her tight, letting her quaking tears fall.

"Cry it out with me, babes. Then go home and call Colm. You need to tell him all you've been feeling, and you need to listen to him. And if the man does his whole stoic sexy superhero thing, use your gift of gab to coax it out of him."

"What if I don't want to be the one coaxing?" she sniffled.

"Babes, you're in love with the *wrong* man then. With Colm, you're always going to have to pry him open just a little. The nice thing is that he always opens for you, because he loves you more than anything else in this world. I've always known that, but *that* night when he carried you into the ED it was cemented. I never saw someone so scared. So desperate. I've been an ED nurse for twelve years, and I've seen a lot of scared people come through those doors. Colm didn't just look terrified of losing you, but of losing himself."

Evie's head tilted up to Leo studying his grief-stricken face. As if he was still there, standing at the nurses' station watching Colm carry her through the electronic glass doors. Most of that night was cut with moments of black, flashes of groggy clarity, and fuzzy images laced with panicked voices. Colm's tight grip holding her hand in the ambulance. His strong arms hoisting her up, ignoring the EMT calling behind him as he sprinted into the ED. Leo's calm, but concerned voice shouting, "Colm, this way."

"Talk to him, Evie. Just ask him all the questions festering in that pretty head of yours. He'll answer."

"What if he doesn't? What if we can't fix us? What if being in Costa Rica has made him realize he deserves better than this broken girl?"

"You're not broken."

"I feel broken. Leo, he's barely touched me since last year. We've had sex once since then and he insisted on a condom like he didn't trust me or didn't want to run the risk of…"

"Evie, ask him these things. It's not fair to him for you to assume his answers. It's also not fair to you to paint yourself with those colors. Talk to him. Listen to him. Above all, listen to yourself. Especially your heart, because I'm pretty sure it's telling you I'm right." His arms clenched her.

Evie closed her eyes and tried to hear the soft voice of her heart over the crashing waves of frustration and doubt pulsating inside her. She heard nothing but silence.

"My heart's not speaking to me."

"It's probably pissed at you right now. You took away its favorite playmate," Leo huffed a small laugh.

"Playmate?"

"Colm's heart. Although, I'd imagine it hasn't gone far. It just may be a little lost right now and needs its other half to whistle to him to help him find a way out of the maze you're both trapped in right now."

"Maze? Have you been reading self-help books again?" Evie snickered through sniffles.

"Maybe." The corners of his lips lifted in a smirk.

"You went a whole twenty-four hours without giving me your opinion on something. That may be a record." She swiped away her tears flashing a watery smile.

"Well, between my uncharacteristic self-restraint and your tears, I think we've earned a treat. How about we go get Queen Elizabeth and hit up Nick's on Second for butter cake?"

Hours later, Evie sat curled up with Queen Elizabeth on the couch thinking about Leo's advice to listen to her heart. While Evie was good at listening to others, listening to herself could prove difficult. It meant going quiet. It meant going deep within herself to visit the parts that she didn't like to go to. The parts that were sad, angry, and missing. The parts of herself that frowned and shouted. The parts of her that could be a little selfish. The parts of her that were ugly.

The parts she feared if others saw, they wouldn't like. Then they'd know she wasn't special.

"Ok girl, we're doing this."

She turned off the music and closed her eyes. With a deep breath she waded into the dark quietness to hear what her heart wanted. Instead of hearing her heart's desire, she heard an insistent knocking.

Evie hoisted Queen Elizabeth into her arms and went to the door.

"Hello? Who is it?" she called, peeking through the peephole.

"Evie, it's Jonathan."

"Jonathan?" She placed a wiggling Queen Elizabeth on the floor and unlocked the deadbolt. "It's after nine. Is everything—"

She opened the door and came face-to-face with an iPad, Colm's face on the screen.

"Go on a date with me, please?"

CHAPTER TWENTY-FIVE

In The Goodbye- Colm
Present - Two Seconds Later

Maybe this wasn't a good idea. It had seemed like a good idea this morning to enlist Jonathan's help to get Evie to talk to him, but the shocked eyes and slack jaw painted on her face made him doubt his plan. What had seemed like a romantic gesture now felt more like an ambush.

"You want to go on a date? But you're in Costa Rica."

"Yeah, I said the same thing," Jonathan mumbled under his breath.

"You're not helping, Jonathan," Colm chided.

"Sorry. I'll be quiet."

Colm held the iPad as if they were her slender shoulders. "Evie, you said you felt alone even when I was there. I can come home if you want me to. I'll be on the first flight out…"

"No. You've committed to the school down there."

"I'm committed to you first."

There was a tiny, almost unnoticeable, rise of her lips—a hope of a smile.

Buoyed by that almost-smile, he continued. "I can and will fly home if you want, but if we're going to fix this, we need to feel connected even when apart. I don't want my coming back to be a Band-Aid. I want us to fix us. I think using this time and physical distance to find each other again will help. I want you to feel me even when I'm not there to hold you."

Evie's arms wrapped around her body in an almost-hug. He wished those were his arms around her. That within them she'd know she was loved, that she was the most important thing to him. That even though he felt like half the man he should be, without her he felt less. That she was his anchor. Without her, he drifted alone, never truly belonging.

"I get it," Evie murmured. "We use the next thirty-seven days to fight for us. Taking away the distractions of physical proximity and our everyday life to focus on reconnecting."

"Yes." His voice breathy, as if he had been holding his breath for days.

"What happens at the end of the thirty-seven days?" Evie's fingers found her butterfly necklace and tugged.

"I come home. If you're at the airport when I come down the escalator, then we go forward together. If you're not..." Colm's throat bobbed, "...then I'll move out and we'll say goodbye."

"Buddy, no..." Jonathan sighed in warning, stopping his own words.

Evie looked up from the screen. They had both clearly forgotten about the human tripod holding up the iPad.

"What if you don't come down the escalator?"

Colm knew what she was asking. What if he didn't want to come back together at the end?

"I don't know," he confessed.

The idea of not being there was unfathomable, but it could happen. This wasn't about him winning her back. It was about them winning *them* back.

Evie's fingers tugged and rolled her necklace. With each twist of the pendant, Colm could see the thoughts rolling around in her. The questions. The concerns. The doubt. And maybe even a little hope.

"Ok." she finally said, resolve shining in her blue eyes.

"Ok." Colm said.

Never had two letters meant so much to him. They meant hope. They meant it was time to fight.

PART 2

THE FIGHT

CHAPTER TWENTY-SIX

In The Fight- Evie
The Next Day

"So, let me try to understand this. You broke up for twenty-four hours and then decided to long distance date to get your relationship back?" Josephine asked, face scrunched in dismissive annoyance.

"I think it's romantic," Martin said, placing his hand on his cheek and looking starry-eyed at Leo, who was moving through the clusters of patrons towards the bathroom.

The four were happy-houring at Beacon, a lighthouse-shaped bar in Rainbow Harbor. Nestled on the wood planked patio overlooking the waterfront, Evie filled them in on the new plan.

"But you broke up with him for a reason. You haven't been happy in months. I get that you have been together for a while, but maybe it's time to move on," Josephine said, sipping her martini.

"That's harsh, Peterson."

Martin never called Josephine by her first name. At first it had seemed a fun endearment, but it was not. There was a not-so-quiet tension between them. The two often sparred and were on the opposite sides of any discussion. Evie and Leo frequently found themselves playing referee.

"That's Peterson-Zimmer now." Josephine flashed her wedding ring at Martin, the emerald cut yellow diamond gleaming in the early evening sun. Turning to Evie, she continued her interrogation. "So, will you all be addressing these problems or just hiding them behind your smiles and his silence?"

"Like a dog with a bone," Martin muttered.

"Was that a roundabout way of calling me a bitch?"

"If the collar fits."

With a wave of her hands, Josephine dismissed Martin like pesky fly before turning back to Evie. "So?"

"Yes, we're going to discuss the issues," Evie said.

Josephine frowned, blowing out a disappointed breath. "Evie, I know I'm the hard one, and not as close to Colm as Leo and Martin, but I come from a good place. I just want to see you happy. To get everything you deserve in your life."

"I know." Evie reached across the table to squeeze Josephine's hand.

There was a hard candy shell to Josephine. Most people read her tough skin and pull-no-punches comments as bitchy, yet male colleagues that carried themselves like Josephine were seen as strong leaders and decision-makers. Men to follow. It was sexist, but she was determined to support Josephine and others in fighting it where she c could. Evie may not be as steely as Josephine but she'd sweetly correct or speak up. Papa had told her soft voices can still scream and rail against injustice.

Josephine's hard exterior was part of her protective nature. There was a reason she'd become a doctor. To care for others. To protect. Even though she wasn't a cupcake-wielding hugger like Evie, that didn't mean she wasn't as loving, she just showed it in different ways.

"I just don't get it." Josephine shifted in her seat ducking further under the oversized red umbrella.

"It's not for you to get. Just support your friend," Martin scolded.

"Down tiger," Leo said, kissing Martin's cheek as he arrived back at their table.

"Yeah, down tiger or I'll get the whip," Josephine hissed, batting her brown eyes.

"I told you she was a part-time dominatrix." Martin elbowed Leo. "I bet she charges rich businessmen a thousand dollars an hour for the pleasure of her insults."

Josephine leaned across the table squeezing Martin's cheeks and flashing him a saccharin smile. "To think, I do it pro bono for you."

"Ha!" Martin pushed her hands away and turned to Evie. "So, when does this whole long distance dating start? Knowing the two of you, there is probably a fourteen-point plan."

Evie tugged her butterfly necklace and regretted saying anything. Too much attention on her, and Josephine's continued disapproval wasn't helping. It had all made sense last night. Jonathan had taken Queen Elizabeth for a walk while Evie and Colm ironed out the details.

Saturday would remain their date night. Each would take turns planning that week's date. Evie had assumed they'd just be on video chat like they had been, only they would actually talk, but Colm said they should be special and more than just sitting on couches or beds looking at a phone. Besides the weekly video dates, each day they'd email or text each other a memory, something they'd never told each other, something that made them fall in love with the other, or something they hoped for in their relationship.

It all seemed simple, even though, it wasn't. They'd have to unknot so many feelings that had festered over the last year. Evie knew the ones tangled within her and wondered what she'd find in Colm.

"Let's leave Evie alone," Leo said, turning his gaze to Josephine. "Did I tell you Martin wants us to buy a house in Orange County?"

"I didn't realize you were *so* bougie," Josephine said, flipping her long blonde hair.

"Says the woman that wore a Vera Wang dress for her wedding," Martin scoffed.

Leo bent close to Evie and whispered, "That should get them off you for a bit."

"Thanks." She pressed a peck on Leo's grinning cheek.

"I can't. I'm done with you," Josephine said, tossing her hands up in the air and turning away from Martin. "Oh, thank the sweet little baby Jesus here comes some reinforcement."

Evie looked up from the menu to see Wyatt stride through the driftwood arbor entrance of the patio. His white shirt rolled at the sleeves and red tie loosened at his unbuttoned collar. A carefree smile rested on his face as if he hadn't just come off a twelve-hour shift.

"That man is a walking wet dream." Martin blushed, flashing an apologetic smile at Leo.

"Not my type." Leo dismissed with an eye roll.

"Wyatt is *everyone's* type. Gorgeous. Successful. Charming. Right, Evie?" Josephine glanced at Evie, who offered a non-committal shrug.

"Hey, guys," Wyatt smiled stepping up to the table.

"Wyatt, I didn't know you were coming," Leo said through a tight smile.

"I didn't know either. Josephine texted me as I was leaving the hospital. It's been a day so drinks with friends sounded too tempting to pass up." His eyes landed on Evie as he spoke.

"Too bad we didn't know. We're at a four-person table and there's no room at the inn. This place is a madhouse. I don't know if we'll find a larger table."

Wyatt glanced around the chaotic patio with limited seating options. "Oh."

"Nonsense," Josephine insisted popping out of her seat. "Wyatt, take my seat and I'll go work my magic with the manager. I've given him enough free medical advice over the years that he owes me. You'll have to sit next to Martin, but at least you'll have Evie across from you. Her conversation skills far more refined than Marty over there."

Martin glowered at Josephine.

Even if Josephine hadn't had years of prescribing antibiotics and telling Jonas, the manager that yes, he should get that mole checked out, he'd not tell Josephine no when she requested a table. Few people could tell Josephine no. Including Evie.

There was a row of too-short dresses in her closet that Josephine had talked her into buying over the years. The length never an issue for Colm. After each shopping trip, he'd grin wickedly and ask her to model the dresses for him. It often led to sex. A Josephine shopping trip six months ago led to the first and last time they'd had sex since the miscarriage.

Colm insisted on a condom. There were risks. At least that's what he'd said. The sex was slow, tentative, guarded, distant, and sad.

"Evie should totally apply. She'd be fantastic!" Martin exclaimed, pulling Evie out of her memory.

"Apply for what?"

"The Assistant Director position is coming open. Winters took a position in San Diego and leaves in a month.

They want to find someone before he leaves," Josephine explained.

"I agree Evie would be amazing, but would she want to do that?" Leo's brow furrowed in disbelief.

Josephine pointed a manicured red fingernail at Leo. "She's sitting *right* next to you. Perhaps ask her."

"Well, Evie?" He cocked his head towards her.

"I don't know. I mean I've only been a department head for a year. They normally hire former chief financial officers." Evie shrugged.

"True, but you have experience that no CFO has," Josephine encouraged.

"Fashion sense?" Leo deadpanned.

"She does dress better than any CFO I've ever met, but no. You have both clinical and administrative experience. You understand the world of the clinicians in the trenches with patients and you've been a department head dealing with personnel, budgets, logistics, and strategic planning. You're the total package."

Heat climbed up Evie's neck at Josephine's praise. "Thanks."

"You should apply, get it, and then in December after Keeney retires, I'll secure the chief of staff gig and we'll shake up that boys' club in the hospital's executive suite. Sorry Wyatt." Josephine turned to Wyatt with an unapologetic smile.

"No apology needed. I could never best you in any match Josephine."

While women and people of color made up a large percentage of the entry level nursing, clerk, housekeeping, and social work ranks of the hospital, most of the leadership and managerial positions tended to be mostly male and white. Evie and Josephine had bonded over having to work twice as hard as male colleagues and combating the discrimination and undermining comments tossed their way as young female leaders in healthcare.

"I don't disagree. Having Evie up there would be amazing. Josephine, you'll be terrifying," Leo laughed. "But leadership roles come with a lot of demands. Executives have minimal personal lives."

"Those are *your* hang ups. That's why you've remained in the ED." Josephine pointed her martini's toothpick-speared olive at him.

"True. I like my four ten-hour days and three days off a week to go surfing or have getaways with my sexy fiancé."

Mouths fell open around the table.

"Fiancé!" Evie squealed.

"After seven years he's finally making an honest man out of me," Martin announced pulling a silver ring engraved with the infinity symbol out of his pocket and slipping it on his left ring finger.

"When did this happen?"

"Leo proposed on a sunset picnic at Seal Beach Saturday evening."

Evie placed her right hand on her heart, gushing, "You guys. So romantic! Why didn't you tell me earlier?"

Leo gave her a look that said *really, girl?* When she had shown up Sunday, she was a mess. Leo and Martin wouldn't have said, "So sorry you broke up, but we're engaged."

Josephine ordered a bottle of prosecco and they toasted to the happy couple.

An hour later, Evie slipped into the front seat of her car. It was almost eight p.m. The coming night swallowed the fading beams of sun. A deep red and purple clung to the horizon. Evie sat taking in the vibrant picture of a dying day and rising night sketched in front of her. The image drifted her back to the first time she'd watched a sunset with Colm.

It was their second date. After the trip to the Japanese

gardens and dinner at a Greek café they'd walked hand-in-hand to the beach a few blocks from Belmont Shore. The early September evening found the pier quiet with only a few people sitting on benches holding fishing poles or cups of coffee and taking in the beach scene. The weathered planks below creaked as they'd strolled. At the end of the pier, they stood with Colm's arms around her waist, Evie's head nestled below his chin. They watched the sun say goodnight with burnt orange yawns.

"It's almost as beautiful as you," he murmured, the heat of his breath sprinkling promised kisses along her ear.

"How'd you get so sweet?" Evie mused in laughter.

"My mama dipped me in sugar when I was a baby."

"Oh, my word, you're ridiculous," she cackled, feeling the amused rise of his lips pressed against her cheek.

Guided by the memory, Evie snapped a picture of the sunset and sent it to Colm.

Evie: Martin and Leo got engaged Saturday night during a sunset picnic.

Colm: Amazing! I'll message both.

Evie: Do you remember our first sunset?

Colm: At Veteran's Pier in Belmont Shore?

Evie: Yes. I was just thinking of it.

Colm: Do you remember our fifth sunset?

Evie: No.

Colm: It was after our first mini golf date. We sat in my car. You were telling me about how Queen Elizabeth was still relevant. As you spoke, the colors of the sunset outlined you in this orange halo. Like a fiery crown as if you were a goddess from an Ancient Greek Epic. I remember thinking how beautiful you were. I pointed to the sunset, and you turned. You stopped talking as we sat quietly watching the sunset. Then when the sky grew dark, you turned and without missing a beat started back

up about Queen Elizabeth. The only thing I wanted to do was kiss you, so I leaned in and kissed you.

Evie: Wow.

Colm: That was one of my favorites of our sunsets. Although numbers fifteen and thirty-five are up there, too.

Evie: How many sunsets do you remember?

Colm: All of them.

With a smile, Evie slipped her phone into her purse. There was a deep well of the unspoken within Colm. If there were favorite sunsets within him, what else was hidden behind that stoic face?

CHAPTER TWENTY-SEVEN

In The Fight - Colm
Three Days Later

Leaning against the back counter in the classroom, Colm's lips curved up. A giggled debate raged between two students about whether or not horses could be purple.

"They could only be white, black, brown, or grey," a little boy with dark hair insisted.

"No, José. Mine's purple," said a rosy cheeked little girl with a too big for her face smile. "It's my drawing so I can make it any color I want. Even a rainbow with glitter."

Like butter on toast, Colm's smile spread. Evie's words whispered in his ear. *Everyone wants to sparkle.* How often had she said that while sprinkling cupcakes or putting on jewelry?

With the clap of hands and a smile, Sylvia called the children to the oversized carpet in the front of the room. Chairs screeched and clattered as crayons were tossed into the silver bucket in the middle of each of the two round tables in the classroom. Children shuffled, skipped, and ran to their assigned place on the classroom carpet. It was time for each child to present their drawing based on this morning's science lesson on animals.

Tossing a rogue brown crayon into the bucket, Colm noticed José still sat, his drawing of a horse outlined in brown incomplete. A furrowed brow scrunched the little boy's smooth features.

"José, come join us," Sylvia said in Spanish.

José looked at his picture, then to Sylvia, who stood with a patient smile on her face in the front of the class surrounded by eager children sitting crossed legged clutching their drawings. Colm recognized a familiar anxiety crawling across José's features.

He knew that feeling all too well. There was a task. Finish the picture and present. How could José present if he hadn't finished step one? The little boy's prickling fear pulsated in Colm. A shared understanding and fear twined about them.

"José, come." Sylvia clapped a little harder.

"Señora, I'm not done." José said, picking up his crayon and coloring.

"It's okay José. It doesn't have to be done."

"But—"

"José." She interrupted, her tone firm but sweet.

His forehead creased in determination. He gripped the crayon and pressed it against the construction paper. With gentle strokes brown filled in the outline of his horse.

Colm raised his palm to Sylvia, mouthing, *I got this*.

With a nod, she turned her attention back to the other students that sat crossed legged on the rug in front of her.

Colm sat beside José and allowed the quiet between them to settle before he spoke in Spanish. "Your picture is coming along nicely."

"Thank you," his tiny voice said, never breaking his

concentration as he took a green crayon to draw the grass the horse walked upon.

"How will you know when the picture is finished?"

"Señora said to use the whole paper to draw our picture. When the whole paper is full."

It was an answer Colm may have given when he was a child. Hell, at thirty-five it may still be an answer he'd give. He didn't know if José was on the spectrum. There'd need to be a formal assessment from an expert, but he knew what it was like to be so literal with instructions. To process things differently than others. It was why José was insistent that horses could only be brown, black, white, or grey. Not everyone on the spectrum saw the horses of the world in brown, black, white, or grey, but they shared an affinity for the linear, literal way things appeared, not how they could be.

As the other children tucked their pictures into backpacks and straightened their areas to leave for the day, José showed and explained his picture to Sylvia. Colm and he named the horse Brownie. What else would you call a brown horse? It was a boy horse that ate grass and liked the sun.

When José returned to his seat, picture in hand, the little girl with that too big smile said that she liked his picture. When she held up her completed picture to José to ask if he liked it, he said, "Horses aren't purple." She just giggled. Colm chuckled at the interaction.

Sylvia lined the students up to walk them to the front of the school for dismissal, and Colm ducked out of the room to find a quiet corner. He pulled out his phone and texted Evie.

Colm: Can horses be purple?
Evie: Of course.
Colm: Have you seen a purple horse?

Evie: No, but I saw a pink chicken at the county fair when I was ten.

That did not surprise him. Of course Evie would believe a horse could be purple. The purple horse people of the world needed the brown, black, white, and grey horse people. And conversely, they needed the purple horse people.

"Are you sexting your girlfriend?" Sarah said with a salacious grin, sneaking up behind him.

"We don't sext!" he groaned.

"Not yet, but if you follow my wise counsel, you shall be sexting her panties off by this time next week."

"Nope," Colm protested with huffed laugh, slipping his phone into his pocket before returning to the classroom.

Like a yipping puppy, Sarah followed close behind. "But you are texting your lady love?"

"Yes."

"More than 'Hope your day is good'?"

"Yup."

Colm was half exasperated with Sarah's endless prodding, but also grateful. Jonathan didn't get this long distance thing and thought he should get on the next plane home. Antonio had given lots of encouragement, but also questioned his not flying home.

Without much explanation, Sarah just said, "I got you. Let's woo the fuck out of her." Colm was happy to have someone that wasn't questioning him but was cautious about what defined "wooing the fuck out of her." Some of Sarah's suggestions were borderline sexual harassment even for one's girlfriend of five years. Not all of her recommendations were filthy enough to warrant a shower after listening to them, though. The best, and the one he liked the most, was texting Evie every single time he'd thought of her. The text thread since this morning showed that Colm thought of her *a lot*.

"Good Gigantor. It's a good thing you have me," Sarah

said, flicking his forehead as he leaned against Sylvia's desk waiting for her to return.

"Like a nagging mosquito," he grumbled, swatting her away and trying to focus on what he wanted to say to Sylvia about ways to help José.

"Listen, when you're not with your love it's important to let them know when you think of them. I know everyone wants the big gestures from the movies, but it's the little things that make you feel loved. It was with me."

"You were in love?" He arched a disbelieving eyebrow.

"I was."

"What…" He stopped when he saw her lip quivering.

"It's okay."

Colm wasn't sure if the reassurance was for him or herself, but she continued.

"We're friends. You've shared a lot with me. Only fair. When I was eighteen and a freshman in college, I met Derreck. He was a junior. I fell hard for him. Like stupid love. You know those friends that make you want to puke with their over-the-top sweetness? We were them."

Colm tried not to smirk, but he did.

"I take it from your face you and Evie were one of *those* couples too?"

He nodded.

"Well, we were madly in love. After he'd graduated, we flew to Vegas and got married. Neither of our parents were happy. I had two years left of school. My parents thought I'd quit. My mother is a law school professor and my dad a librarian, so you can see higher education is important to them. But I didn't. Derreck would never let me quit something so important to me. His parents thought he was too young to be saddled with a wife. Even one as fabulous as me."

"Did that impact the relationship?"

"No. It made us hold on to each other more. Derreck did ROTC to pay for college. After he graduated, he left for Army Ranger school. Then after that he was stationed at different bases for training exercises or deployed. We were married for five years and only saw each other for a total of six months during our marriage. Most of our marriage was stolen weekends, Skype calls, emails, and love letters. Like we were a couple from a different century. I'd buy special stationery and spray my perfume on it. It was so lame, but my heart soared each time I'd open a letter on lined note-book paper with his neat handwriting."

Sarah's entire face lit with the memory, flushing the sweet blush of a woman in love. She went on talking about how each letter didn't just say "I miss you" or "I love you," but illustrated it with words scrawled across paper. He'd write about things that happened in the day-to-day that tied to them in some form. To a shared memory. To a shared dream of the future. To something that made him fall in love with her each day even when apart. Even though Sarah went to bed most nights alone, she felt as if Derreck's arms held her tight.

"It was his second tour in Afghanistan. The last letter from Derreck arrived one week after he died. He was supposed to come home in another month. He was to be stationed at Fort Drum in Upstate New York, and I was already settled there. I had an apartment for us and found a teaching position. After Derreck died, I went back home to my parents in Oakland, California."

"I'm so sorry," Colm said, placing an arm around her.

A single tear rolled down her face. Only one, as if she had no more to offer.

"I am sorry I lost Derreck, but not sorry for the pain I sometimes still feel. I know it hurts because I was loved so hard. I never questioned for a moment that Derreck loved me. That he was meant for me. Even if it was only for a short time. Fifty years with Derreck wouldn't have been enough. It's been ten years since he'd died, but there is never a moment where I don't feel how much he loved me. But also, I'm not going to be Miss Havisham from *Great Expectations* mourning my lost love in my wedding dress for the remainder of my days."

"Wasn't she jilted at the altar?"

Sarah elbowed him. "Not the point."

"Sorry."

"I will always love Derreck, but I hope one day to find someone else that I can love again. It won't be like how I loved Derreck, it will be different, but equally as perfect. In the meantime, I will use my Love Guru knowledge to help you."

Colm smiled and tucked Sarah into his embrace. "Thank you for sharing this with me."

"You're welcome."

"And thank you for helping."

"Thank you for agreeing to come be my wingman tonight at El Gato Azul."

"I didn't realize I had."

"You don't expect to get my wealth of wooing knowledge for free, do you?"

CHAPTER TWENTY-EIGHT

In The Fight - Evie
The First Second Chance Date

I t was the first date night since Evie and Colm decided to try again. Colm was planning tonight's date. The only thing she knew was to be ready at eight p.m., dressed for a romantic night out.

"What to wear?" Evie puzzled to Queen Elizabeth who sat patiently in front of the opened closet.

She tapped her fingers against her rainbow terrycloth robe, her hair wrapped in a towel. Once she decided what to wear, she'd know how to style her hair. When she'd texted Josephine earlier for fashion advice, she'd suggested yoga pants and a hoodie. *You'll just be sitting on FaceTime*, she'd messaged. Evie knew there was an eyeroll accompanying that statement.

Josephine was less than supportive of this. On Friday, she'd stopped by Evie's office to hound her about the assistant director position. The posting would go up Monday, closing Friday.

"I'll think about it over the weekend," Evie said, hoping that would appease Josephine.

"Is she still harassing you about that?" Leo laughed, walking into Evie's office and taking the leather chair next to Josephine.

"Shouldn't you be in the ED scaring residents?" Josephine clucked twisting in the chair to face him.

"I'm on a break. Plus, I told them if they didn't behave, they'd get *no* juice boxes."

"In medical school, they'd prep us to fear our attendings when we got into residency, but the true terrors are nurses. Not only do you eat your young, but everyone else."

"Don't forget who you doctors come running to when the shit hits the fan," he tutted.

"Like a witch from a Shakespeare play."

"As entertaining as this is, I need to finish my workday and then get home to Queen Elizabeth," Evie chided with a sweet smile.

"Looks like there's a full house here." Wyatt appeared at the door holding two cups from the coffee cart.

Evie knew one was for her. Since Monday, each day an English Toffee latte appeared on her desk towards the end of the day. Lucy, her secretary teased, "The hottie from internal medicine dropped this off for you." The gesture was sweet, but she started to wonder if Leo was right. Wyatt hadn't made any moves, but there were overtures. Like the yellow Post-It stuck to yesterday's cup that read *Thinking of you.*

"Is one of those for me?" Leo snarked, pointing to the cup.

"No. For Evie," Wyatt said, defiantly striding through the room to hand Evie the cup.

"Thanks."

His fingers brushed hers as she took the latte. "You're welcome."

"We should probably let Evie get back to work," Leo announced, standing up. "She needs to get home to plan her outfit for the big date with Colm tomorrow."

"Ugh," Josephine groaned. "I'm out. Come on Wyatt. You can buy me a coffee before we go on rounds."

"Bye." Wyatt barely got the words out before Josephine pulled him out the door.

Leo crossed his arms, scowling. "I'm happy she dragged him away so quickly, but she is *not* subtle about her displeasure about this long-distance thing. This seems hostile even for Josephine."

"She's a mama bear protecting her cub. She worries and doesn't want to see me hurt," Evie defended, closing out of her computer.

"You're not a cub. You're an adult woman who can make her own decisions."

"As long as they're the ones you approve of," Evie snarked, pulling her purse out of the cabinet to leave.

"Babes, you understand me so well." He looped his arm around her shoulder. "So, what are you wearing for your date?"

Twenty-four hours later and Evie still had no idea what she was going to wear. There were two options. There was that red dress she'd worn for their first FaceTime date, but it reeked of failure. Next to it was the slinky silver number. She hadn't worn it since that afternoon they'd had sex six months ago. She didn't even wear it during Josephine's bachelorette weekend in Vegas, telling Josephine she'd accidentally forgotten it. As good as she felt as Colm's stare lit her on fire before they'd had sex, the dress dripped with the feeling of being broken, untrustworthy, or too risky.

Her deliberations were interrupted by the ringing of the doorbell. Tightening her robe, she padded downstairs, a barking Queen Elizabeth scampering behind.

Evie opened the door to find Jonathan with two giant tote bags, and Toni, from Mama Gurga's, standing beside him. "What on earth?"

"We're here to get things ready for your date," Jonathan said sheepishly.

"Toni, it's a Saturday night. What about the restaurant?"

"Mama can handle it for one hour," Toni said, kissing her cheek.

Over the last year, Toni and Gina—Mrs. Gurga—had doted on Evie and Colm. It was six months before they'd gone back to Mama Gurga's, and even then, they wouldn't eat in, it was too hard. Colm would just pick up their favorite dishes twice a month. There'd always be a slice of pumpkin cheesecake for dessert. Even when it wasn't pumpkin season, and even if not ordered. Gina would never let Colm pay, no matter how much he insisted. There was a pang of guilt for not coming back inside. It wasn't the café's fault what happened.

"Go get dolled up and don't come downstairs 'til eight o'clock," Jonathan instructed, placing the tote bags on the kitchen island.

"What's wrong with you?!" Toni scolded, swatting Jonathan's head. "Dolled up? She's already a doll."

"You're both sweet." She scooped up Queen Elizabeth.

"Leave Her Majesty. I'll be escorting her on her evening constitutional tonight, so you can focus on dating your boyfriend," Jonathan said, raking his fingers through his hair.

An hour later, Evie stood in front of the full-length mirror in the bedroom admiring herself. It was a first second chance date, so she went with the dress she'd worn on their first date. If they were going to find each other again, she'd use breadcrumbs to help. Pieces of their story. Of the time they weren't just falling in love but becoming something more. That's what she wanted to get back to, the more.

When *hello* held so much promise and *goodbye* was a word they'd never spoken.

"Bella," Toni cooed from the kitchen as Evie stepped into the room.

"Dude, you're not Italian. You're Albanian," Jonathan snarked.

"It's part of my shtick." Toni crossed to Evie taking her hands. "You look stunning. I must get back to Mama or else she'll think I ran off with you. Have a wonderful date and tell Colm we miss him…We miss you both."

"Thank you." It wasn't enough but was all she could offer.

Not only had Toni done this, but that night he'd rushed from the kitchen to take care of her after she'd fainted. She had flashes of conscious memory of still being at Mama Gurga's before the EMTs arrived. Of Toni's steady hand holding hers and saying, "We have you both."

"Welcome to Corgi Café. I'm your host, server, and abused sous chef, Jonathan," he said in a French accent bowing to Evie as Toni left. "Let me take you to your table."

With a quiet disbelieving laugh she took Jonathan's arm and he led her to the backyard. Enclosed in a brick wall covered in vines, it featured a small cobblestone patio and garden space now full of blue, white, and pink hydrangeas. Japanese lanterns hung crisscrossing from the top of the wall and the house. Tealights floated in a clear glass bowl in the center of the patio table, their flickering light dancing in the twilight.

"Madam," Jonathan drawled, switching from a French to British accent holding out the patio chair for her to sit.

"This is amazing." She sat down across from Colm's smiling face on the iPad across from her.

"As you can see your date is already here," Jonathan said, pushing in her chair.

"Hello." There was an unexpected flip of her belly.

Colm wore a button up white shirt, navy tie, and sported a fresh haircut. "Hello," he grinned.

Jonathan pulled a bottle of watermelon cider out of a metal bucket filled with ice and poured it into the pint glass beside her. "This is an excellent vintage from Sandia Peak for the lady."

"From our New Mexico trip?"

"I tracked it down and Jonathan went to get it."

"We're full service at Chez Corgi," Jonathan boasted.

"I thought it was Corgi Café?" Evie corrected with a giggle.

"We've rebranded in the last two minutes." He shrugged. "At Chez Corgi we specialize in one dish for dinner and one for dessert. Voila." Jonathan lifted the metal cover off the plate in front of Evie revealing boxed mac and cheese and hotdogs.

"Oh, my goodness," she laughed. "You got Toni to make Papa's dish? He's a master chef!"

"Yeah. Part of him died a little, but Colm didn't trust me to make it. He thinks my mac and cheese is always mushy."

"Colm, this is…" Evie had no words. It was the sweetest thing. After the first time she'd cooked for him, he'd promised to make her mac and cheese with hotdogs like Papa had made her, and he had made it from time to time. She'd come home after a long day at the hospital to find a bowl waiting for her.

"It's been too long since I made this for you. Although, I guess I still haven't made it for you since Toni did it."

"Hey, buddy, I helped," Jonathan said with a pout.

Colm cleared his throat. "Jonathan, what did we talk about?"

"Sorry buddy. I will leave you two to enjoy your meal, while I take Her Majesty for a walk. Evie, dessert is on the top shelf in the fridge. After I walk Queen Elizabeth, I'll lock up and leave you two alone."

"Thank you, Jonathan." Evie grabbed Jonathan's forearm as he turned to leave. "You're a very good friend."

"He's the best. Thank you, man," Colm echoed.

Jonathan scooped Queen Elizabeth into his arms giving them a wry grin. "Just let me borrow this cutie to pick up ladies at the dog park and we're even-steven."

The door clicked shut and Evie and Colm were alone. Soft instrumental music played from a speaker in an open window overlooking the patio. Awkwardness crept in and threatened to take them back to the strained chats of before. This week had felt better with the more freely flowing of text communication, but they were so out of practice of *really* talking. The things that needed to be said hung between them like curtains not letting them truly see one another. Find one another.

Tapping her fingers against the table's cool glass surface, Evie wondered how to start. Dive right into the deep, or wade in inch-by-inch?

"You look beautiful, Evie," Colm finally said.

"Thank you. You look handsome."

A pleased grin played on Colm's lips as he stared through the iPad. He also sat outside, leafy branches waving in the breeze behind him. A soft white glow illuminated his strong jawline, emerald-isle eyes, and freshly cut hair. Evie loved to run her fingers through his freshly cut hair. The barber would shave at the base of his head. It felt like velvet against her fingers as they swept along the back of his head.

Colm tugged on his tie, smiling. "Well, someone told me I should pack at least one nice outfit just in case."

Her lips quirked. "Are you wearing the slacks or are you rocking shorts below the waist?"

"Wouldn't you love to know."

With Colm's mischief-filled smile, Evie relaxed. They'd ease into this. No dropping of emotional bombs. At least not yet.

Evie scooped up a bite of macaroni and hotdog and her eyes lit up. "These are real hotdogs."

Colm had always made this dish with vegetarian hotdogs.

"Yeah. They're real hotdogs."

"Why?"

"You're not a vegetarian." Colm paused; thoughtful inquiry draped over his features. "Why do you always cook or get vegetarian meals when we go out?"

"So we can share."

"We don't always have to share."

"But I want to share." There was a defensive tone to her words.

"And that's fine, but if you wanted the non-vegetarian dish that would be ok. I just don't want you to settle for something you don't want just to make me happy," he murmured. "We don't need to share the food to share a meal together, if that's what worries you."

Was that what she'd done? Just cooked and ordered food to fit with him? At first, it felt like the kind thing to do to make him feel comfortable. The only time she had meat with him was on their first date, or out with friends. Was it about making him comfortable? Making him feel like he fit? Or making her fit?

"What made you ask about why I get the vegetarian options?" Evie asked, placing her fork down.

"When I told Jonathan to get regular hotdogs he said, 'I thought she was a vegetarian like you?' It hit me that he's only ever seen you eat vegetarian, because he's mainly hung with you when I'm around. Then I thought that I only see you eat vegetarian unless I join a happy hour with your friends late and see a split burger on your plate that you're sharing with someone or when you talk about that sushi place down the street from the hospital. It may seem weird to fixate on this, but planning this meal made me realize that you're sacrificing for me. You already sacrifice too much for me as it is. I don't want regular hotdogs in your papa's dish to be another thing you give up for me."

"Colm, I'm not—"

"But you are," he cut in. "We skip parties that I think you *really* want to go to. We leave events early when I think you probably wanted to stay. I want to be the man that can stand by your side the entire night. The man that can charm your friends. The man that isn't feeling like crawling into bed under the blanket after an hour at a party. I want to be *that* man for you, but I can't be."

"I've never asked you to be that man."

"I know."

"Colm, you're right in some ways but so wrong in others. Yes, I've wanted to stay longer at parties. I'm your classic extrovert. I love being around people, but I love being with you more. I was happy with our plan, because at the end of the night those things I thought I wanted more of were washed away as soon as you held my hand walking with me to the car. As soon as we came home and curled up together or took Queen Elizabeth for a walk. I didn't think of those things anymore, because I was happier with you than dancing one more dance or talking to one more person."

"Evie, please don't be so understanding. I don't deserve it."

"Colm. Please don't patronize me. I know my feelings, please take them seriously. I'm not being Happy Evie about this. Two things can be true at the same time. Yes, I can wish to have stayed at those parties longer, but I can also be happy I left them with the man I love. Our plan that *we* developed to face these social situations together worked, but over the last year you pulled out of our plan. It was nine months ago when you last went to something with me. You stopped going with me altogether."

"I know." He looked away. "I thought you didn't want me to go anymore."

"Why would you think that?"

"You used to ask, 'Would you go with me?' Over the last year you'd just say, 'You probably don't want to go.' Of course, most of the time I don't want to go. Not because of you, but those events are dreadful to me. So, when you asked, I answered honestly that I didn't, but thought you'd still ask me to go. Instead, you'd say, 'that's what I thought.' Then you'd just go without me. You never asked me to come with you anymore."

Evie followed the memory map of the last year. Opening Josephine and Mandala's wedding invitation, the first words out of her mouth had been, "You're not going to want to go." Colm's response was "They're more your friends." He hadn't said no to going with her because she'd never asked. Most of the things over the last nine months he never said he wouldn't go with her. He just said he wouldn't want to.

"I always want you," she said, inhaling deep the warm summer night air, allowing it to fill her to speak the words that knocked on her lips to be let out. "But I don't want to always have to ask. To be so specific like that."

"I'm sorry. I know it's frustrating that I'm so literal or don't often read beyond what is specifically said."

"I know it frustrates you, too," she said, and he nodded. "Can we just make it a blanket rule that I always want you to go with me unless I say, 'Colm, I want to go by myself?'"

"Yes." His answer was quick and decisive.

She smiled. "I know you don't like to go to these things, but you did for me. Did you see that as a sacrifice?"

"No."

"Neither did I, when we left something early."

She reached across the table and placed her hand where his would be if he sat across from her in person and not on the iPad. With a warm smile he reached his to where they would meet.

"I wish you'd said you were feeling like this sooner."

"I should have. I should have done a lot of things." Regret invaded his features. "When you said you couldn't do this anymore it gutted me. Not just the idea of losing you, but that you were right. I don't think I could have done it much longer, either. The not being us. You were right. We've not been us since last year."

"Well, we don't have to do it anymore. That's what this is about. Finding us again. Right?"

"Yes."

"So, we were both feeling unwanted and both unintentionally pushing what we wanted away."

"Yes. Like you say, two things can be true at the same time." His lips curled.

"Well, I'm pretty wise," she said with a small cheeky grin before sipping her cider.

"Evie, I'm also sorry I made you feel like I didn't take your feelings seriously."

"Thank you." Evie pulled her hand back and picked up her fork. "It's a sensitive point for me right now."

Colm leaned back too and picked up his fork. "Why?"

Evie spewed the whole story about feeling like people at work didn't take her as seriously as she'd like. It wasn't a new topic of discussion for them. There'd been blips of this during her career at Grace Memorial. It wasn't just Wyatt's comment that had triggered the resurgence of self-doubt. When Evie mentioned to Lucy, her secretary, that she was thinking about applying for the assistant director job she'd said, "You're too sweet for executive management." Then on Friday morning, during the kudos section of their morning report there were crickets until Dr. Keeney chuckled, "I thought Evie would have a kudo for someone's tie at least," and everyone laughed. She did that silent non-laugh laugh, but cringed inside.

"Nobody will take me seriously as a candidate for the job," Evie sighed. "Maybe it's my own fault."

His forehead creased. "Why would it be your fault?"

"You know, the cupcakes, bright colors, and the cheerleader personality I apparently have. Did you know some of the surgeons refer to me as Sandy? You know from *Grease*?"

"That's ridiculous. You're not even a blonde."

Evie tried not to smile, but it wasn't working. "I'm serious, Colm."

"I am too. The comparison is flawed on other levels. Sandy ends up changing herself at the end of the movie to get the guy. You'd never change who you are for anyone or any job. Nor should you."

"Thanks. I just don't know about the job."

"You'd be amazing, but do you want it?"

Evie closed her eyes trying to listen beyond the voices telling her the job wasn't for her. That nobody would see her as the assistant director. That to others she would only be the supporting cheerleader, not the team captain. All the words hissing within her like vipers only spoke of how others saw her. Not of what she wanted.

"I do."

"Then go for it, baby. I know you. If you want something, it will happen. Let people underestimate you. While they're doing that, you'll win the race. You always do. Remember when you applied for the director of social work? People thought you were too young. Too whatever. But here you are. It doesn't matter if the doubters take you seriously. What matters is that you do."

Evie smiled. Colm had done mock interviews with her

preparing for the interview with Dr. Keeney for the position. He even wore a suit, sitting at their dining room table calling her Ms. Johnson as he flipped to the next index card in his pile with the questions he'd researched online. After the mock interview and his thorough critique, he even more thoroughly sexed Evie up on top of the table, the index cards below her naked body as he, wearing only his red striped tie, drove into her until they collapsed in a sated heap. Evie teased that his index cards were ruined. Ten weeks later, they'd gone to Mama Gurga's to celebrate her promotion.

Was that when we'd gotten pregnant?

Evie bit her lip. They still needed to talk about that. It was the gigantic pink glitter elephant holding a *We Need to Talk* sign in the room. But she wasn't ready. Not yet.

CHAPTER TWENTY-NINE

In The Fight - Colm & Evie
A Week In Texts

Sunday

Colm: We said one of the things we'd do is text a memory or something we've never told the other. Here's mine. *Prayer Hands Emoji.* Ricardo and I are at a coffeeshop in downtown. He's chatting up a girl from his school. The confidence dripping from this kid is astounding. It made me think about how nervous I was when we met at Jitter Bean Coffee. I spent way more time than I normally would milling around the counter debating about approaching you while you waited for your drink.

Evie: I know. I was watching you from the corner of my eye the entire time.

Colm: *Grinning Face Emoji.*

Evie: Here's something I never shared with you. I only offered to buy the drinks for Stanley and you because I thought you were cute. I noticed you standing outside, holding the door for a woman pushing a stroller. I stepped out of line so I could be closer to you in line. I knew from that small act of kindness that you were someone I wanted to know.

Colm: I had no idea. So, when you approached me at the table, it wasn't because there were no more seats, then?

Evie: No.

Colm: *Grinning Face Emoji.* Boy, am I glad I didn't go to Coffee Bean that day.

Monday

Colm: Today, Señor Rivera Pabon, the school's principal, asked Sarah and I to go with him to San José next week to speak at an educational conference about the curriculum we're building.

Evie: Amazing! Congratulations! How do you feel about it?

Colm: Nervous. While my Spanish has gotten good while I've been here, I don't know about doing a whole presentation in it. Also, public speaking. *Scared Face Emoji.*

Evie: Will Señor Rivera Pabon and Sarah be co-presenting? To help share the load?

Colm: Señor Rivera Pabon said he'd help with translation. Sarah's Spanish isn't the best. She makes me go out with her to bars to play her Spanish-speaking wingman.

Evie: Adorbs! She's your Jonathan down there.

Colm: She is totally the female Jonathan!

Evie: Well, if that's the case, thank goodness that she

has you. Jonathan would get himself in so much trouble without you to pull him back sometimes. Frankly, I'm concerned what shenanigans he's gotten up to since you've been gone.

Colm: Don't tell Sarah, but sometimes if I don't get a good vibe from the guy then I purposely mistranslate things, telling her he's married, gay, or has herpes, so she loses interest quickly.

Evie: Terrible!

Colm: If you saw some of the guys that hit on her, you'd get it. They often look like rejects from that terrible show you watch about the pump rules?

Evie: *Vanderpump Rules.* Don't pretend you don't know. You always seem to be sitting in the living room when I watch.

Evie: Back to the presentation. I know date night is Saturday, but do you want to add an additional FaceTime for Sunday afternoon and you can practice your presentation with me? I know I don't speak good Spanish, but I can listen.

Colm: Sí.

Evie: Is that Spanish for "Yes, my gorgeous goddess?"

Colm: Sí. *Winky Face Emoji.*

Tuesday

Colm: Thank you.

Evie: For what?

Colm: When I called Mom this afternoon to wish her

happy birthday, she told me you were taking her to dinner tonight and had sent flowers to her from us.

Evie: No need to thank me. We do this every year for her.

Colm: But you didn't have to do it. Mom said you'd confirmed the plans with her last Monday, which means you still planned to do this even after we broke up. Before we decided to try again.

Evie: I love your mom. I also don't like breaking my promises.

Colm: Thank you. Even if you don't think it's a big deal. It is. Most people don't stick around after they say goodbye.

Evie: But we're not saying goodbye yet.

Colm: We're not. Hopefully not ever. But you didn't know that then.

Wednesday

Colm: Thank you for sending the selfie with Queen Elizabeth at the dog beach this evening. I like the matching happy grins on your faces. It made me think of the first time we took her there when she was still a puppy.

Evie: You were such a helicopter corgi dad the entire time! It took me ages to get you to let us take her off leash, and even then, you followed a step or two behind her.

Colm: I had to look after our girl. *Smiley Face Emoji.*

Evie: Leo says that you do that with me. That when we're out places and I run to the restroom or something, your eyes follow. That even if you glance back to Martin and him, your eyes always flick back to where I went.

Colm: Queen Elizabeth may be our girl, but you're mine. This may be caveman of me, but I want to protect you. To look out for you.

Evie: You know I can protect myself, right? There were twenty-six years of my BC life where I protected myself.

Colm: BC life?

Evie: Before Colm.

Colm: I know you can protect yourself. It doesn't mean that I don't want to do it too.

Thursday

Colm: I know we're meeting on Sunday for you to hear my talk for the conference, but I'm freaking out a bit. Sylvia asked me how the prep was going, and I felt like I was going to vomit.

Evie: Remember to close your eyes and think of England. If you stay grounded in the why you are doing something you can face the how and what.

Colm: You're right. This is important. What Sarah and I built will help so many teachers and in turn students. It's why I came here. Over the last year and a half of teaching, I've felt lost in the monotony of the day-to-day. Being here has reignited my passion for teaching. It's inspired me to redesign my curriculum when I get back. Although I'm still scared.

Evie: It's okay to be scared. It's like when we hike up

those steep climbs. I'm terrified but it's worth it for the view at the end.

Friday

Evie: I'VE SUBMITTED MY APPLICATION!!!!

Colm: That's a lot of caps and exclamation marks. Are you excited? I can't tell.

Evie: Ha! *Face Sticking Out Tongue Emoji.*

Colm: Seriously, though. I'm proud of you, my little chatterbox.

Evie: Thanks. I'm not going to lie that I'm nervous.

Colm: They should be the nervous ones.

Evie: Who?

Colm: Anyone going up against you. I know you worry people don't take you seriously, but they should. You're a powerhouse. You're like a gentle river. People are in awe of its beauty but miss how it shapes the world around it.

Evie: For a man that says he's not good with words, you often leave me speechless with the wonderful things you say.

Colm: It's funny how you talk even when you're speechless.

Evie: Aren't we sassy.

CHAPTER THIRTY

In the Fight – Colm
The Second Second-Chance Date

For the first time in months, Colm had been himself
again. More importantly, he and Evie were more
*them*selves again. After the initial awkwardness and ripping
off the first of many "Let's not talk about it" Band-Aids
they'd eased into how they used to be. The conversation
flowed. It was a good start.

"Knock knock," Antonio said from the open doorway of
Colm's room. "I'm here to collect you for your date."

Colm still had no idea what tonight entailed. The only
thing he knew was that Sarah and Sylvia had been speaking
in hushed voices at the end of each school day since Tuesday.
During last week's date, Colm had shared more about Sarah.
On previous calls there'd been an undercurrent of hostility
that dissolved once he told Evie more about her. Evie had
apparently reached out to Sarah via social media and enlisted
her help planning tonight's date.

"Oh, you'll need your ticket." Antonio clicked his tongue and handed Colm a construction paper ticket.

"The Backyard Cinema?"

"I see your gears spinning," Antonio chuckled leading Colm downstairs to the backyard.

Ricardo smiled as he stood guard at the French-style door in a blue polo and khaki pants. An index card with *Ticket Taker* written in black sharpie was taped to the right breast of his shirt.

"Hello sir, welcome to Backyard Cinema. Do you have a ticket?" His face lit with the joy of this little game of pretend they played.

"My ticket," Colm said, unable to battle his amused smile.

"Very good. I'll escort you to your seat. I believe your date has already arrived."

Fairy lights hung from the top of the six-foot limestone wall enclosing the yard. In the center of the yard the wicker loveseat faced a small inflatable movie screen. The matching coffee table held a giant bowl of popcorn and metal bucket with two bottles of IPA cooling in ice.

"This place is great, isn't it?" Evie's voice filled the backyard, and her big smile took over the entire screen of the iPad as she looked at him from atop a pile of pillows.

"It is. How'd you find this theater?"

"Oh, I have some connections in San Ramón," she winked. "Ricardo, please tell your mom and dad I said thank you." Ricardo had just pulled a beer out of the bucket and handed it to Colm.

"Of course, Señórita Johnson." Ricardo's head bowed. A bashful blush swept his cheeks.

"Ricardo. Thank you." Colm twisted, catching the spying smiles of Antonio and Sylvia standing at the open door.

"Thank you all." It was hard to believe that five weeks ago they were mere strangers.

"The movie is ready. Just press this button on the remote and it will start," Ricardo pointed to the green button and with another bashful glance at Evie, he shuffled into the house.

Colm turned to watch the door shut and noticed the curtain pulled open slightly before masculine hands tugged away prying female eyes.

"Are they spying on us?" Evie whispered; her head ducked on the screen as if she were hiding.

"Nope. Looks like Antonio wrangled them." Colm looked up noticing the lights in Sylvia and Antonio's bedroom turn on.

"They're *so* sweet. Colm, I'm so happy you're staying with them."

"They are. They're like the families you see on sitcoms."

"How is that for you?"

"It's good. I think Antonio is reminding me what kind of man I want to be."

"What kind is that?"

The kind that doesn't fail the people he loves. The words coiled in his throat, but he did not utter them. Instead, he said, "A good man."

"You are a good man."

Colm could drown in those words if he'd only let himself wade into their comforting waters.

"I think Ricardo has a little crush on you. His cheeks were red like apples when you talked to him," Colm said, changing the subject.

"He's adorably sweet, but too young."

"So, I guess you're stuck with me."

"Guess I am," Evie said, her blue eyes sparkling with sass.

The butterflies were back in his stomach. They'd been

scarce in the last year. Over the last few months, there'd been a few cautious flutters, but tonight they twerked like backup dancers in a music video.

"So, I have my popcorn and beer. Do you—"

Evie held up a Big Gulp and a bag of Peanut M&Ms. "You betcha."

Every movie night it was the same treats. Evie with her candy and Coke Zero. Colm with a pint of IPA and popcorn. She'd insist she didn't want popcorn, but halfway through, her hand would always sneak into his popcorn, so he'd always get the large. Even when they'd have movie nights at home, they'd have the same treats.

Colm preferred movie nights at home. Nobody talking during the movie but Evie. At home they could also pause the movie to refill snacks, use the bathroom, or kiss. There were a lot of kissing breaks during romantic movies.

"So, what are we watching?"

"Only the *most* romantic movie of all time…." Evie did a drumroll with her hands. "…*The Notebook*!"

Laughter burst from Colm. In five years, they'd never made it past the kissing in the rain scene. He had no idea how the movie ended. Each time they attempted to watch it, as soon as Allie and Noah kiss in the rain, Evie would pounce on him. To be honest, sometimes he suggested they watch it not in hopes of finally knowing what happens in the end, but for the pouncing. With the slide of Eve's hand up his thigh and her lips nuzzling his neck moments before that scene, he knew they wouldn't make it to the credits. The film would be paused. Evie would straddle him, and their kisses would grow deeper until Colm scooped her up to the bedroom or Evie impatiently took him on the couch. There was something about that movie that made Evie an extra ravenous seductress. *The Notebook* was his favorite movie that he'd never actually seen.

As the movie faded into the credits, he finally understood why droves of people loved it. Why Evie got starry-eyed, gushing that it was the most romantic movie ever. Even he had an ache in his chest. Three love stories weaved into a single story of one couple. There was first love, when Allie and Noah were teens before World War II. Then there was the second chance at love as adults coming together after the war. And there was the tragically sweet love of them as seniors living in a nursing home, Noah's body failing, while Allie's mind failed. Despite the sadness, they found each other over and over again. That was the message Colm took. That was the dull ache in his heart. Hope. They found each other as teenagers, again as adults, and finally as seniors, to say goodbye.

Picking up the iPad, he stared deeply into Evie's still-watery eyes. "I love you so much Evie Johnson. I'll always find you."

"I love you too. What does that mean?"

"I know we lost each other over the last year. I lost you and I think I lost me too. I know we're not there yet, but I am feeling more me…more *us*."

"Oh, Colm," Evie paused, her fingers fiddling with her butterfly necklace.

Over the years he had learned the different ways in which she'd reach for that necklace. Nervous tugs. Happy squeezes. Thinking fiddling. Sad grasps. Tonight, her fingers grazed the smooth edges in consideration.

"Me too. Leo said we've been lost in a maze since last year since…" she sucked in a deep breath. "…since mom died. Since I miscarried."

He didn't like her saying "I" miscarried. It assigned blame to herself for what happened. When, if anyone was to blame, it was him.

"I'm sorry I wasn't strong enough when mom died. I'm

sorry." Her voice cracked. "That night I broke. I never wanted to be a burden. Something you were stuck with. Something you had to take care of. Who wants a broken doll to play with? And that's what you got."

"No." He shook his head. "You're not broken."

"You say that now, but you barely touched me after. The one time we had sex you insisted on a condom—like you didn't trust me, or I wasn't worth the risk. I guess I can't blame you. Who would want a broken girl? Nobody. That thought just kept coming back. Each time you'd push me away. Each time you'd sleep on your side of the bed."

"Evie." He gripped the side of the iPad as if holding her shoulders, anchoring her to him. Or perhaps him to her. "When you fainted that night, I was terrified that I would lose you. I wanted to hold you close and never let go. But that night when we came home, you turned from me. Because I didn't protect you. Because I didn't take care of you."

"It's not your job to take care of me."

"And it's not your job to take care of me, but you do. You take care of everyone. You talk about not being strong enough when your mom died, but what I remember is the woman that was on the phone with Terrance when I came down the morning after, comforting him. Baking blueberry muffins to take to Leo as a thank you for his help in the ED. Calling the funeral home to make sure your mom's wishes were carried out. Despite your heart being tattered in a million pieces with everything that happened that night, you still took care of everyone else. You always have. You're the fucking strongest woman I know."

He paused before continuing. "You used to ask me for things. For help. Not because you needed it, but because you wanted it. You stopped asking. You stopped wanting—"

"No." Her one word punctuated by stern conviction. "I

always wanted. I just didn't want to be your burden. Your obligation. I know that's why you insisted on the condom, because you didn't want to risk being stuck."

"God damn him!" he gritted through clenched teeth.

She blinked. "What? Who?"

"Your fucking father for making you think this. For planting these seeds that if you're not perfectly content and happy people won't want you. I love you, Evie Johnson. I want you. Not because you're perfect. You hog the covers. You leave pots and pans soak in the sink too long. You talk through movies. You get every barista's life story before ordering, no matter how long the line behind you is. You watch those trashy reality shows. You don't see how fucking amazing you are. Nor how strong you are. You're not perfect, but your perfect for me."

"Colm." His name came out scratchy.

"I almost lost you. I wanted the condom not because you weren't worth the risk but because I'm not. I didn't want to risk something happening to you because I got you pregnant. Evie…" Salty tears pricked his eyes..

It all cracked wide open. The tears rolled down his face like a raging waterfall.

"When you collapsed at Mama Gurga's, I felt like my heart was ripped out. I didn't know what to do. How to help. How to make it stop. I was so scared. I'm still scared."

"But I'm here. I'm here," she cried.

"I know, but there's a voice in my head that keeps wondering for how long. Telling me I don't deserve you." Colm let the truth slip out. The fear that one day Evie would be gone.

"Goddamn *him*!" Evie shouted.

Colm nodded at his words of anger repeated by her to him. The seeds of self-doubt planted in him by his father, as well.

Colm feared being left behind. Of not belonging. Of losing the belonging he had with Evie. Most of all, he feared that he'd be like his father. Leaving behind the people that loved him in the wake of his selfishness. There were moments over the last twelve months that he feared that that was, indeed, coming true.

"I am so sorry Evie. I'm sorry that I went upstairs that night when I should've stayed with you or carried you with me to our bed. I'm sorry I didn't turn when you left for the wedding. Most of all, I'm sorry that I didn't get out of that car and run to you. Hold you. Stay with you. I'm so fucking sorry I left. I should have never left. You needed me and I left. Just like my dad."

"You're not like your dad. He left. You're here. You're still here," Evie said with fierce conviction.

"I feel like him."

"When I said I couldn't do this anymore, you fought for us. Does that seem like something your dad would do? You never let go. We're here tonight because of you. Because you fight for the people you love. I can tell you these things, but you need to tell them to yourself."

With a deep breath Colm sucked in her words. He thought back to the weeks after his dad left. There was no plea for a second chance. No apology. Nothing. Just the silence of where he'd been.

Colm had left, but she was right. He was still here. Costa Rica was an escape. But he couldn't escape the truth. His heart remained with Evie. Even thousands of miles away, he was still there. Still with her.

"I'm sorry too, Colm. Sorry that I pushed you away. I thought I was lifting your burden, but I realize I only added to it...and to mine. By not being what we were. A team. I just wanted to be strong for you. After the miscarriage, I didn't want to lose you because you had to take care of me. Like with my papa," she confessed.

"He had a heart attack."

"I was so scared that night. We'd had bad storms and tornado warnings before, but nothing like that night. He held on to me so tight as I screamed and cried. I thought we were going to die. He just kept holding on and telling me it was all going to be okay. I know it's ridiculous, but I sometimes think if I had been stronger that night that his heart wouldn't have given out. That if it hadn't needed to work so hard to calm me, that he wouldn't have died."

Colm's chest twinged with a longing pain. His arms ached to embrace her and fold her into him, allowing the beat of his heart to lull her into a sweet dream and away from these cruel thoughts.

"You know that's not true. He didn't die because you were scared. You were a little girl and tornados are scary."

"I know that rationally." She swiped at her tears.

"And I hope you know, and if you don't, please listen to me. There may be more tornadoes like the night your mom died, and *we* miscarried. It's okay to be scared. To lean on me. I'm not going anywhere. Not ever again."

"I know."

"I love you, Evie."

Colm raised his hand as if to touch her through the screen. But he couldn't. Her tears remained unwiped. Her wayward dark strand untucked. Her small smile unkissed.

"You were reaching to touch me, weren't you?"

"Yes."

"You forgot I wasn't there in person."

"Yes."

"I did the same thing last week when I reached for your hand during dinner."

"I think it's a good sign."

"Yeah. You can't reach for what you can't see. I think we're seeing each other again. More importantly, I think we're letting ourselves be seen again. Truly seen," she murmured.

"Yeah."

"Colm, I think we both have daddy issues."

He laughed.

"I also think we have some unresolved grief. It may be a good idea for both of us to talk to someone other than just each other about these things."

"Like a therapist?"

"Yes. Not a couple's therapist, but individual ones for each of us to work on these things that keep creeping into our relationships. Not just with each other, but with ourselves and others. I think we're both more impacted by our dads than we'd like to admit sometimes. I still want us to talk to each other about these things, but I think a professional may help."

"I think that's a good idea." He blew out a heavy breath.

He could almost see the victorious smirk on his mother's face. She had dragged him to child therapists after dad left, but he would just sit there with his arms crossed, not speaking. She finally gave up, but every few years she'd sprinkle the suggestion like paprika into chili.

"Well, I *am* brilliant."

An amused grin took over Colm's face as confidence sparkled in Evie's glistening eyes. Like the moon, her confidence waxed and waned. But when it was full, it lit her up, making the darkness that threatened to engulf her from the hurts of the past dissolve in its bright glow.

"I do love you," he said.

"And I you."

"What about a couple's therapist?" Colm placed iPad Evie back on the pile of pillows.

"Let's see what happens in three weeks. Then we can go from there."

"Ok, but I want you to understand this. I will be at the top of that escalator at LAX." The resolve in his voice was unmistakable. He would be there.

CHAPTER THIRTY-ONE

In the Fight – Evie
Five Days Later

The sun filtered through the former firehouse truck bay-turned indoor/outdoor seating area of Stop, Drop, and Sushi Roll. The Asian/American fusion restaurant was a favorite lunch spot for Evie, Leo, and Josephine when they had the luxury to sneak out of the hospital for an actual sit-down lunch.

"Rumor has it the director wants HR to have the top candidates for potential interviews sent to him by next Friday. So, I think we should go shopping Saturday for possible interview outfits," Josephine winked, forking a piece of black-pepper-encrusted edamame.

"I appreciate your confidence in me, but why don't we wait 'til I get an actual interview before we do any shopping," Evie said, dunking her green bean fries into the wasabi dipping sauce.

"Fine." Josephine took a sip of her iced tea. "But maybe

we could go shopping anyways. It's been ages since we've done solo 'ladies that lunch' time."

"I don't see what the difference is between time spent with me and your solo lady time," Leo clucked.

"We talk about our periods *way* more," Josephine deadpanned.

"I'm a male nurse. Eighty percent of my fellow nurses are ladies. There's nothing you can say about periods that I haven't heard."

"I'd love to have some lady time, but how about Sunday? I have plans for Saturday," Evie offered.

It had been ages since Evie had one-on-one time with Josephine. The last six months were dominated by last-minute wedding dress fittings, meetings with the wedding planner, taste-tests with the caterers, the actual wedding, and the honeymoon. Not to mention Josephine's father's family from Texas and mother's family from Denmark being in town. The soon-to-be brides had been shuttled between big family events for thirty days up to the wedding leaving little to no time for shopping trips, lunch dates, and yoga classes with Evie.

"Are Saturday's plans *date* related?" Leo's tone was reminiscent of a child taunting someone that they had a boyfriend.

"Maybe." There was a heating of her cheeks that she had *no* problem with.

After Saturday's taming of the giant pink glittered elephant in the room, the heaviness that weighed her down over the last year had lifted. Not only had she shared the tsunami of emotions drowning her from inside, but so had he. Learning that Colm's pulling away over the last year wasn't a rejection of her but was a fear of losing her was eye opening.

It would be naïve to think that the talks they'd had since

agreeing to long-distance dating each other would magically poof everything away, but it put them on the right path back to each other. Colm's agreement to talk to a therapist to deal with both the fallout from his dad and grief about the miscarriage was huge. It was as huge as Evie's agreement to do the same thing. She'd scheduled her first appointment for next week. Colm had researched some possible therapists for himself and would connect when he returned from Costa Rica.

"I take it from the blush it is," Leo said with a smug raise of his left eyebrow. "How's it going?"

"Really good. We are talking about so much."

"Has he told you why he emotionally skipped-out of the relationship for the last year?" Josephine narrowed her brown eyes.

"He didn't emotionally skip out."

"Please, he's barely shown up for anything this year. Hell, the last time I saw him was your Corgmas party and he kept disappearing. You go to more things alone than any person in a relationship that I know."

"True, I was at a lot of things alone, but—"

"Oh Evie, I hope you're not settling. You deserve better." Josephine cut in with a dismissive flick of her wrist.

"You're being harsh, Josephine," Leo warned.

"And you're not being harsh enough, Leo. What happened to being Evie's ride-or-die? You're being more bros before hoes with your boy Colm."

"Screw you, Josephine," he flared.

"Whoa!" Evie raised her hands as the two glared at each other. "There's no need for any of this. Josephine, I'm not settling for anything. Colm and I have had a lot of good conversations. I better understand where he was at this past year, and he better understands where I was. We're finding a path forward together."

Josephine crossed her arms over her chest and leaned back in the red leather chair as Evie explained. She didn't want to share everything. There were some things that would remain between Colm and her. What she did share was that the miscarriage shook him. That the last year of growing distance was fear-based on both their accounts. Not wanting to be a burden, she overcompensated by doing more on her own, and he felt unwanted because of that, and was so terrified about losing her that he pulled away.

"It doesn't make sense. If he was so scared of losing you, why would he push you away?" Josephine scoffed.

"You weren't there that night, Josephine. You didn't see. Colm was a wreck. Hell, I even had a good long cry in the bathroom after. When Colm carried her in…" Leo's words choked.

Evie grabbed his hand and gave it a squeeze.

"I know I'm a nurse and I've seen worse things come through the ED doors, but when it's someone you love—it shakes you to the core."

Josephine's face softened. "I'm sorry Leo. You're right. I wasn't there. I wish I had been." Her voice pinched sadly. "I'm not trying to be unfeeling about this. I just think there's more to this. More that he's not saying." Reaching across the table she placed her hand on Evie's and Leo's. "I know how I can be. I just want what's best for Evie, and for you, Leo. Even if you are marrying Marty McFly."

"I'm going to tell him you said that."

"I count on it." She winked.

"He looks *nothing* like Marty McFly," He pouted.

"Josephine, I appreciate your concern. I know you come from a good place, but trust me to make my own relationship decisions. Colm and I have worked a lot of things out. We'll continue to do so. I feel like we're getting back to who we'd been before last year. I'm happy again. Trust in that."

"Ok," Josephine sighed in agreement.

"Babes, you will be an unbeatable candidate for that assistant director gig. You got Josephine to back down. Mandala can't even do that."

Josephine tossed a napkin at him. "I'm not *that* stubborn."

"Mules are more acquiescing."

"You know Leo, if she was a man, you wouldn't say that." Evie tsked, giving Josephine an "I got you" wink.

Josephine fought fiercely for the people she loved. Granted a little too fiercely at times, but the tenacity of her fight was only dulled by the depth of her love.

"If she was a man, I'd say she was being an ass," Leo deadpanned.

CHAPTER THIRTY-TWO

In the Fight – Colm
The Next Day

When Señor Rivera Pabon had said they'd be presenting a session at a small educational conference in San José, Colm had pictured a meeting room at a hotel with twenty or thirty people, *not* an auditorium for two hundred. And not just any people, but school administrators and teachers. It was the largest crowd Colm had ever spoken to.

All the fears thrummed through him. Falling over his words. Forgetting his words. Too many questions. No questions. Bored eyes and blank stares.

Just close your eyes and think of England. Evie's sweet encouragement from Sunday's practice session came back to him. It was something she'd say whenever either of them needed to do something hard that they were nervous about or didn't look forward to. Queen Victoria had said this to one of her many daughters before her wedding night, when the young princess was scared about consummating the marriage. The first time Evie shared this was a hike in their first year of dating.

"Does thinking of England make sex better? Are you thinking of England when we have sex?" Colm said with an arched right brow as they traversed a steep climb at Chino Hills State Park.

Despite her fear of heights, she had never turned back on the more rigorous hikes, single file cliff walks, or rocky slope climbs. She'd just inhale, muttering, "Think of England."

"Ha! No, it's about reminding yourself why you're doing something. Remembering what's important to you. If you hold on to the why, then you can face any fear."

Smiling at the memory, Colm slipped his phone out of his pocket, opening the photos and found one of the two of them atop Sandia Peak in Albuquerque. Sweaty-faced and exhausted, but proud of their accomplishment. It had been their biggest climb—until the mountain they climbed now. The one leading back to each other. Back to them.

"Think of England," he murmured, running his thumb across their picture.

"Ready?" Señor Rivera Pabon asked, walking up with Sarah, who was tugging at the sleeves of her cardigan.

"Yup," Colm affirmed, slipping his phone back into his pocket.

"Perfect." He clapped his hands together. "I'll let them know they can announce us." He turned, disappearing into the darkness of the stage wing across from them.

Sarah moved next to Colm. "Aren't you nervous? You look so calm. I feel like I may vomit at any minute," she said, fiddling with a button on her sweater.

"Just close your eyes and think of England."

"What?"

"It's something Evie says. Stay focused on why you're doing something rather than what you're doing."

Sarah nodded. "Makes sense. Helping kids with different learning abilities and styles be successful."

"We got this." Colm squeezed Sarah's shoulder.

"You're a good wingman, Colmy Bear," she teased.

"I can't believe she told you that awful nickname. No good is going to come out of this new friendship between the two of you."

"Oh, hush." Sarah jabbed his ribs with her finger. "So, who's this Jonathan? She mentioned wanting to introduce me to him when I come visit you two."

"Nope. No good will come of that, either." One Jonathan and one Sarah in his life were enough. The two of them together screamed a future of fuckhat captions on surprise Instagram pictures of him.

Although he did like the idea of Sarah visiting "you two." It meant Evie would be at the bottom of that escalator. Tomorrow would mark two weeks left in Costa Rica. Two date nights done via video chats and then the next would be at home. Home with Evie. He could already feel her tiny but strong arms hugging him tight, her floral bakery scent invading his nostrils like the most desired conqueror. He couldn't wait to taste her sugary lips and hear her sleepy singsong good morning as she rolled over to him.

Nope. There would be no rolling over. She'd wake up in his arms. There would be no more of this his side and her side bullshit. They'd be in the middle. Where they belonged.

Before any of that, though, there was one more thing that needed to be done. One more unspoken thing to be discussed.

Just close your eyes and think of England.

CHAPTER THIRTY-THREE

In the Fight – Evie
The Third Second Chance Date Night

Sneakers. No hat. Be ready at six p.m. These were the only instructions provided for tonight's—well, *today's* date. It wasn't yet the night of date night. Evie stood in tan shorts, a loose robin's egg blue camisole tank, and white sneakers. The mercury inched close to ninety-eight degrees today. Despite the cool ocean breeze when jogging along the bike/running path that snaked against the coast from downtown to Belmont Shore, it was a steamy Saturday.

Queen Elizabeth and Evie had spent most of the day indoors curled up with *The Wedding Date* by Jasmine Guillory. Colm teased her for her love of romance movies and books, but he also enjoyed the benefits of the steamier ones. This book had steam rising from almost every page. The combination of their renewed closeness and the sexual chemistry and antics wafting from the paperback on the coffee table had Evie counting down. Only fourteen days until Colm walked through the door.

Between the endless stream of text conversations and their date nights that stretched into the early hours, Colm's presence saturated each moment of the day. Even when not talking to him, she knew he was there. For her and with her.

That aside, there were still things she missed. The feel of her fingers in his hair. The scratchy cheeks he'd rub against hers after he'd gone a few days without shaving. The taste of coffee left on her lips when he kissed her before leaving in the morning. His strong arms wrapping her snug as they slept in the middle of the bed.

In two weeks, she would stand at the bottom of the escalator at LAX and she'd look up to see Colm at the top. To the world he'd wear a stoic smile. To Evie, she'd know it was the smile of the happiest of men. There'd be a moment of playing it cool as he descended, his eyes fixed on her, but as his feet touched the floor, she would run squealing into his arms. She'd never been cool, so why bother pretending?

Evie was pulled out of her fantasy by a knock on the door. Queen Elizabeth merely raised her head and huffed her annoyance at the nap disruption.

"You really are a terrible guard dog," Evie giggled. "Don't tell daddy I said that. He'd never let me live it down that he was right about your un-guard-dog character."

"Milady." British Jonathan bowed with a cheeky grin as the door opened. When he came back up, he replaced his chauffeur's cap, looking very much the part in his black aviator sunglasses and black suit.

"Oh, my word!" Evie laughed. "You look like the bad boy driver from the wrong side of the tracks come to steal my daughter's heart."

"Hear that, Queen Elizabeth? I'm here to steal your heart."

The corgi's head popped up at Jonathan's voice and she trotted over to him for pets.

Evie shook her head. "Too late."

"Aww, the ladies love me." He winked, bending to scratch her large caramel ears. "You may want to bring a sweater, just in case. You ready?"

"Yup." Evie plucked a cardigan from the hook by the door. "Where are we going?"

"You tell me," he said, handing her an index card.

"What?"

"Colm dictated clues to help guide where we're going."

"A date night scavenger hunt." Evie's face bloomed in a smile.

This was adorable. There was no other word that would do. Colm would likely blanch outwardly, but inwardly be pleased at being called adorable.

She read aloud, "Remember, size does matter, and you know where to go to get the right fit."

Jonathan pinched his nose. "Size matters? Oh god. I'm not taking you to buy a vibrator for some kinky phone sex thing, am I?"

"Jonathan," she scolded, swatting him with the index card. "No. Even better!"

It was Mad Hatters, Evie's favorite hat shop in Shoreline Village along the boardwalk. Granted, it was the *only* hat shop. Evie was a hat girl. There were several racks in the guest room/office dedicated to her hats. Not to mention two shelves in the small, attached garage full of hat boxes. The bigger the better. An oversized sunhat was the perfect march for a twirl-worthy short sundress or flowy long maxi. Walking into the Wonderland-inspired shop with teapot shaped hat racks and tables draped in white linen topped with silver serving platters covered in hats, Evie was greeted by Leo wearing a Mad Hatter purple suit, white gardenia boutonniere, and black top hat.

"Does Colm have something on you guys? How does he

keep roping you all into these things?"

"Dude, you look ridiculous," Jonathan jested, flicking Leo's green bowtie.

"Well, at least I'm not the help," Leo counted with a smug smirk.

"Touché."

"To answer your question my dear, we're his boys. So, we've got his back. Also, I'm your ride-or-die, so I've got yours. You'd be shocked at the lengths I'd go to for the people I love," Leo said.

"Thanks," she sighed, hugging him.

"Yo! What about me?" Jonathan whined, his arms wide.

"You're so needy," Leo clucked, yanking Jonathan into a group hug. "Alright, let's pick you out a fabulous hat."

Twenty minutes later, Evie left with a giant pale pink sunhat with baby blue flowers. It was a little sweet and over-the-top but seemed to go with her outfit perfectly. Perfect for any outdoor activity. Colm had clearly put a lot of thought into this date.

The next card presented to Evie read *It's gonna be a gouda night*.

"To Brie Myself, Jeeves!" Evie cheered, commanding Jonathan to drive them to the wine and cheese shop in Belmont Shore.

"Jeeves? Colm owes me big," Jonathan muttered, opening the back door of his SUV.

Evie had offered to ride in the front, but Jonathan was leaning into his role. Except for being called Jeeves. Perhaps even Jonathan had a limit for what he'd do for a friend.

"Thank you for all of this, Jonathan. If you're free next Sunday, can I take you to brunch as thanks?"

"Nutella French Toast at Crema Café," he said rubbing his flat stomach happily before shutting the door.

The bell chimed as Evie walked through the picture

window front door of Brie Myself. The red and black checkerboard floors gleamed as the early evening sun streamed through the floor-to-ceiling windows. Black bistro tables were filled with patrons chatting, sharing cheeseboards, and sipping wine.

"Ooh La La! Look at this vision of loveliness," Martin purred with a French accent as he greeted Evie in his all-black ensemble and cranberry beret.

"Seriously! How deep is Colm's team bench?" Evie asked with a sassy lilt.

After muddling through Martin's terrible French accent and flip-flop use of English, French, Spanish, and German words, the attendant behind the mahogany counter presented Evie with a picnic basket that had instructions to not open until she arrived at the final destination. This, of course, was also taken care of by Colm, who so far hadn't appeared on this date. The anticipation of seeing him thrummed through Evie.

The final clue took Evie to a small boat dock off Naples Island, a coastal neighborhood next to Belmont Shore in Long Beach. The air was still warm as the sun slowly strolled to sleep.

Summer's hot breath kissed her skin as she walked towards a man dressed in a striped black and white T-shirt and black slacks holding a sign that read, *Colm's Little Chatterbox*. A giggle escaped Evie.

"You must be Chatterbox," The man said, tucking the sign under his arm as he reached for the wicker picnic basket. "I'm Bert, your gondolier. Your date will join us shortly."

He helped her onboard and to a plush red leather bench in the center of the boat, placing the picnic basket on a low table draped with a red checkered tablecloth in front of the bench.

Bert pulled out an iPad and connected it to a portable

charging station and turned to Evie to explain, "I usually have music playing from this as we move, so there's a continuous power supply to ensure your date is with you the entire time. Here we go."

With a few clicks, Colm's grinning face appeared.

"Hey Colmy Bear," Evie winked.

"My little chatterbox," he smirked. "I love the hat."

She grabbed the brim swaying her head back and forth modeling it. "Oh, this old thing?"

An amused gleam twinkled in his eyes as he watched her vogue with her hands outlining the hat.

"It was very sweet of you. This whole scavenger hunt was amazing. Colm! I have no words."

His face lit with laughter at how many words she used to say she had no words.

"I know. I know. I'm never actually speechless," she laughed self-deprecatorily.

"It's just one of the many things I love about you."

Heat flushed her cheeks pink. "Thank you…And thank you for all this. It's so sweet." Evie gestured around her. The hat. The boat. The picnic basket. It was all thoughtful and kind. It was all Colm. "Oh, the picnic basket. Let me open."

The basket was wicker on the outside but insulated inside with several ice packs. Evie pulled out a small cheeseboard wrapped in plastic. Different cheeses, dried meats, sliced strawberries, crackers, grapes, and flavored almonds covered the dog-shaped cutting board. Colm explained they didn't have a corgi one, but this was as close as he could find. It was still adorable. There was a bottle of chilled Prosecco with a stemless plastic glass. For dessert a mascarpone and chocolate tart.

"Colm, how did you come up with this idea?" she asked as the gondola glided through the canal.

Couples strolled hand-in-hand along the stone paths

flanking the calm canal waters. Children stood on tiptoes peeking at the drifting boats over the iron fence at the stone path's edge.

"You've mentioned wanting to do this for years. Especially at Christmastime to see the houses decorated at night. I don't know why I've never taken you. It's not Christmas, but I thought we'd start with sunset and then next time... Christmas lights," Colm explained, a hopeful expression on this face.

"Yes, but hot chocolate and cookies for that picnic."

"No gingerbread latte?"

Evie grabbed her chest in mock horror. "Oh, my word, don't tell the Gingerbread Man I forgot about my beloved gingerbread latte."

"Your secret is safe with me."

As the boat drifted, so they too drifted between conversation and companionable silence. The sunset's rainbow of amethyst, red, and orange cascaded across the dimming sky, and the gondola swayed in the water as they took in the last moments of waking day. She could almost feel his arms around her holding her close, the firmness of his chest and the beat of his heart lulling her into relaxed happiness. She imagined the spicy fresh scent of his cologne washing over her, and the minty heat of his breath placing promised kisses on her as he spoke.

"It feels like you're here. Like you're really here," Evie murmured, closing her eyes to stay in that waking dream.

"I keep turning to kiss you and have to remind myself you're not physically with me," Colm admitted.

"I miss you, but not how I've missed you this past year. I miss touching you. Holding you. Kissing you. But I don't miss you. I don't miss us. Not like I did." A single tear zigzagged.

"Baby, please don't cry," Colm choked.

"No. These are happy tears. I feel like I have you back again. Like we have us back."

"Me too."

"Last week you said with a hundred percent certainty that you'd be at the top of the escalator. Well, I can say with two hundred percent that I will be at the bottom. So, you best stock up on ChapStick, Colmy Bear! There is going to be an obnoxious LAX PDA make-out session when you step off that escalator in two weeks. I have so many kisses stored up for you."

Bert snorted, turning away from Evie and iPad Colm.

"That nickname," Colm said bemused.

"You love it."

"Because I love you."

"And I love you," Evie sighed. Twisting around in her seat, she said, "Sorry, Bert. I know we're being disgustedly sweet. We've been accused of causing diabetes in the past."

"It's okay, Chatterbox. It comes with the territory. At least it wasn't a proposal gone wrong. I once had a guy propose thirty minutes into a two-hour sail. She said no. It got awkward. This I prefer," he chuckled.

"Evie…" Colm started, a slight seriousness to his tone.

"Yeah…What—" Evie burst into laughter as a Duffy boat pulled up beside them, Martin at the helm. It was decorated with Christmas lights and Jonathan strummed an acoustic guitar while Leo sang "To Make you Feel my Love." All three men wore matching white shirts, red bow ties, and suspenders with barbershop quartet style hats.

Evie turned iPad Colm to see the scene. "Look baby, sailing buskers."

"Ha!" Bert barked.

"Seriously, how did you get these guys to do this?"

"This I did not orchestrate. They've gone rogue," Colm groaned.

CHAPTER THIRTY-FOUR

In the Fight – Colm
Four Days Later

"Your friends have gone viral," Sarah chirped, plopping next to Colm at the orange picnic table on the perimeter of the school's outdoor cafeteria.

"I'm aware," he mumbled as she pulled up the video of Jonathan and Leo serenading Evie on her phone.

Someone captured the entire thing on their cellphone from the stone path overlooking the canal. The video showed up on several social media sites with the hashtag, *only in the LBC*. One of the nurses in the ED had seen it and recognized Leo, who then sent it to Colm and Evie. Leo thought it was hilarious. Martin was happy he was only the driver and not caught on camera. Jonathan joked that it may score him some dates, like he needed help with that.

"So, Jonathan is the one playing guitar, right?"

Colm nodded at Sarah's question.

"Cute, but the one singing is a dish I'd like to taste," she purred.

"I'll let him know, but his fiancé, the guy driving the boat, may not want to pass that dish," Colm quipped.

"Boo to him for not being single, but yay to you for making a joke. I'm liking this 'Happy in Love' Colm. Much better than the 'Grumpy in Love' one I first met," she said in a taunting baby voice, squeezing his cheeks as he jerked away.

"Yet you still persisted to force me into a friendship."

"What can I say, I'm a saint. Shrines will be erected to my benevolent greatness." An air of magnanimous self-satisfaction wafted as she batted her eyes and pressed her right hand to her chest.

Colm shook his head and scooped up more gallo pinto. The simple rice and bean dish with fresh salsa had easily become his favorite go-to lunch since coming to Costa Rica. Sylvia made it most mornings for breakfast with an assortment of fresh fruit and pastries. She'd shown Colm how to make it. He'd started making it for breakfast for the family and bringing leftovers for lunch. Evie asked for the recipe, but he'd refused, insisting that he'd make it for her when he came home.

At three p.m. California time in a week and a half, he'd have Evie in his arms. He had so many plans for when he got home. He'd be gentlemen enough to wait to enact several of his plans until they were behind the closed doors of their townhouse. Plans he planned to repeat—*a l*ot—in between welcome back dinner with mom and friends, hitting the dog beach with Queen Elizabeth followed by walking with both his girls to Pietris for Evie's English Toffee latte and his Greek coffee, going on long kiss-filled hikes, and jaunting off on a few weekend getaways since they'd missed their annual summer trip this year. So many plans.

Colm grinned at this. *We have plans.*

"So, did you talk to her about that thing?" Sarah asked, interrupting his daydream.

"Umm…" Colm swallowed.

He hadn't given specifics to Sarah. It didn't feel right to share with her something he'd not fully shared with Evie yet. He'd just said there was something else. Something that needed to be discussed before they fully moved forward.

Colm had started to say it after Bert, the gondolier, mentioned that proposal. The whole night flooded back to him, the guilt still gnawing on him like a dull-tooth zombie, teeth not sharp enough to instantly shred and kill, but slowly rip and tare. As lost as he was in the euphoria of Evie's declaration that she'd be at the bottom of that escalator, Colm knew he'd never truly be free until he atoned.

"Bad form, my dude," Sarah chided with a shake of her head. "I don't want to bring you down. I know how happy you two are again. Your girl uses so many exclamation marks and heart emojis when she talks about you. Oh, BTW we've moved on from DMing to texting. I think you're stuck with me. She may be my new bestie."

Colm's face pinched, but Sarah dismissed him with a flick of her wrist. "My point is, I know when we're happy we don't want to rock the boat but sometimes the boat needs to be rocked so we know it's seaworthy. I know you've had a lot of big conversations already. What's one more?"

"I know." It was the last of the unsaid things. The last Band-Aid to rip off.

CHAPTER THIRTY-FIVE

In the Fight – Evie
Later that Day

Evie's pink heels clicked happily against the grey-blue terrazzo floor of Grace Memorial's lobby, three large boxes of pizza in her hands. The ED had been swamped most of the day. Too many patients and not enough doctors, clerks, nurses, and social workers meant the staff in the ED were exhausted. Some of the day shift crew had stayed over to help with the remaining patients. Evie had spent several hours there today helping with patients and had ducked out to pick up some food for the staff. When the ED was like this, it was hard to get away for lunch breaks.

Evie would drop off pizza to their breakroom in the back and relieve the current social worker. Once they returned, she'd round on the inpatient wards to check on the staff there.

"Well, hello stranger," Wyatt said, striding up to Evie, his lab coat flowing like the cape of a superhero.

"Wyatt." His name said more as an accusation than a greeting.

There had been limited interaction with Wyatt since last week. Outside of a brief hello or head nod during morning report or passing in the hall, they'd not really seen each other. There'd be English Toffee lattes left on her desk during the week, but no Wyatt. Evie wasn't sure if it was just coincidence or if she was avoiding him. There was a pang of guilt at that. Wyatt had been kind and sweet since meeting.

There was a gnawing discomfort about him since that day in her office when his flippant comment left her with the sense of being seen as a little ridiculous and Leo's comment about him sniffing around her. Yes, the clapping outburst statement was a joke. Yes, he'd said he respected her. Yes, he'd never made any romantic overtures or moves. But…there was a but—something that swirled and kicked in her belly, warning to be careful.

"Here, let me help you with those," he said reaching for the boxes of pizza.

"No. I have them," she protested.

"Nonsense. It's not a problem." Are these for the ED? I heard they'd been slammed. Josephine mentioned you've been down there helping most of the day."

"Yeah," Evie said, yanking at her butterfly necklace before falling into step beside Wyatt as they walked towards the ED.

"Now, you're bringing them pizza. You really are too good to be true."

"I'm not *that* good." she mumbled. There was that warning kick in her belly again.

"Don't be so modest. This is the type of leadership I was talking about. Encouraging. Empathetic. Not above rolling up your sleeves and getting in there with the frontlines. I'm with Josephine. You'll make an amazing assistant director. She mentioned you put your hat in the ring."

"Yup," Evie said, feeling the tension relax. This wasn't the conversation of a man with romantic intentions. Just one colleague giving kudos to another.

"Are you going to Josephine's shindig on Friday?"

Evie went to answer, but was interrupted by a shouting Leo, "Thank God! Nourishment!" He lifted his arms in the air as if in thanks to the pizza gods from behind the charge nurse desk in the center of the ED bullpen.

The room buzzed with activity. Between hallway consultation about patients, nurses shuffling doctors between rooms, and arguments over the phone with inpatient staff to get someone a bed upstairs, staff teased with good natured ribbing, plucked candy from the dish at the clerk's desk, and groaned about needing a drink or giant scoop of ice cream after this day.

"Look! Dr. Kurtzman brought us pizza instead of getting us the eight beds we need to admit our patients," Leo hollered eliciting a round of "boos."

"Ha…Ha," Wyatt mocked. "Actually Ms. Johnson bought the pizza. I'm just the muscle."

"Sure are," someone hooted.

Someone else whistled.

"Hey! Don't make me have HR come down here to do another sexual harassment training." Leo rose, placing his hands on his hips like the six foot schoolmarm he'd grumble about having to play in the ED.

"Wyatt, you can put those in the breakroom. The troops know they're here, so they'll come a-running. Thank you for your help. I'm going to relieve Michael, so he gets a break." Evie smiled, turning.

"Hey, you never answered my question. Josephine's party?"

"Yup. I'll be there."

It was after eight p.m. when Evie got home. Martin had volunteered to walk Queen Elizabeth knowing Evie and Leo were slammed. In just over a week Martin wouldn't have to pitch hit with Queen Elizabeth anymore because Colm would be home. Each time she thought that she felt like jumping and screaming like she was a kid again finding out that they'd have breakfast for dinner. God, she loved brinner nights.

Colm teased her for calling it that, but despite his mocking when she'd come home to veggie sausage breakfast burritos he'd smile, "I thought you'd like some brinner tonight."

Showered and changed into a silky sleep cami and shorts, Evie stood at the open closet surveying her clothes. It was part of her evening routine. Time to decide what to wear tomorrow. As she was pulling out her navy pinstripe pencil skirt, the mirrored door started vibrating. Her feet swayed as everything tilted violently left and right. Queen Elizabeth whimpered.

"Earthquake," Evie said in a calm tone. "It's okay girl."

She scooped the shivering corgi into her arms and dashed to the doorway, pressing tight to it as things shook. Several shoe boxes flew out of the top shelf of the closet onto the floor. The clatter of picture frames tumbling from bookshelves filled the room.

After several seconds, everything stilled. Evie remained pushed against the doorframe holding Queen Elizabeth, soothing her whines with slow strokes of her silken coat and quick kisses to her head while she waited in case there were sudden aftershocks. It had been strong enough to knock several loose things down, but for the most part everything looked okay, and the power was still on.

Within seconds, texts came in from Leo, Josephine, and Jonathan checking in. They were okay. She replied that she was fine too. Then she texted Scarlet, who was okay, just annoyed that it preempted the TV show she was watching.

Evie turned on the bedroom TV to hear the local news coverage of the earthquake. It had been a 5.3—strong enough to do a little damage, but nothing major. She got Queen Elizabeth settled down to chew a fresh rawhide in her bed and started picking up the things scattered on the floor.

As she was replacing the contents of a box that had fallen out of Colm's side of the closet, she found a small black velvet box. She tossed it back in with the other things, but curiosity bested her. With a click she opened it to discover an emerald cut pink sapphire ring with tiny clear sapphire butterflies dotting the silver band.

Her jaw went slack.

Was this for her? Was he planning to propose? Her heart raced. *Why hadn't he? Did she want him to?*

Evie startled, dropping the ring box as her phone came to life with an incoming video chat request from Colm.

"Baby, are you okay? Is Queen Elizabeth? Mom texted that there was an earthquake."

"Yeah. We're okay. She's in her bed with a rawhide. I'm just cleaning up some things," Evie explained, not taking her eyes off the ring box.

"Was there a lot of damage?"

"No. Just loose stuff that fell. I'm picking up the last."

"Are you sure you're okay?"

Evie broke the stare off with the ring box to look at Colm. If he was here, he'd be in this room. The ring box would be in front of them both. The conversation would happen. That had been the problem. Not having the conversations. Just pushing things down. Pretending. The last few weeks taught her that talking made it better. Even the hard things. *Especially* the hard things.

"Colm, this fell out of a shoebox that toppled out of the closet," she said, holding the ring box in front of the phone.

His mouth went slack. "Evie."

"How long has this been here?" Her voice kept steady.

"Since *that* night."

Evie nodded. "Dinner wasn't to just celebrate my promotion, but to propose."

"Yes."

Josephine had been right, there was something more. He had the ring, but never asked. He had said she wasn't broken. That to him she was strong. Not a burden to take care of. He said he wanted her. But he never asked.

"I know why you didn't propose that night, but why not after? You said you feared losing me, but wouldn't this bring some sense of security? Unless…" A choking lump threatened to stop her, but she swallowed it down painfully. "…it wasn't about being scared of losing me, but about a forever with me."

"No." Indignation flared in Colm's eyes.

"It's okay if it was that. It makes sense." There was an attempt to sound reassuring, but her voice wobbled.

"No," he roared, making Evie flinch. "It wasn't you. Never you. You are my forever. It was me. I don't deserve you."

"But you do. Why do you insist on that narrative? Colm, it—"

"Because I stole her from you," he interrupted, slamming his fist against his chest. "Your mom knew I was proposing that night. I told you to wait to call her back, because I was scared that she'd let it slip. Ruin my plan. My *fucking* plan! Those two missed calls from her that night—what if you had called her back? You could have said goodbye. You could've helped her. If I had told you to call…she may still be alive. Our *baby* may still be alive."

His face crumbled; heavy tears rolled. As if he'd kept these ones just for this. Like the good china of tears brought out only for the truly heart wrenching occasions.

Like a jagged knife his words sliced into Evie's heart. His guilt radiated through the phone. It all clicked together. It all made sense. The guilt had slowly consumed him over the last twelve months. A vicious voice inside him telling him this was all his fault. That he was a bad man. That he wasn't worthy. Sorrow seeped through her seeing the pain that he carried.

That night, Colm had apologized and she had said it was alright, because it was. But in the haze of her own grief, she hadn't heard what he was saying. It was a plea for forgiveness, the seedlings of guilt already sprouting.

"Colm, look at me," Evie said.

His head was bowed, his hands over his face, sobbing.

"Look at me." A soft fierceness to her tone.

He looked up, his eyes a turbulent sea of emotion.

"Those two missed calls weren't from mom. She was already dead. They were from the good Samaritan that found her car in the ditch. They'd used mom's phone to try to get a hold of family while waiting for the ambulance. They'd left a message. I didn't listen to it 'til weeks later, thinking it would be the last time I heard her voice. I just wasn't ready to hear her voice for the last time."

"But what if it had been…"

"What if? What if? You think I don't ask myself that all the time? It wasn't her. If it had been, I still wouldn't have called her then. Not because you said to wait, but because I wanted to wait. Think about how many times you'd say, 'We're on a date,' and I'd still call mom in the car. You'd just roll your eyes and laugh. If I'd wanted to call her, I would have."

Colm sniffled, swiping at his eyes.

"Baby, the miscarriage wasn't your fault. You didn't cause it. I didn't cause it. Neither of us are at fault. It just happened. What *is* our fault is not properly grieving. Not talking about it. To each other or to anyone else. That's what we're both guilty of. Nothing more."

He nodded, the tears still coming. Evie soothed him, telling him to cry, to let it out. To expel the guilt that snarled away his ability to move forward. His ability to love himself. To let himself be loved. To love her the way he wanted to, without any fear.

"This is what good men do. They blame themselves. They take responsibility, even when it's not theirs to take. You are a good man, Colm. You're my man."

Evie held the phone inches from her face, as if clasping Colm's face. As if her breath could caress him through the screen in a ghost of a kiss as she spoke. As if the heat of her body wafted through the phone, tucking him into the embracing knowledge that he was good. That she loved him. That he loved her. That they loved each other.

"I'm sorry I didn't tell you about the calls not being from mom. Colm, if I'd known…I'm so sorry."

"You didn't know because I didn't tell you." Colm closed his eyes. "I should have talked to you. Why did I stop? We used to talk about everything. We were a team."

"I think we were both consumed by wanting to not burden each other that we forgot that part of being a team is sharing the load. We're talking now and that's what matters."

"I never want to stop talking to you again."

"I never want to stop talking to you either."

"I love you so much."

"I love you, oodles and boodles," she said, a sweet silly grin on her face. It was a little goofy, but they needed that.

"My silly little chatterbox. You are my forever. Please know that. Please never question that."

Forever? There'd been vivid daydreams about a future with Colm for years. She'd imagine them greyed and wrinkled, her stirring batter in the kitchen, him sneaking behind her and looping his arms around her, a lifetime of family photos surrounding them.

"Colm…"

He raised a hand, stopping her words. "Please don't say anything right now. Not about me being or not being your forever. Just wait."

"Wait 'til when?"

"The bottom of that escalator at LAX. We'll meet there. Then we'll start our forever."

"What do we do in the meantime?"

A wry grin spread. "We continue dating."

CHAPTER THIRTY-SIX

In The Fight - Colm
Two Days Later

"So, you proposed," Sarah said, pulling her thick dark curls into a high ponytail while they waited outside Señor Rivera Pabon's office.

Colm's forehead creased. "No," he said, leaning against the wall. Its coolness felt good after helping Sylvia with the kids on the playground during their afternoon recess.

"You told her she was your forever."

"That's just a fact, not a proposal."

"A fact that you *proposed* she confirm by showing up at the arrival escalator at LAX." A smug smile stretched across her face.

Colm opened his mouth, and then closed it again. Had he proposed? On accident? Can you propose on accident?

He shook his head. "No. It's not a proposal unless you say, 'Will you marry me?' There also needs to be a ring."

"Oh, but my dude, there was a ring."

Fuck. He proposed. That's not how it should have gone.

Not through tears on video chat. There should be candles. Romantic music. A speech. That's what he'd planned for the first proposal. Not this.

"This will not do." He raked his fingers into his short blond hair.

Sarah placed a comforting hand on his bicep. "It's all good. It doesn't matter how you ask, only how she answers. You want forever with Evie, right?"

"Of course."

"Ok. You said when she shows up at LAX, then you start forever. We have eight days. Let me help you plan a proposal redo," she said with a thoughtful tap of her chin. "So many ideas. My love of swoony romance novels is going to come in handy. Boy, you are so lucky you have me."

"Colm. Sarah," Señor Rivera Pabon called, hurrying down the hall. "Sorry, I'm late. I have news. Two of the administrators from last week's conference are interested in adopting the curriculum we've built."

"Sweet!" Sarah wiggled and danced, her dark locks bouncing.

"Careful Medusa." Colm flinched, stepping away from her swinging strands.

"This is why I keep mine short," Señor Rivera Pabon joked, running his fingers over his thinning hair. "Come in my office and let's discuss. Both administrators want to meet with you next week before you leave. We can set up conference calls."

Colm nodded and smiled, but inside he was hatching a plan. A plan for forever. God, he loved plans.

CHAPTER THIRTY-SEVEN

In The Fight - Evie
Later That Night

E vie stood on the sidewalk waiting for Jonathan. Nights like this she missed Westin, Missouri. The small town with little light pollution offered a blanket of stars each night. On summer nights as a little girl, she'd sit with criss-cross applesauce legs in an oversized Adirondack chair on Papa's back porch, spoon clanking against a ceramic bowl filled with cookie dough ice cream as she'd look up at the stars dotting the black velvet night. Papa would point to different constellations telling the stories from Greek mythology. Evie's favorites were always the love stories, but none of them ever seemed to end happily. Lovers separated by war, death, and then forever in the stars, always reaching for one another.

"Your chariot awaits," Jonathan drawled, rolling down the passenger window as he pulled up.

Jonathan was accompanying her to Josephine's party tonight. Partly because Leo and Martin were spending the weekend in Lake Arrowhead with Martin's parents and partly because Jonathan had a thing for Josephine's little sister Nina. They'd met a few times over the years. She was one of the few women immune to Jonathan's charms. So, of course, he was smitten.

"What, no chauffeur hat tonight?" Evie asked, waggling her eyebrows.

"Mess up this perfectly coiffed hair? Don't you dare," he warned, ducking and batting her hand away as she reached to tousle his sandy strands.

Fifteen minutes later, Jonathan parked in front of Josephine's downtown building. Josephine loved to entertain, whether it was a large party with dancing, a fancy dress dinner, or a casual brunch. Each year she'd even throw a classy canine cocktail party in honor of Queen Elizabeth's birthday. She'd find any excuse to put on a fancy dress and play hostess.

The party was on the rooftop garden/pool area. Olive trees twinkled with lights throughout the Greek garden inspired décor. Solar lights lined brick paths that wove between the oversized potted plants, bistro tables, and iron benches surrounding the kidney-shaped pool.

Guests sat at tables chatting over plates of tapas, lounged poolside with goblets of red wine, and swayed to music on a makeshift dance floor. Like the queen she was, Josephine held court at the center of the party, her statuesque physique accentuated by a strapless ruby red jumpsuit.

"Evie," Josephine greeted with a peck to her cheek. "You made it. I see you brought Jonathan."

"Yep. You look gorgeous, as always," Evie cooed.

"Josephine." Jonathan kissed her cheek. His eyes darted around the clusters of people. "Is Nina here?"

Josephine pointed with her tumbler of scotch toward a small group on the dance floor. Nina's strawberry blonde curls bounced as she danced to Lizzo in a hot pink tulle skirt and lavender top. Just like her big sister, Nina drew all the light to her. Both sisters were gorgeous but had personalities that took charge in different ways. Josephine's commanded. Nina's was effervescent.

Like a moth to a flame, Jonathan soon found himself on the dance floor with Nina. Much of the night he fluttered between hanging with Evie and flirting with Nina, who flicked him away like a rogue piece of lint. It would have been sad if Evie hadn't observed Nina's secret glances at Jonathan when he wasn't looking. It was like a strange game of cat and mouse where he chased, having no idea he was actually the mouse.

"Looks like Marla's making a move on Wyatt." Josephine rolled her eyes, gesturing with her drink at a buxom brunette flirting with a smiling Wyatt.

"He doesn't look too unhappy," Evie observed with a laugh.

Wyatt's eyebrow arched with intrigue as the second-year oncology resident cooed and giggled, gliding her fingers across his bicep. Relief swept over Evie. Leo was wrong. If Wyatt was sniffing around her, he'd be here. Not there.

Josephine's eyeroll was deafening. "Men are so easily distracted by big tits squeezed into a top that's a size too small."

"Wasn't Mandala wearing a rather tight top when you first met her at that art show?" Evie teased.

"Oh, hush." Despite the dismissive hand gesture, a gentle blush resided on her cheeks. "Any news on the assistant director gig?"

"The director's secretary called late this afternoon. The director will be on vacation next week, but they locked in interviews for the week after."

Josephine gripped Evie tight and squealed, "I told you!"

"Told you what?" Jonathan asked returning to Evie's side after Nina deserted him for a tall man in black rimmed glasses.

"Like the boss she is, Evie will be interviewing for the assistant director position at the hospital in two weeks."

He gave Evie a high-five. "Nice job!"

As the party wore on, Evie offered to take empty platters to Josephine's condo. Truthfully, she'd wanted a break, but didn't want to ask Jonathan to leave. At the moment, he sat on a bench with Nina, deep in conversation. He'd flashed her an "I'm finally making headway" smile a few minutes ago. There was no need to force him to leave yet, even though she was fatigued.

It had been a long week. Between the busy workdays and long late-night chats with Colm, she was exhausted. They'd talked again last night until almost one a.m., though it hadn't been as emotional as Wednesday, which felt like the last hurdle in the marathon they'd been running. All hurts had been laid out on the table. No more secrets weighed either of them down or kept them from moving forward.

Forward to what end, Evie still wondered. To forever? It was like a new pair of shoes. A little snug once on and in need of breaking in. Did Evie want to break it in? Did she want forever?

"There you are." A smooth baritone slinked into the quiet kitchen where Evie stood rinsing porcelain platters.

"Wyatt. Having fun?" Evie asked as she placed the last platter in the dishwasher.

"Yup."

"You and Marla seem to be hitting it off. She's pretty cute."

"She's okay." He shrugged, leaning against the kitchen island across from Evie. "Not really my type."

Evie laughed. "What? I think Marla's everyone's type. She's gorgeous."

"I prefer a more subtle beauty," Wyatt murmured, stepping close. The space between them heated as he reached to tuck a fallen piece of hair behind her ear.

"What are you doing?"

"Something I've wanted to do since the wedding." Wyatt closed the space between them, dipping his head. Hot breath laced with scotch fell on Evie's lips in a prelude to a stolen kiss.

She pushed him away. "Stop!"

"I know you feel it too. There's something between us," he insisted, leaning back against the kitchen island.

"I have a boyfriend."

"That's not a denial. That's an excuse. He's an excuse," Wyatt said, undeterred. He stepped forward.

Evie gave him a warning glare. "Colm is not an excuse."

"I think he is. I think you're settling. Maybe he feels safe, but do you want a life of safe or a life of love?"

"You don't know me. You don't know Colm. You don't know us," she snapped, pivoting to walk away.

He grabbed her arm. "I know that he left you when you needed him the most. What kind of man does that? I was the one holding you while you cried at Pietris."

Evie yanked her arm away. "What kind of man tries to steal someone's girlfriend?"

"The kind that knows that girlfriend's deserve better than a man who emotionally checks out after she loses her mom and miscarries in the same night. I would never do that to you, Evie. I'd never leave you."

The venom and cruelty of his words were a gut punch. "I never told you about the miscarriage. How do…" Her words faltered. "Josephine."

How much had Josephine told Wyatt? What was her

motivation? There was nothing sloppy about Josephine. While everyone else played checkers, Josephine played chess. Evie had always assumed they'd been on the same team. Until now.

"I'm sorry. I shouldn't have said that about the miscarriage. I'm sorry."

"Not as sorry as I am for trusting you." She glowered.

"Hey. Hope I'm not interrupting." A cheerful Josephine sauntered into the kitchen carrying two empty trays.

"I don't think you mind inserting yourself," Evie sneered, crossing her arms over her chest.

Josephine placed the trays on the counter, her face pinched. "What's that mean?"

"Why don't you tell me? What have you been telling Wyatt about me? About Colm? What's your angle?"

"Evie…"

"You have said enough, Wyatt. You're dismissed," Evie hissed with a dismissive flick of her wrist.

"Evie, that's rude. That's not like you," Josephine chastised.

"What's rude is pretending to be my friend while you try to sabotage my relationship. The little comments. Filling Wyatt's head and sending him in like a relationship destroying heat-seeking missile. I've tried to ignore it. I've made excuses, but it hasn't been just during our rough patch. You've never liked Colm. When we got your wedding invite, he'd said, 'They're more your friends.' He was right. You've never given him a chance."

"He's not what you need. You need a partner that will match your brightness. Not shade it. I just don't want to see you settle."

"Settle?" Evie's voice raised.

"Yes. You're dynamic. He hides in the corner. You can talk to anyone. He barely says two words."

"Yes. He's those things and so much more. If you gave him a chance, you'd know that. Colm is my forever. That's not something you settle for. That's something you reach for and hold on to."

Evie spun and walked out, certain of her truth. She was ready to leave behind the self-doubt and the pain of the last year. She knew what she wanted. A forever with Colm.

"Evie, wait!" Josephine called, her heels clicking loudly as she chased, leaving Wyatt standing in the kitchen. Grasping Evie's arm, Josephine halted her steps. "I'm your friend. You must believe I just want to see you happy. What's best for you."

"Friends don't do what you did. You not only tried to destroy my relationship, but you didn't trust me to make my own decisions. To choose my own happiness. What kind of friend is that? I don't want people in my life that don't respect me."

"I respect you."

"If you did, you wouldn't have done that. We're done. Goodbye." Evie walked out the door.

CHAPTER THIRTY-EIGHT

In The Fight - Colm
The Last Chance Date Night

Seven was Colm's new favorite number. In seven days, Evie would be wrapped in his arms, not just smiling at him from his iPad. Tonight's date night was a cooking class. Of sorts.

Sylvia stood peacock proud wearing a chef's hat with her faithful sous chef, Antonio, clucking, "Yes, Chef." For the last date night in Costa Rica, they would learn one of Sylvia's recipes to replicate at home. Besides the gallo pinto, one of Sylvia's best dishes was her vegetable empanadas.

The iPad at the townhouse in Long Beach allowed Colm to watch Evie flutter around their kitchen in her cartoon corgi apron over a short pink dress, hips swaying as she chopped vegetables. Her dark hair tumbled down her slender shoulders. A tiny blue stepping stool used to reach top cabinet items. The music of Queen Elizabeth's stubby feet scampering across the hardwood floor.

In seven days, he'd be in that kitchen, leaning against the island listening to Evie's melodic voice chattering away. Reaching above her to grab things off the top shelf making that step stool unnecessary. Looping his arms around her middle as she chopped vegetables. Pressing kisses to her neck as Queen Elizabeth blinked up at them. Lifting her onto the counter, her legs coiled around him as he drove into her. God, he was like a teenaged boy thinking about Evie.

"Sylvia, this is so yummy," Evie gushed, closing her eyes with another bite.

He smiled at Evie's praise of Sylvia for the food she'd made back in Long Beach. It was totally his Evie.

He and iPad Evie sat across the table from Antonio and Sylvia, eating the fruits of their labor. A flickering candle danced between them in the air conditioned breeze.

"Evie's an amazing chef," Colm boasted, watching her big smile beam with gratitude.

"You've mentioned," Sylvia chuckled. "Evie, we've heard so many wonderful things about you. You may be Colm's favorite topic of conversation."

"Amor, that's how men in love are," Antonio's sweet chide accompanied a sweeter kiss to her temple.

"You two are adorable! How long have you been married?" Evie asked.

"Twenty-six years of marriage, but thirty years together."

"Wow. What's your secret?"

Antonio snaked his arm around his wife, pulling her close. "We've never stopped dating. Like a plant, love is something that must be watered so it lives. It keeps growing. Continuous dating is love's fertilizer."

"You know fertilizer is shit, right," Sylvia teased with a cheeky grin.

"Your mother always said I was full of it."

"You are, but you're full of so much more." Their big smiles pressed in a quick kiss.

After dinner, Evie and Colm went upstairs. Laughter filled each step as he ascended the stairs, watching the shaking movement of the iPad as Evie mirrored his steps at their townhouse. It was only seven p.m. in Long Beach. The sun still streamed through the tiny picture windows along the stairway wall.

In their rooms, they lay atop their beds. His in Costa Rica. Hers in Long Beach. Losing themselves in conversation with each other. Making plans for after he came home. His excitement about the two schools interested in the curriculum he and Sarah had built. His pride as Evie talked about her upcoming interview for the assistant director position.

The only lull in the conversation was the sadness as she talked about what happened last night at Josephine's party. There was a not-so-subtle desire to go full vengeful-Viking on this Wyatt, but the greater threat to Evie was the fight with Josephine. It weighed heavy on her. It weighed heavy on him.

Since they'd met at Corgmas five years ago, there had been a stiffness between he and Josephine. Most conversations got translated through Evie. Josephine's prickliness and his natural standoffishness went together as well as pickles and peanut butter on a sandwich.

That aside, Josephine had been a good friend to Evie through the years. Always encouraging her, and fiercely protective. He had witnessed it on a few occasions. At a happy hour two years ago, a surgeon from the hospital referred to Evie as "Little Miss Sunshine" when she walked away to use the restroom. Before Colm could say anything, Josephine verbally slapped him with a cutting remark. And last year, she'd flown to Missouri to attend Diane's funeral, staying a few extra days to help.

"Baby," Colm started, wishing he could run his fingers through the dark hair that hid the collarbone he loved kissing. "I know you're hurt by Josephine. You have every right to be. But she's been a good friend through the years."

"What she did was so wrong."

"I know, but sometimes people do wrong with good reasons. It doesn't absolve the wrong, it doesn't change what happened, but it helps us understand. I don't think Josephine was trying to be cruel or malicious. I can understand going about things in the wrong way, a way others don't quite understand. Sometimes that even you yourself don't understand."

"You're too sweet," Evie sighed. "Josephine comes for you —for *us*—and you're advising understanding."

"I know. You're a bad influence on me," he grinned. "You always say two things can be true. I think Josephine was in the wrong with her actions but justified in her reasons. It came from love."

"Are you saying I should forgive her?"

"No. I'm not telling you to do anything but be open to listening and following your heart. Whatever you choose to do when it comes to Josephine, I support and love you."

"I'm not going to lie, the social worker in me is *so* turned on by you right now. I want to jump your bones so bad," she giggled.

Colm's lips tugged up in a devilish smile. "Yeah?"

"Yeah," There was a sultry quality to her voice.

"If I was there, I'd take those pink lips of yours in a slow kiss." He lowered his voice while watching her fingers trace that heart shaped mouth.

"What else would you do?" she asked, breathless.

"I'd trail kisses down your jaw, to your neck, to your collarbone." Heat prickled down his body. "I'd slip the straps of your dress off your shoulders and pull it down."

As the words flowed, his arousal grew watching Evie bring to life the scene he sketched. She pushed down her pink sundress to reveal a lacy white bra. As if her hands were his, she unclasped it. It wasn't her delicate fingers rolling those taut pink nipples but his rough ones. Not her pinching, but his mouth nipping and licking them as her breath hitched.

It was his strong hands lowering her onto the bed, bunching the dress at her middle and tugging lacy panties down. His hands spreading her open, not hers. His tongue licking down her center, drinking up her sweetness, not her finger guiding her through the waves of pleasure.

"Colm, I want you inside me," she pleaded.

Unzipping, he freed himself. "Are you ready for me?"

"Yes."

Their eyes locked as they moved in tandem toward release. It wasn't his hand sheathing his arousal, but her wet heat clenching around him.

"Colm, I'm almost there," she whimpered.

"Come for me, baby. I've got you."

Her face contorted with the euphoria of climax, and seconds later his own orgasm shuddered through him.

Their eyes remained tethered as they came down together, breathless and satisfied. It had been months since he'd had sex with Evie. Over a year since he'd had *this* kind of sex with her. The unguarded and open sex they'd had before the miscarriage. The connected sex, where both were fully present. Captured in each other.

"That was amazing," Evie exhaled, beads of sweaty satisfaction dotting her forehead.

"I know."

He'd masturbated thinking of her before. Not just over the last months of dry spell, but even in the years before. The years full of regular sex. Yes, he was that guy. The one whose girlfriend got him off more than any actress or random woman in too-tight yoga pants at the gym. The dream girl that starred in his fantasies lay mostly naked on top of their bedspread right now, skin pink from orgasm. An orgasm he'd caused. The thought sent a cocky pride through him.

"If you thought that was good, just wait 'til next week."

CHAPTER THIRTY-NINE

In The Fight - Evie
Four Days Later

With a happy sashay, Evie strolled into the office. "Afternoon Lucy. How's your day going?"

Lucy looked up from her computer. "Aren't you chipper? You've been on cloud nine all week. Does this have to do with Colm?"

A hot flush jigged up Evie's body at the mention of his name. Who knew they were phone sex people? The last four nights in a row Evie drifted to sleep sated and dreaming of the deliciously filthy scene Colm's words painted of the things he wanted to do to her.

"Just excited he's coming home soon." Evie blushed and went into her office.

"The nonstop flush and gettin' some smile on your face almost makes me think he's already home," Lucy called from her desk.

"How about you put a 'gettin' to work' smile on your face instead of harassing me?"

Fifteen minutes later, Lucy popped her head into Evie's office. "You have a delivery." Walking in, she plopped a bouquet of chocolate chip cookies on Evie's desk. "Is it from Colm?" she asked as Evie read the card.

Nope. A tight smile set.

It was from Josephine. Since Friday, Josephine had texted *I'm sorry* every day. Now, she'd sent an apology arrangement of Evie's favorite cookie. The betrayal of Josephine's actions curdled in Evie's stomach making her nauseous at the sight of the cookies. The fact that Josephine was ruining her favorite cookie infuriated Evie even more.

"It's from a grateful patient's family," Evie lied, ripping the card up and tossing it into the trash. "Feel free to put it in the reception area and email all social work staff to stop by to grab a cookie."

"Ok. Do you want one?"

"Nope. Not hungry," Evie said through a fake smile, as she turned to her computer.

"If you're sure," Lucy said, turning. "Hey! Cookie?"

Evie looked up at Lucy's greeting. Wyatt stood in her doorway holding two cups of coffee.

"No thanks, Lucy."

"Your loss." She shrugged. "Well, I'm going to put these down and then get a coffee. I'd grab you a latte Evie, but I see your delivery boy has one for you. Back in ten," she said, leaving the office.

"What are you doing here?" Evie's hackles rose.

Wyatt sighed, "You're not responding to my messages, and I wanted to apologize."

Like Josephine, Wyatt had texted several *I'm sorrys* and a few *I had too much to drinks*.

"I was clear at the party," Evie glared and crossed her arms over her chest.

"I know. I overstepped. I thought there was something

between us." His hands motioned between them. "I realize that it was completely one sided. I want to apologize for my actions. I know this means a friendship between us is unlikely."

"It's impossible," she asserted.

A wave of dejection swept over his face. "I know. I told you when we first met, I was impatient. I should have just waited instead of pushing."

Her eyes narrowed. "Wyatt there's nothing to wait for. Even if Colm wasn't in the picture, I couldn't be with someone like you."

He flinched at her words.

"I think it's best if, besides work-related things, we no longer interact."

"I know. I'm not going to pretend this isn't a gut punch, but I understand," he murmured, placing the cup on her desk before pivoting to leave. Stopping at the door, he looked back with a sigh, "While Josephine told me things about you and Colm, she never pushed me towards you. In fact, she reminded me repeatedly that you had a boyfriend. That day she dragged me out of your office, she lectured me about pushing up on you while you were still with Colm."

"Did she send you here to tell me this?" The indignation unhidden in her tone.

"No. This is me. I made such a mess of things with you. I couldn't look myself in the mirror knowing I destroyed your friendship with Josephine. I'm truly sorry."

"Thank you for apologizing. I know you're not a bad guy, just not my guy."

There was good in Wyatt. Two things could be true. Someone could be good and still do bad things.

"I truly wish you and Colm the best. I hope he is your forever and you're happy," Wyatt said.

As Wyatt disappeared out the door, she tossed the drink in the trash declaring, "You hope. I know."

CHAPTER FORTY

In The Fight - Colm
Day Sixty In San Ramón

Colm sipped coffee at the table. Ricardo asked a million questions about Denver, where he'd be heading in the fall for his yearlong student exchange program.

Between bites of mango, Antonio chided with an amused grin, "Stop pestering poor Colm on his last breakfast with us."

"Sorry," Ricardo apologized.

"It's okay," Colm reassured. "I've never been to Denver, but perhaps Evie and I will visit while you're there. You can show us the sights."

"Evie?" A blush filled Ricardo's cheeks.

Yep, he's crushing on my Evie.

The thought of "His Evie" spread happy warmth through him. Sixty days ago, "His Evie" felt so far away. Now, she lived inside him again. Burrowed back into his heart. Her presence felt even thousands of miles away. In ten hours, he'd be able to touch her, not just feel her. They'd start their forever.

Thanks to Sarah and Antonio's supportive counsel, this proposal would be done right. At the bottom of that escalator, he'd bend to one knee and ask the question he should have asked so long ago. A year and five weeks ago in Mama Gurga's bathroom, he'd worried about her response. Today, there was no fear. He knew she would be there. He knew she would say yes.

"You ready?" Antonio said, placing his hand on Colm's shoulder.

"Yeah. Let me grab my bags."

Colm placed his cup in the sink, taking one last look at the kitchen. As happy as he was to go home and enjoy breakfast sitting across from Evie at their dining room table, there was a sad ache at saying goodbye to Sylvia, Antonio, and Ricardo. They'd absorbed him into their family, giving him a glimpse of what life could have been if he had been a boy like Ricardo with a dad like Antonio, and also a sneak peek of a future where he could be a man like Antonio, going to the bakery daily for his sweetheart and sweetly chiding his child to remember their manners.

"We're going to miss you," Sylvia sniffled, wrapping Colm in a tight squeeze. "If you decide to accept the offer, please know you have a place to stay."

The administrator of San Ramón's schools wanted to hire Colm and Sarah to continue their consultation for several schools in the city. Much of it could be done remotely, but they'd like them to come back in person next summer for another sixty days just as they'd done this year.

Sarah jumped at the chance, but Colm said he'd need to think about it. He'd discussed the offer with Evie Thursday night. He wanted to help, but the idea of leaving her again left him queasy. The time in San Ramón had reignited so much more than just his passion for teaching. At the same time, though, it also represented his running away.

San Ramón had been both one of the worst and best decisions he'd made. It took him from Evie, but also brought him back to her.

Two things can be true at the same time. Evie's words whispered in his ear as he walked to Antonio's car.

Despite the very long drive, Antonio insisted on taking Colm to the airport in San José. With final hugs from Sylvia and Ricardo, Colm took one last look at the yellow brick house he'd called home for the last sixty days. The house grew small as they drove away. He turned forward to his forever.

CHAPTER FORTY-ONE

In The Fight - Evie
That Same Day

I n front of the closet Evie tapped her feet, while an unhelpful Queen Elizabeth lounged on the bed. The age-old struggle of what to wear filled the room. How fancy? How sexy? How sweet girl-next-door? There was a ten-minute internal debate about a flowy skirt with no panties to facilitate easy access after she'd drag Colm into the nearest bathroom stall at the airport. She'd concluded that while they were clearly now phone sex people, they weren't public sex people. The cleanliness of LAX bathrooms did not elicit a burning desire in Evie's lady parts.

Evie turned at the sound of the doorbell, and trotted downstairs in her robe, Queen Elizabeth too consumed with her napping to follow.

Terrible guard dog. Evie chuckled.

"Please don't shut the door," Josephine begged.

"What are you doing here?"

"Making amends. Evie, I was so very wrong. You're

completely right. I never gave Colm a chance. I had an image of who I thought you should be with and when Colm didn't fit that, I wrote him off. I was so wrong about him," Josephine said, her voice cracking with emotion.

"What brought on this reversal?"

"Colm reached out to me this week."

Evie gaped.

Josephine continued. "He sent me a text Wednesday saying he forgave me. Saying that he understood that I was just trying to protect my friend. That he'd not been the man he should've been over the last year but is striving to be that man again. The man you fell in love with. He also apologized saying he'd never really tried with me either and that the state of our relationship was on him, as well."

"What?"

"Yeah," Josephine said in awe. "I couldn't believe it. I was so wrong on so many levels. Colm is a good man. I was wrong to judge him based on, frankly, superficial reasons. Trust that Mandala has given me quite the talking to. Even more, I am sorry that I didn't trust you. You're right, I wasn't a good friend."

Evie shook her head. "No. You're a good friend who just went about things the wrong way. Wyatt told me you didn't push him on me. That you reminded him that I had a boyfriend and to back off."

"Yes, but I shouldn't have told him the things I did. That's on me. I was wrong about so many things," she sighed.

"Thank you. I appreciate you owning your actions," Evie said, her stance softening. "In the future, please allow me to make my own decisions. It doesn't mean that you can't raise concerns, but you need to trust me."

"Future?" A small hopeful smile bloomed.

"Yeah."

"Before we hug on it, I also want to add an additional

stipulation. When Colm gets back, and after the two of you lock yourself in the bedroom for the next week, I want to take him to dinner. Just him and I. It's time for me to truly get to know him. I want to grow old and fabulous with you, so I need to bestie-up with your forever. Do you think he'd be open to that?"

"Yeah. I think he would," Evie smiled and wrapped her arms around her friend.

Growing up her mom would say "Forgiveness costs nothing but pays in dividends." Yes, Josephine made mistakes. But mistakes made from a place of love were forgivable. Holding on to anger after Josephine's vulnerable amends would only hurt Evie. And there'd already been too much hurt.

"Aww, look at this lady action!" Leo whistled from Josephine's car.

"Leo?" Evie's right eyebrow ticked up.

"Hey babes, now that you two are ladies that lunch again, we're here to get you ready for the big reunion." As Leo jumped out of the front seat, an unknown woman and man emerged from the back.

"Yeah, so that's Sasha, my hair stylist, and Raymond, who did my makeup for the wedding. They're here to glam you up —my treat," Josephine said. "I want you to know I'm fully onboard. If I need to get a Team Colm shirt, I'm sure Leo has one I can borrow."

"Damn skippy," Leo said, carrying three garment bags. "We've got outfit options for you. All guaranteed to knock his pants off."

"Thank you." Evie looked at Leo and then to Josephine. "Both of you."

Three hours later, Evie walked through the sliding glass doors of the arrivals area at LAX. The strappy white heeled sandals and flirty sleeveless pale pink dress Josephine had chosen were perfect for their first hello of forever. This dress was the same color as the one she'd worn at Jitter Bean Coffeehouse at their first meeting. Sasha fashioned Evie's brunette locks into loose silky curls.

She chose to wear the teardrop emerald earrings Colm had bought her in Vancouver. She hadn't worn them since that night, and it felt important to wear them today to symbolize that they'd move forward. Hands clasped. Hearts open. Towards their forever.

His flight, which had been delayed per the airline app, would be landing in about twenty minutes. Evie figured that once he was off the plane and cleared customs, he'd be on the escalator by five fifty p.m.—six at the latest.

At five twenty p.m., the app showed the plane landed. She could barely contain her excitement as she stood at the bottom of the escalator searching the faces of the newest wave of arrivals as they descended.

At six fifteen, there was still no Colm.

Six thirty. She texted. No response.

Six forty-five. She called. Direct to voicemail.

Seven ten. Seven thirty. Eight p.m. Still no Colm.

Eight forty-five. An apologetic United representative said that since she was not technically family, they could not provide passenger information.

Evie sat in a daze at baggage claim, searching the arrivals board for any incoming flights from Costa Rica. Maybe he missed his flight and wasn't able to text. Maybe he'd broken his phone. Maybe he'd forgotten it. Maybe it was stolen.

At nine o'clock, Evie stood at the bottom of the escalator to greet the eight fifty-five arrival from San José, but by ten p.m. it had become painfully clear.

He hadn't come.

Only if you looked closely would you see the tears rolling down her cheeks. There were no loud sobs. No bloodcurdling wails. At least on the outside. On the inside she roared.

At eleven o'clock Evie unlocked the front door and was greeted by Queen Elizabeth.

"He's not here, girl," Evie sniffed, scooping the dog up.

Evie sat on the couch and held Queen Elizabeth close, allowing her soft fur to catch her hard tears. None of this made sense. Where was he? Had something happened? He'd promised. Colm always kept his promises.

Social media provided no answers. Neither did texts or voicemail. Nothing about or from Colm. According to Instagram, Sarah's flight left two hours after Colm's, so she probably wasn't home yet. Evie called Scarlet. She hadn't heard from him since this morning, but said she'd call United. "Surely, they'll give me info. I'm his mother."

At eleven forty-five p.m. Evie's phone rang.

"Evie," Sarah's voice quaked. "There's been an accident."

CHAPTER FORTY-TWO

The Fight - Colm
Earlier That Day

T he car crept closer to the San José airport through the snarled traffic. Aggressive drivers pushed in and out of limited curbside spots. Honks, roaring engines, and shouting people muffled through the windowpane as Colm peered out. Thank God they weren't doing curbside drop-off.

Antonio secured a spot in short term parking across the busy street from the airport. Despite protest, there was an insistence by Antonio to park and escort him inside.

"How will I face Evie if you miss your flight?" Antonio laughed, pulling Colm's bags out of the trunk.

Warmth filled his chest. *This is what it would be like to have a father.*

There'd been a collection of stand-in paternal figures throughout his childhood, but never was there a wish for a replacement dad. Until now. An older man that worried about him. That took care of him in small ways, like carrying his duffle and making sure he made it to security at the airport. That offered support, comfort, and advice. What might it be like to call this kind man with the caterpillar' eyebrows and impressive mustache dad?

"Antonio, I don't know how to thank you for everything you've done for me," Colm said, feeling the emotion squeeze in his chest.

"Mijo, your friendship is thanks enough," Antonio said, pulling him into a hug.

The use of the Spanish word for "my son" drew a quiet tear, blinked away before Antonio could notice.

Antonio led through the clusters of bustling people like a mother duck, all the while clucking about the best places to eat at the airport. Colm followed, pulling his suitcase. While Antonio insisted on taking his carry-on, he'd wrestled the suitcase out of his bulky clutches.

At the crosswalk, a little girl with brunette curls was clutching a stuffed rabbit, her tiny arms snaked around the neck of the tall man holding her. The father and daughter a sweet vision of what his future could be. A little girl with Evie's big smile and his green eyes. A smoothie of all their best qualities. Tiny arms wrapped around his neck chattering away as Evie walked beside.

The signal flashed to proceed. Antonio, engaged in a one-sided conversation, moved forward. As the little girl bounced in her dad's arms, the bunny tumbled to the ground. Horror invaded her little face, but before a single cry came, Colm bent and plucked up the bunny.

Tapping the tall man's shoulder, he said in Spanish, "She dropped this."

"Thank you," The man sighed with relief. "She'd be a terror on the flight without her stuffy." And they disappeared into the current of people.

"Colm, I thought I'd lost you," Antonio turned and

chuckled, hands on hips in the middle of the thinning crowds in the crosswalk.

"Sorry," he called as he strode to catch up, turning at the sound of a loud honk. Time slowed. A rusty blue pickup barreled towards Antonio, the truck's driver honking and shouting out the window in Spanish, "The brakes!"

"Antonio!" Colm shouted, sprinting towards him.

Antonio's eyes went wide as Colm pushed him out of harm's way. Antonio hit the ground with a loud "Ooof" that drowned out the screams, honks, and shouts swirling around them. Colm let out a relieved breath, his racing heart slowing.

He's safe.

He looked up just as the truck made contact. Pain sliced through him. He heard Antonio call his name as he soared into the air, weightless.

The rough pavement bit into his back as he landed. Something cracked. Warm liquid spread underneath him. Everything hurt.

He looked up into the blue sky—or was it Evie's eyes? *Evie…I'm coming…*

CHAPTER FORTY-THREE

In The Fight - Evie
Three Days Later

For three days Colm had been unconscious. Antonio had ridden to the hospital with him in the ambulance. Doctors said there was internal bleeding, broken ribs, and brain swelling. He'd been in surgery for hours. His phone had been destroyed when the truck hit him.

No one in Costa Rica had known how to get a hold of Evie. Neither Antonio nor Sylvia had her number. Sarah had called Evie as soon as she arrived in San Francisco and turned on her phone filled with desperate calls from Sylvia.

Evie had gotten on the first flight from LAX and arrived in San José at one p.m. the day after the accident. A grief-stricken Antonio met her at the airport.

"I'm so sorry, Evie."

"This is not on you." Evie assured, embracing him. "He wouldn't want you to blame yourself. You're safe. That's what's important."

Colm's mom flew in later that same day. Josephine,

Jonathan, and Leo ignored Evie's protests and also came. Martin volunteered to stay with Queen Elizabeth.

"I'm a doctor. I'm going to make sure he gets the best treatment," Josephine declared as she arrived at the hospital, wrapping comforting arms around Evie.

Both Leo and Josephine exerted their obnoxious "I'm in healthcare" selves at the hospital, frustrating and terrifying the staff. Thanks to Josephine's connections, a neurologist from Sloan-Whitney Healthcare, one of the nation's top healthcare systems, consulted remotely on the case. At this point it was a waiting game. Brain activity was there. He just wasn't awake.

Scarlet placed her gentle hands upon Evie's shoulders. "Honey, you should take a break. Go to Josephine's hotel. Get some rest."

"No. I'm fine. I'm where I need to be. Where I want to be," Evie said with kind defiance.

There'd be no leaving until the end. Whatever that end looked like, they'd face it together.

"How about I go get us something from the cafeteria?" Scarlet offered, squeezing Evie's shoulders before she left.

"You should talk to him," Josephine said, walking into the room.

The hospital enforced the two-person visitor policy. Team Colm assembled in the waiting room down the hall and took turns weaving in and out, but Evie remained.

Evie looked up at her friend's sad but determined face. "Yeah?"

"He can hear you. I know he can." Bending to Colm's ear she said, "Colm, I'm giving you *one* more day to sleep this off, but you need to wake up by tomorrow. You need to prep our girl for her job interview. Plus, you and I have dinner plans. I know how you hate to not follow through with a plan."

A tear of gratitude fell from Evie's eyes. "Hear that, baby? Josephine means business."

"Talk to him." Josephine placed a hand on Evie's arm. "He'll hear you. He'll come. I know he will."

Alone, Evie's fingers skated across Colm's warm hand, his skin pale from days without the sun. Machines beeped. Feet shuffled outside the door. Wires and tubes tethered Colm's body to this space. Body present, but the rest missing.

"Josephine told me to talk to you. We know I'm good at that. I'm your little chatterbox. But talking *to* you isn't as much fun as talking *with* you."

Holding his hand tight, Evie's eyes closed as she talked. About nothing. About everything. About how he'd saved Antonio, ensuring that Sylvia kept her love, and their children their father. About how there was a whole team of people here. For him. For them. Hoping that the light of her words would cut through the darkness where he wandered, like a beacon leading him back. Back to her. Back to them.

Raising his hand, she kissed his fingers. "Baby, I know you're lost right now, but I'm here. Follow my voice and you'll find me. You said you'd always find me. I'm here. I'm waiting. I'm not going anywhere," she said, pressing his palm to her cheek.

"I'm here." A quiet voice rasped.

Evie's head jerked, tears tumbling down her face.

"Please, don't cry."

"Colm! You're awake!" she cried, clutching his hand. "You're awake."

"I'm here," he whispered.

"My baby," Scarlet gasped, dropping a tray of food as she'd walked into the room to see Colm stirring. "Nurse. He's awake. Come quickly!"

"Mom?" Colm's eyes squinted in the harsh fluorescent lighting, and he winced as he tried to sit up.

"Easy Señor Gallagher," a nurse cautioned, walking into the room. "I'm going to ask you all to leave, so we can get the doctor to examine him."

Colm clung to Evie's hand, his eyes pleading for her to stay.

"They need to examine you. I'll be right outside. I'm not going anywhere. You're stuck with me Colm Gallagher." Evie bent, pressing a soft kiss. "I love you."

"I love you. Forever," he murmured.

"Forever."

CHAPTER FORTY-FOUR

In The Fight - Colm
Two Weeks Later

F ive days after waking up, he was released from the hospital. They'd remained in Costa Rica for another nine days to allow more time to heal before the long flight home. Leo, Jonathan, and Josephine flew home two days after he woke. Scarlet followed a few days later.

They stayed with Sylvia and Antonio. Evie and Antonio walked to the bakery every day and brought pastries to their sweethearts. Much like Diane, Evie took over Sylvia's kitchen, and filled the house with her melodic chattering and the sweet aroma of baked goods.

Though his ribs ached, each night he held her tight in that double bed. They'd even made love this morning before leaving for the airport.

It was slow, with tentative movements of her hips atop of him. It was quiet. Both muffled moans so nobody heard them. The pain of his still healing ribs replaced with the euphoria of being connected again. Nothing between them, anymore. No secrets. No hurt.

No fucking condom.

Evie didn't miss her chance for the job thanks to Josephine, who made a few calls. Her initial interview was done via video conference two days ago. Yesterday, they'd informed her that she and another candidate would have a formal interview with the hospital board next week.

On the six-and-a-half-hour flight from San José to LAX, Colm conducted a mock interview using the practice questions he'd researched, their hands intertwined the entire time.

As they prepared to deplane, Colm reached for his duffle in the overhead, flinching slightly.

Evie wagged her finger. "No. I'm carrying this," she chastised, grabbing the duffle. "I'm strong enough to carry both our baggage."

"You sure are," Colm smiled, dipping to kiss her.

As they moved through the crush of LAX crowds towards baggage claim to meet Jonathan, Colm squeezed Evie's hand. It was strong, despite its size. People that questioned Evie's fortitude because of her sweet exterior were blind. Inside this tiny package was a skyscraper of a woman. Towering in her strength and ability to withstand the fiercest of winds.

They stepped onto the escalator together. When they reached the bottom, Colm pulled Evie to the side.

"This is where we were supposed to meet," he said gesturing around them.

"We're here now. That's all that matters." Evie placed a hand on his cheek.

"Yup." Colm took the duffle from her and dropped it to the floor at their feet.

"Evie Johnson, you're the strongest woman I know. You are kind, loving, goofy, sweet, beautiful, and my favorite person. My teammate. My forever."

He pulled a blue velvet box out of his pocket. Ignoring the tweak of pain in his ribs, he bent to one knee and took her hand in his.

"Colm…"

"Evie Johnson, will you let me be your forever?" he asked, opening the box.

It wasn't as fancy as the one that still sat in the shoebox in their closet. He'd give her that one too. This was a simple silver band in the shape of the Irish Celtic Knot symbolizing union. Symbolizing forever.

"Yes!" Evie squealed.

Happy tears fell as Colm slid the ring onto her finger. It was a little loose, but he'd have a lifetime to make it a perfect fit. Like she was for him, and he for her. Neither perfect, but perfect for each other.

.

PART 3

THE FOREVER

CHAPTER FORTY-FIVE

EPILOGUE

The Forever - Evie
One Year Later

Evie leaned back in the brown cushioned chair at Mama Gurga's, admiring a canoodling Leo and Martin in their tuxedos. Leo pressed sweet kisses on his husband. The flickering candles washed them in a soft light. Mama Gurga's was the most romantic restaurant in Long Beach. She'd said it many times to Leo during the months of wedding planning.

Mama Gurga's transformed with tables draped in white linen and the dancing light of long white candles flanking red roses in crystal vases. Fairy lights hung along the ceiling and outlined doorways.

Evie's hand rested on the empty seat beside her. From time-to-time the seat beside her would be empty, but never for long. Over the last year, she and Colm found their stride again. With months of individual and joint therapy they'd emerged stronger.

"Is this seat taken?" A deep voice teased.

"It's yours. Always."

Colm looked down with adoring eyes. The tuxedo jacket he'd worn earlier hung over the back of his chair. Sleeves rolled up and tie loosened, he was the picture of all her fantasies. Some of those would become a reality tonight.

He placed two glasses in front of them before he sat. "I grabbed these for the toasts." He placed a protective palm on her abdomen. "How are you feeling?"

"You know if you keep touching my belly, people are going to *know* what's in there," she whispered conspiratorially.

Two and a half months along. Everything was going well, but they were waiting until after the first trimester to announce. They'd only told Scarlet, Leo, Martin, Josephine, and Jonathan.

Colm and Josephine had grown closer with weekly dinner dates, conspiring on how to bubble wrap Evie for the next six and a half months.

With Evie's role as assistant director and Josephine taking over as chief of staff after Keeney retired, their offices were next door, so there were frequent check-ins, Post-It reminders to take prenatal vitamins, and random healthy snacks left on her desk.

Josephine had also helped Evie convince Colm to fly to Costa Rica to consult with the schools in San Ramón during the last two weeks of June. During the school year he'd consulted remotely and flew down for spring break with Evie in tow. Josephine reminded him that there was a deep bench in their team for support and Evie would be well cared for, so he'd joined Sarah for two weeks to provide in-person consultation.

"I'm sorry," Colm said, moving his hand, but Evie grabbed and rested it back.

"I've got our little pumpkin. They're safe."

"I know." His eyes twinkled with certainty.

"That best be sparkling water and not cider in those glasses. Too much sugar in cider." Josephine pointed, striding to the table in a metallic gold dress.

"Of course, Jo. I always listen to doctor's orders," he smirked, fist bumping Josephine.

He'd started calling her Jo and she seemed to delight in it, though no one else was allowed to do it.

"Toast time," Leo and Martin said in joint excitement, plopping into their seats.

Leo leaned over to kiss Evie's cheek. "Babes, you were right about this venue. It's perfect. Intimate. Romantic."

A whispered hush fell over the room as Toni's booming voice called everyone's attention to where Jonathan stood holding a champagne flute.

"Don't tell Martin, but this wedding may be nicer than ours," Leo whispered to Evie.

Evie beamed, looking down to her lap draped in the satin of her wedding dress where Colm's hand clasped hers. The ring he'd proposed to her with and the original engagement ring he'd meant to give her at Mama Gurga's claimed the ring finger of her left hand. He wore a matching silver Celtic knot ring on his left hand.

"I've been working on this speech for six years, ever since my best bud showed up with the goofiest grin on his face over a girl he'd met at Jitter Bean Coffeehouse. His Evie. She's not just the love of his life, but his partner in it. As Colm's best friend I can embarrass him with stories. Like how he was almost friend-zoned by *not* kissing Evie on their first date."

The room erupted in loud chuckles.

"I could talk about how he gushes about her like a teenaged girl swooning over Harry Styles."

More laughs.

"The only thing embarrassing about Colm is the amount of riches in his life. The greatest being the love he shares with Evie, who is just as smitten with him. I bet she has a notebook with 'I heart Colm Gallagher' written in glitter pen all over its cover."

There were loud laughs and hoots of agreement.

"Join me in raising a glass to Colm and His Evie, and to Evie and Her Colm," Jonathan toasted.

Cheers erupted. Hands clapped. Silverware clanked on glasses, demanding the bride and groom kiss. The small room overflowed with loved ones cheering as they kissed. Sylvia, Antonio, and Ricardo clapped. Scarlet's adoring eyes glided across the table at her son and new daughter. Sarah leaned at the bar, sipping a cocktail, victory drawn in her smile. Mandala kissed her wife's cheek. All their people. Their team filled the room.

"Come on man, you call that a kiss?" Toni hollered from the hostess stand where he stood beside his wife. "Give her a good one!"

Colm winked wickedly before taking Evie's mouth in a deep penetrating kiss. Thank goodness she was sitting. That kiss turned her legs to jelly.

"Woohoo!" Toni cheered.

The room roared with whistles, hoots, and laughter.

As the kiss ended, Evie cupped Colm's face. "I love you, Colmy Bear."

"I love you, my little chatterbox."

"Forever?"

"And a day," he grinned.

There would be seasons of happiness and seasons of sorrow. Seasons of storms and seasons of calm seas. Each changing season of forever weathered…together.

The End

Sign up for Melissa's newsletter to be the first to know about new novels, blog updates, event, and more.
Visit Melissawhitneywrites.com to sign up.

Keep reading for a sneak peek at Finding Home, Book 1 in the Home Series, coming Summer 2024.

SNEAK PEEK: FINDING HOME

About the book:

Eleanor "Elle" Davidson wants to click her fashionable heels three times and escape the small town she'd grown up in. For fourteen years, Elle used every reason to avoid the tiny hamlet that had formed her. Too many ghosts, too many questions, and far too many secrets. But her presence has been requested for a family wedding and a birthday party for the man who was more father than her own had ever been, and she's out of excuses. Now the only question is whether she can survive the next thirty days in Perry, NY.

She hadn't counted on running into the handsome local veterinarian, Dr. Clayton Owens, a man who knew her as Eleanor, but is falling for her as Elle. Will the blossoming romance with Clayton be enough to help Elle free her heart from the prison of her past or will she do what she's always done...run away?

FINDING HOME
CHAPTER ONE

"Ah! There is nothing like staying at home, for real comfort."
Jane Austen, Emma

"Explain this to me like I'm four," Viet said. "You'll go to your hometown for a week for your cousin's wedding, fly back here, and then fly back again for another week for your uncle's fiftieth? All within the same month? Do I have that right?"

Willa ran a manicured finger around the rim of her glass. "Why don't you just stay in New York the entire time?"

"I can't take a month off!" Elle scoffed.

Eleanor "Elle" Davidson regretted her rare decision to leave her downtown L.A. office before seven to make happy hour with her friends. Viet and Willa's tag-teamed badgering was akin to the Spanish Inquisition. Only with more rosé and less physical torture.

"Aren't you the boss?" Willa signaled the server to bring another round.

"Yes." Elle looked around as if Sloan-Whitney, the healthcare company she worked at, had secret HR spies at the bar. She bent closer and whispered, "I'm the boss bitch." And there it was… She was officially tipsy.

"Yes, Queen!" Willa snapped her fingers.

"I may lose my feminist card for that one."

"More importantly, aren't you the National Director of *Virtual* Medicine? If anyone should be able to work remotely, it should be you." Viet tipped his glass toward Elle.

Willa shimmied and raised her hands in the air. "Brilliant! Would you Airbnb your place? My cousin is a visiting nurse and needs a short-term rental in August. I can guarantee he's very clean."

"What?" Elle tried to blink away the rosé fuzziness.

"Your cousin Ned? Yes, please! He's hot, despite his old man name." A pale blush swept across Viet's face.

"He's also single and hetero-leaning." Willa winked.

Like a modern-day version of Jane Austen's Emma Woodhouse, Willa Andrews was ever the matchmaker. Just like Emma, she was bad at it. *Really Bad.* Over the years, Elle had been subjected to a string of Willa curated meet-cutes. None of which were cute.

"I do love that Ned is a boy nurse." Elle batted her hazel eyes, the rosé warmth spreading across her limbs.

"He prefers man nurse."

"And what a man!" Viet raised his Old Fashion.

"Thank goodness he's my cousin by marriage or this would feel a little Lannister Family Rules to me," Willa joked.

"Back to my opening thesis. Elle, it makes sense. You've been trying to get your headquarters to be more open to remote work. You could pilot it." Like the highly-paid corporate lawyer that he was, Viet laid out his argument.

"You just want to use your spare key to catch Ned in his underpants." Elle aimed her now empty glass at Viet.

"I think Willa may be more apt to do that as she

mentions how they aren't related by blood each time his name comes up." Viet waggled his finger at Willa, who flipped him off in response.

"Besides, you *hate* flying. When we went to London last summer, you needed three glasses of wine to get on the plane. You especially hate non-direct flights. Don't you have to take two flights and a wagon train to get to Perry, New York?" Willa mocked.

It was unoriginal, but Elle gave her the finger.

"Also, Uncle Pete," Viet murmured, playing his trump card.

Damn it. Elle closed her eyes. Guilt churned in her belly.

Her best friend of eighteen years knew Elle better than anyone. Even if he didn't know all of her. Who did, after all?

He knew how important her surrogate family of Uncle Pete, his wife Janet, and their son Tobey were to Elle. A simple silver framed photo of Elle in a cap and gown beside a grinning Pete and Janet, while a smirking Tobey gave her bunny ears, was the lone family picture displayed in her condo.

Pete, Janet, and Tobey were far too important to Elle to be dealt the last fourteen years of bad excuses that she used to not visit. They deserved better.

"Ok," she whispered her defeat.

"Hand me your phone." Viet held his hand out, palm up.

"Why?"

Viet's forehead puckered. "Eleanor Marie Davidson."

"Oh, you got full-named." Willa laughed, sipping the fresh cocktail that had poofed into existence without Elle noticing.

Perhaps, the wine fairy would bring Elle a fresh glass to numb the dread of being forty minutes from the nearest cocktail bar for four full weeks. More importantly, to dull the anxiety about being in a town where painful phantoms of her past haunted each corner. How much rosé could she pack in her luggage?

"Fine," she grumbled and dropped her phone into Viet's hand.

"I'm texting Uncle Pete to tell him the news."

"Wait, I need to get my boss to sign off." Elle reached for the phone.

But Viet was faster. "You're a boss bitch. You'll make it happen."

"Fine." She puffed out a breath. "Willa, let Ned know he can stay at my place."

"Oh, I texted him five minutes ago. He's pumped."

"What if Viet's emotional terrorism hadn't worked?"

"Plan B was for you to fall in love with Ned via forced proximity."

"You read too many romance novels." Elle took Willa's drink from her and sipped.

Stupid alcohol. She narrowed her eyes at the cocktail, scrunched her nose, and handed it back. It was the three glasses of rosé's fault that she was doing this. At least, that's what she'd tell herself.

"No such thing! I've had some of my best orgasms thanks to Denise Williams." She fanned herself with the cardstock menu. "Anyways, I'll find you a *dream* Airbnb to live in while you're in Perry-dise. I wonder if I can find one with a hot farmer waiting for a city girl to melt his pants off with her steamy sass!"

"Check the filter options," Viet deadpanned.

"This will be more like a Stephen King novel, only Carrie returns to get doused with even more buckets of blood." Elle rested her head on the table. The cool smooth wood sobered her to what a terrible idea this was.

"Except in this version Carrie returns as a badass healthcare executive with killer fashion sense and a hot bod." Viet grinned, placing Elle's phone beside her head.

"Totes! Also, you style your hair *way* better than in high school."

Face pinched, Elle raised her head. "Why did I show you my senior yearbook?"

"It will be fine." Viet placed a warm palm over Elle's hand. "You're going home."

Only she wasn't going home. She was going back to where she'd grown up.

ACKNOWLEDGMENTS

It truly takes an entire village to bring a book to readers. When I sat down in February of 2023 to write this story, I had *no* idea all that would be needed to bring Evie and Colm's story to you my dear reader. There were so many people instrumental in helping me bring *In the Hello and in the Goodbye* to you. I'd like to take a moment to acknowledge them.

First, thank you to my dear husband who held my hand, kissed my forehead, rolled his eyes, laughed with me, and soothed my tears on my author journey. I love you, baby. Thank you for supporting me in telling this story.

Katie Graykowski thank you for your kind support with guiding me in the process of indie publishing. Publishing is very much the wild, wild west and you've guided me safely.

Thank you to the legendary Juliette Cross, who connected me with my first editor and my writing mama bear, Gemma Brocato. Your willingness to help aspiring writers is only surpassed by your ability to weave the sexiest, funniest, and most heartfelt love stories!

I could spend 100,000 words talking about how amazing Gemma Brocato is. Having edited the 300,000 word (no joke) dumpster fire that was my first novel, she knows I can do it! Thank you for taking a chance on me and forgiving me for cheating on you with this book. I can't wait for the world to see the books we've partnered on!!

I have had such supportive friends, but I want to high-light a few that made this book possible. Jen Anwar, thank you for pushing me to write this story. Jen Tsan thank you for being the best damn human ever and helping me with all the technical stuff this geriatric millennial struggles with! I can't wait for your next book.

Meghan Fischer, I would be lost without you. Thank you for being my thoughtful alpha reader for this and all my manuscripts thus far. You were the first person that said, "I think you're a writer" and I hope one day my own belief in myself matches what you have for me. Remember I will always find you (inside joke).

I'd like to acknowledge my editor Brenda Athey, who put the smile on this story (www.notestomyselfediting.com). As well, thank you to Su from Earthly Charms for the beautiful cover for this book (www.eartlhycharms.com).

Thank you to Deb Mcllroy for your support and guidance.

I'd like to thank the members of the bookish/bookstagram community and authors that are serving as members of my ARC Team. I have been blessed by your presence and kindness on my journey to bring this book into the world. I only hope I can honor your support with my work.

I saved the best for last. I want to thank you, my dear reader, for reading this book. As someone whose TBR is out of control, I know how many options there are for you. I am deeply grateful that you've taken the time to read Evie and Colm's story. I hope this is just the start of our journey together and thank you for reading.

The Home Series

Finding Home (Summer 2024)

Coming Home (Late Summer 2024)

Making Home (Fall 2024)

ABOUT THE AUTHOR

Melissa Whitney is your typical Jane Austen fangirl with a deep love of the perfect cup of tea, a tasty scone, and a swoony love story. She resides in Orange County, California with her soccer-obsessed husband and their three rescue pugs (see IG for all the pug love). When not listening to her latest audiobook or writing, she enjoys traveling with her husband and trusty bestie Cane Austen (her white cane, which is the accessory for all fashionista legally blind ladies like Melissa).

For the last fifteen years, she's worked in healthcare. Like so many of her fellow healthcare workers, the stress of the pandemic had her leaning into the things that made her happy. This meant lots of steamy romance novels and coming back to her joy of writing. Melissa's goal is to tell heartfelt love stories that explore issues and themes of mental health, trauma, grief, loss, disability, and other topics in a way that make you smile, laugh, cry, and fan yourself. She wants her stories to reflect actual life. Life's not a rom-com and it's not a tragedy. It can be a little bit of both, so are Melissa's stories. Only her stories come with guaranteed HEAs/HFNs. This is romance, after all!

You can learn more about Melissa's upcoming publications and receive exclusive bonus content, inside info, and connect with her by visiting www.melissawhitneywrites.com and signing up for her newsletter. Melissa can also be found on Instagram at @Melissa_Whitneyauthor and on TikTok @melissasuewhitney.

Made in the USA
Columbia, SC
06 November 2024